STEADFAST STAR
INTERSTELLAR FLEET
BOOK TWO

J.J. GREEN

INFINITEBOOK

Reader Group

All books in the Interstellar Fleet series are written by a human and in British English.

Sign up to my reader group for exclusive free books, discounts on new releases, review crew invitations and other interesting stuff:

https://jjgreenauthor.com/free-books/

The Books of Interstellar Fleet

BOOK ORDER OF INTERSTELLAR FLEET

Book 1: *Talman Prime*
Book 2: *Steadfast Star*
Book 3: *Heaven's Envoy*

Blessed is the man who remains steadfast under trial, for when he has stood the test he will receive the crown of life.

James 1:12

One

Her feet resting on her desk, Carys was about to idly turn the page of her book when her falcon friend, Loki, swept down from her shoulder and did it for her.

"Thanks." She would have petted him, but Loki hated it. He seemed to think petting was beneath him. How had he known she'd read to the bottom of the page? She wouldn't have been surprised to discover he was reading too.

Loki had settled on her shoulder once more, leaning slightly forward, his sharp eyes focused on the book, when the door to Carys's office flew open.

The *Bres*'s purser, Kate Lineton, burst in. Fury burning in her eyes, she snapped, "Ellis, what the hell do you think you're doing?"

Carys slowly straightened up. "Er... working?" She put her book face down on her desktop, leaving it open so she didn't lose her place. Loki's talons gripped tightly.

"Very hard at work," Lineton scoffed. "Is your comm broken or did you deliberately turn it off?"

"Uhh..." Carys's hand crept to the button on her uniform. "Looks like I forgot to turn it on this morning. Whoops."

"Yeah, whoops. You just made me walk across the entire ship to speak to you." Lineton strode to the desk and snatched up the book. "What *is* this thing?" She closed it and peered at the front and back covers.

Carys gave a small sigh. "It's a book. A novel. It's about—"

"It's a piece of old junk. I can't believe anyone would be stupid enough to waste their baggage allowance on a freaking antique. But what else should I expect from a zookeeper?"

"This isn't a zoo," Carys growled softly. "It's an aviary. They're not the same."

Maybe the purser had somewhat of a right to be annoyed. Carys had to admit she hadn't *exactly* been working. But ignorance about something so important and easy to understand as the difference between a zoo and an aviary was not forgiveable.

Lineton tossed the book to the desk. "Zoo, aviary. Who gives a shit?"

Carys's jaw muscle twitched.

"I'm assigning you new duties," the purser announced. "Most of our passengers disembarked months ago at Prime. Your visitor count must be nearly zero. I can't believe I let you slip under the radar for so long. As of today your zoo is closed. Shut everything down and report to the sanitation coordinator within an hour. You can help with the sanobot crisis. One hour, Ellis. I'll be checking."

"What?! I can't shut the place down. Birds are living creatures. They need constant care."

Lineton was already on her way to the door. "Then you'll have to do it in your free time."

"I won't have any free time if—"

"Figure it out."

Lineton was gone.

Carys sank back into her seat. "What a bitch."

Loki pecked comfortingly at her hair.

Carys jerked the mop from the bucket, slopping water over the sides, and thrust it into the wringer. Cursing under her breath and imagining that the lump of sodden threads was Lineton, she pressed and twisted the mop viciously. The water in the bucket was dirty, as grey and murky as her mood. The floor wouldn't be any cleaner after she'd mopped it, but she didn't care.

So what if the sanobots were breaking down left, right and

centre? Why was that *her* problem? She was a bird expert. A raptor specialist. Not a cleaner, and certainly not a cleaner of ship's heads.

An idea popped into her mind.

She smiled.

She lifted the mop and casually tapped the bucket with her foot.

The bucket wobbled.

She gave it another knock, harder this time.

It toppled over, and dirty water flooded out in a wave, soaking her boots.

"Whoa!" a voice exclaimed.

Carys looked up.

Setia Zees was at the open door, gaping at the mess. She was wearing her signature leather jacket, looking cool in dead animal skin as usual. "What the...?" Her gaze rose to meet Carys's. "What are you *doing*?"

The water was disappearing through drainage grids.

Damn.

She'd forgotten about those. "What does it look like? What are *you* doing?"

Setia stepped gingerly across the wet deck towards one of the toilets. "Isn't it obvious? So they have you cleaning now? I heard about the sanobot emergency. Didn't know they'd roped you into dealing with it. I hate to say it, but you don't seem to be doing a very good j..." She halted and regarded Carys with an amused look. "You knocked over that bucket on purpose, didn't you? You're hoping that if you screw up enough, they'll leave you alone. Let you go back to your birds. Am I right?"

Carys shrugged. "It's worth a try."

"Well, good luck. I can't say I blame you. It's not the most glamorous duty."

"If I'd known I'd wind up doing this I'd never have joined the crew."

"Could be worse. You could be living on Talman Prime, World of Endless Rain."

"With a bunch of rich morons. True." Carys picked up the overturned bucket and set it straight. As Setia disappeared into the toilet, she asked, "How's the elf doing? Have you seen her?"

"You probably shouldn't call her that."

Two

Carys waited impatiently in the auditorium, anxious to return to the peace and quiet of her aviary. But the lectern on the central stage stood frustratingly empty and the grumbles and chatter of the waiting audience grew louder.

Rumours of an imminent revelation from Captain Bujold had been circulating the ship for days. The most popular theory was that it had something to do with the reason for the Fleet's hasty departure from Talman Prime. As soon as the colonists were settled in their new homes, the commanders of the *Bres* and her sister ships, the *Balor* and *Banba*, had made embarrassingly quick farewells and virtually fled the system.

The nature of the colonisation could have been sufficient explanation for the fast departure. What a farce. A bunch of ageing business moguls and trust fund babies had turned out to *not* be the ideal candidates for building a new human civilisation in deep space.

Who could have known?

It had been a stroke of luck that Prime had been inhabited by a species suspected to be the cousins of humans, and that they'd forgiven the Fleet for attacking them.

A figure appeared in the auditorium doorway, exciting an immediate hush. Mapper Robins walked to the stage, crossed it and took an empty seat in the front row. Disappointment rippled through the throng. He wasn't going to speak ahead of the captain.

Carys watched the old man. As always, his expression was mild, giving nothing away. No doubt he already knew the subject of the announcement. Skein mappers had been excluded from the decision-making process during the failed genocide on Prime, but since then they had been re-admitted to the inner circle.

The higher-ups had put all the blame for the terrible treatment of the Primians on the late Lieutenant-Colonel Markham, saying the stresses of his position had sent him crazy. Predictably, they were rewriting history. The truth was, all the commanders had gone along with Markham's plans at first, even Bujold. Carys didn't trust any of them as far as she could throw them.

A second figure appeared at the auditorium entrance.

At last!

A wave of quiet spread from the scarred, severe features of Captain Bujold as she regarded the crowded room. When all was still, she marched to the lectern. Her gaze swept the rows of watchers from the lowest to highest tiers of seating. "Thank you for coming, everyone. I am not one for speeches, as you may have already noticed. In fact, I contemplated sending out a shipwide statement detailing what I have to tell you today. But I felt that, on this momentous occasion, a written missive would not do justice to the historic, extraordinary nature of what I am about to impart."

If the captain's arrival hadn't already captured everyone's attention, these words certainly did. A profound silence reigned as Bujold paused.

She continued, "There has been much speculation about the true purpose of the Interstellar Fleet. In the years before our departure, pundits argued that the Fleet's professed objective of settling Talman Prime was a smokescreen for a deeper intent. Three massive starships to only colonise one planet? It was overkill—a remarkable waste of resources."

A rare smile played on the captain's lips. "The pundits were right."

Murmurs of surprise disturbed the stillness.

Bujold waited for the hubbub to subside. "We're many light years into our journey, and our first task of disembarking most of our passengers is complete. I am finally at liberty to reveal the nature of our mission." She rested her hands on the lectern. "What I am about to tell you is not news to some. However, for the rest of you I can confirm whispers you may have heard during your time on Earth. The truth is, during various periods of the history of our world, aliens lived among us. We have also encountered them during classified military expeditions into deep space. I am not talking about the Primians, who we guess probably originated on our home planet and are cousins of homo sapiens. I am talking about intelligent species from extra-solar worlds, who most likely evolved hundreds of millennia before humans even existed."

Discomfort crawled into Carys's stomach and she grimaced. *Not this shit again.*

"In terms of technological and physical development, we are infants compared to these beings. Their capabilities are simply beyond our comprehension. There is no point in explaining those capabilities. That information isn't important today. What I can tell you is that one of these species is hostile, and another appears to be benevolent. The generosity of the latter is responsible for the advances humanity has made in recent years, including most of what surrounds you.

"Another thing I can tell you is, from our limited perspective, these life forms don't appear to have anything to do with each other. They are extremely advanced and ancient, yet they do not have any organised relationship. This may seem as strange to you as it does to Earth's political powers. As far as we can tell, neither these nor any other species has formed a galactic governing body. There are no mutually agreed rules or laws relating to acceptable behaviour or anything to help ensure the safety, well-being or advancement of intelligent life.

"We cannot guess why neither has taken this step. It seems the obvious thing to do. But perhaps our species' habit of creating institutions and forging productive alliances is unique within the galaxy. Or maybe in the far distant past the attempt was made but failed. Regardless, what I can reveal to you today is that the goal of the Interstellar Fleet is to attempt to build this organisation—to lay the foundations of a new galactic federation."

Bujold's tone filled with added conviction as she went on, "Our mission is to visit planets showing signs of intelligent life, contact their governing bodies, and propose that they join with similarly developed species for their mutual benefit. We will start with Polaris, and then move on to the next system, and the next. It will be a long process. The galaxy is vast and may contain thousands of eligible life forms. This is a task that I will not live to see completed. It is outrageously ambitious. It is, perhaps, halfway between ignorant and insane. Nevertheless, we will attempt it."

Her hands fell to her sides and tension left her body like a great weight falling from her shoulders. "That is all I have to say. You will receive a more detailed plan, including your personal role, within the next few minutes. If you have further questions, please address them to the relevant crew member."

She stepped from behind the lectern and walked quickly from the stage. The shock permeating the space collapsed. Clamour erupted. The tidal wave of sound was too much for Carys. She rose from her seat and stepped over legs to leave her row.

A galactic federation?

An endless journey through space?

The Fleet had no final destination?

Worrying about what it all meant, she trotted down the stairs, anxious to leave before getting caught in the general exodus. Setia crossed the stage, heading for Robins. Carys kept her eyes on the two in conversation while she descended. It was impossible to hear what they were saying. Robins looked grave as he spoke and Setia reacted with a frown. As Carys reached the bottom of the stairs they parted and she arrived at the exit the same time as Setia.

"Some news, huh?" Setia remarked. "Have you checked what you'll be doing?"

"What I'll be...?" Carys recalled Bujold mentioning that everyone would have a role. "No, I'll have a look in a minute, though I don't think I'm going to like it. Lineton will probably have me slopping out alien latrines. What were you talking to our mapper about?"

Setia pulled a face. "I wanted to know what his skeins told him about the mission, particularly our time at Polaris."

"I thought you didn't believe in his predictions."

"No, I do, kind of. I think there has to be something in it anyway. I mean, he was right that our activities on Prime had a big impact on how things turned out. If Waylis hadn't ended up on the *Bres* she couldn't have sent down all our data and reverse the direction of the war." She gave an impish grin. "I just like to tease him about it."

"So what did he say about Polaris? What's his forecast?"

"He doesn't have one."

"He doesn't *have* one? Isn't it his job to have one?"

"Every skein he casts comes up wildly different, he says. Even with identical inputs minutes apart. The maps are chaotic and he doesn't know why, doesn't know what the problem is. Says it's the first time he's seen it happen. And it's the same for the mappers on the *Balor* and *Banba*. None of them has a clue what the future holds."

Three

Waylis put her interface down on her lap and frowned. "It's weird. I understand most of your words, but sometimes when I read them together in sentences, they don't seem to make any sense. Your language is hard."

"What are you reading?" Carys idly asked, glancing at the door. Her stint of babysitting the Primian was nearly over. Miriam would be here in a few minutes to relieve her, and not a moment too soon. Carys wanted to get back to her birds, who were far more interesting than any person she'd ever met.

"A poem."

"A poem? Bloody hell. I don't think I can help you with that. Why are you reading poetry?"

"It's an old poem. I'm trying to learn more about Earth history. And Polaris."

Curiosity overcame Carys's boredom. "Okay. I give up. What poem covers both Earth history *and* Polaris?"

Waylis tutted and shook her head in a characteristically human way. There was no question that her species was closely related to homo sapiens, but Carys couldn't rid herself of the feeling that Waylis was distinctly *other*. Not in a creepy way. She was just different. Carys suspected it was this impression that stopped their shipmates from treating Waylis like one of their own, not an obsession with her strange ability as Setia thought.

Or perhaps they had heard stories of elves, brownies, and other mythological beings as children. It couldn't be denied that Waylis looked like she'd stepped out of a fairytale.

Rather than answer the question, she'd walked over to Carys and held up the screen. "The poem doesn't involve Earth history," she mildly remonstrated. "It's just a very old piece of literature. I was looking up information about Polaris, and I learned it was significant to humans for a long time, even before you understood about stars and space."

"It was. In my country we call it the North Star. It was used for navigation because it stays in the same place in the night sky. The other stars appear to revolve around it."

"Exactly. The steadfast star." Waylis pointed at lines in the poem.

By this the northern waggoner had set, his sevenfold team behind the steadfast star.

"Yeah," Carys said. "I have no idea what that's saying." She frowned. "Except maybe the 'sevenfold team' might be the Plough, a constellation that points to the North Star."

"Constellation?"

"A star pattern. People used to group stars into patterns and give them names. Now we know stars that appear to be near each other could actually be thousands of light years apart. And we know Polaris isn't a single star but three in close proximity, astronomically speaking."

"You said that looking at it from Earth it seems to stay in the same place. So steadfast means motionless?"

"No, more like steady, reliable, loyal. That word has a few meanings."

Waylis nodded. "I like it when it's your turn to keep me company. You answer my questions. If I ask Miriam a question she gives me more things to read. If I ask Setia, she makes jokes."

Carys winced. "My turn? You know we're taking turns to stay with you?"

"It wasn't hard to figure it out. Your time with me ends about now, and then Miriam is next to—"

The door opened.

"Hi," Miriam said brightly. "I was just passing and thought I'd stop by for a chat. Fancy seeing you here again, Carys. Have you two been having fun?"

"You don't have to pretend," said Carys. "She knows."

"Oh, er..." Miriam's cheerful expression faltered.

"I don't mind," said Waylis. "I think you're all very kind, and I'm grateful."

"It was Miriam's idea," Carys explained, uncomfortable at being included in Waylis's compliment. In truth, though Miriam had proposed babysitting Waylis, Setia had figuratively twisted Carys's arm to make her join in.

"But you're here," said Waylis, "and you don't have to be."

"Not for much longer." Carys rose to her feet.

She was beating an exit when Miriam said, "Hey, I thought I saw Sheldrake earlier."

Carys halted. "You did?"

The ex-corporal had become an enigmatic figure around the ship. She hadn't seen him for weeks.

"Just a glimpse in the refectory. He was leaving. I was about to shout out but decided against it. Do you think I did the right thing?"

Carys bit her lip. "It's hard to say. We definitely shouldn't draw attention to him. On the other hand, he can't be having much fun sneaking about all the time, worried he's going to get caught."

"Mapper Robins must know he's aboard," said Miriam. "He can see everyone in his skeins. He'll have to let Captain Bujold know sooner or later."

"I bet she already knows. She just has bigger fish to fry."

Waylis giggled.

"What's so funny?" Carys asked. Sheldrake's position was a difficult one. Ejected from military service due to defying orders and attacking a fellow soldier, he had no place on the ship's manifest. Somehow, he'd managed to avoid being forcibly disembarked at Prime. This was probably because of the massive upset over the Colonisation Coordinator, Wulandri, attempting the exact same thing. As far as Carys understood, he'd simply been overlooked.

"What a strange saying," Waylis replied. "Bigger fish. People aren't fish and you don't fry them."

"Uhh, returning to the subject..." Carys went on "...arriving at Polaris is going to change everything. Assuming Bujold knows Sheldrake is a stowaway, I suppose she hasn't bothered with him while we're en route. I don't think she would actually space him. But when she has a planet handy, the obvious solution would be to get rid of him on it. I really hope it doesn't come to that."

The man had a lot of qualities. It was a shame he was persona non grata.

"I hope so too," Miriam said mournfully, "but I don't see a way he can return to soldiering, and what else is there for him to do?"

"Maybe Setia's working on it."

"If she is, she hasn't let me in on her rescue plan."

Loki was calling.

At some point while Carys had been bringing him up, the bird had either invaded her mind or she'd become overly enmeshed with him. She'd never been able to decide. But she needed to return to her cabin. "I have to go."

Leaving the two women, she set off across the ship.

The minute the richest of the *Bres*'s passengers had boarded the shuttle that would take them to Prime, there had been a mad scramble for their cabins. Now their owners would no longer be needing them, luxury suites were up for grabs. Every crew member from third-class engineers to high-level officers like Purser Lineton had rushed to long-coveted dwellings and quickly installed their belongings. In some cases, more than one person had their eye on a particular habitation. There had been arguments. Carys had heard of punches being thrown.

Her requirements were more modest. She hadn't been forced to compete for her new abode. A two-room place, it was a decided step up from her assigned cabin, yet it wasn't particularly extravagant. There was enough room for her and Loki, and that was all she needed.

When she entered her place, he flew from his perch to her shoulder.

She chuckled and crossed the cabin to the counter-top refrigerator. "What have you been doing while I've been gone?"

Naturally, Loki didn't answer. He flexed his feet excitedly while she took out a container and opened it. After picking up a ready-prepared strip of meat, she held it between two fingers for Loki to grab with his beak. The little snack soon disappeared and she fed him another couple of pieces.

When she closed the lid and returned the container to the refrigerator he complained. "*Kee kee kee.*"

"If I feed you any more you'll be as fat as a chicken."

Loki had made a full recovery from the time he'd spent on Prime. When she'd first seen him she'd been shocked by his thin, bedraggled state. He'd barely resembled the healthy young kestrel she'd nursed from an egg. The Primians had managed to keep him alive but they clearly knew nothing about birds, let alone falcons. Now he was back to his usual active, curious self.

She hoped that if Bujold decided one of the worlds of Polaris was suitable for bird life—which would mean the end of the voyage for the aviary-keeper—it would be a good home for Loki.

"I might not have my family, but at least I have you."

He playfully nibbled her ear.

Four

Polaris is a triple-star system comprising Polaris Aa, Polaris Ab and Polaris B. Our sister ships will be visiting Polaris B. The mission of the Bres is to investigate a suspected inhabited world of Polaris Ab, the smaller of the paired suns. Ancient astronomical studies indicated the planet has liquid surface water and an atmosphere that contains oxygen, carbon dioxide and methane, and therefore may harbour life.

However, the Antarctic Project dismissed it as a potential site of colonisation. The planet's gravity is too low (0.771 SG) for long-term survival of a human colony, and there is a high likelihood of challenging surface conditions due to the proximity of Polaris Aa, a massive star.

Most recently, the Fleet's long-range scanners have detected radio signals that seem artificially generated. We have been unable to extract any meaning from the signals so far. All we know is they are transmitting between the worlds orbiting Polaris Ab and Polaris B. We may discover the radio waves are a physical phenomenon unknown to us at this time, not generated by an intelligent species. In which case, we will search for evidence of life and assess and catalogue other planetary data before moving on to our next destination.

Your role in this mission

. . .

Carys glanced sideways at Loki, who, as always, was giving the impression he was reading too. "Here we go."

The next few sentences of the document would reveal her fate—her immediate future. Possibly the fate of the birds under her care too.

She had put off reading the captain's message, sent directly after the announcement about the Fleet's purpose, for days. Just the thought of the ongoing journey made her heart sink. She didn't want to think about the fact that she'd signed her life away. The personalised notification was a stark reminder that she had to do whatever Bujold dictated, whether that meant staying on the ship forever or living out the rest of her life on an alien planet. Neither option held any attraction anymore, yet both were inescapable.

Loki hopped from her shoulder to the interface and pressed the ball of his foot to the arrow. The next page appeared.

"Stars, you're clever."

If he'd tapped with his beak it might not have worked. His foot had a better blood supply.

He gave her a look before fluttering back to her shoulder.

"All right, I'll read it."

Carys Ellis, you are to establish a suitable area for the release of the birds currently held within the ship's aviary. If no suitable site can be found, we will unfortunately be faced with the only alternative solution: euthanasia.

She gasped.

"No! No way!"

There was more, but she didn't read it. Slamming the interface onto her desktop, she leapt up. Loki lost his grip and flapped to maintain his balance, but she barely noticed him. She marched from her office, causing a flurry of wings as she burst into the aviary. The parrots, parakeets, corvids, finches, sparrows, buntings, pigeons, woodpeckers, hummingbirds, toucans, and myriad other forms of avian life scattered at her approach, disappearing into shrubs and rising into the trees and high netting.

The outer door was locked—a precaution against Lineton

disturbing her quiet reading time again. She slammed the release button and the portal swept open. Her passage through the ship was a blur. She glimpsed startled faces and people moving hastily out of her way. In record time, she arrived at Bujold's office.

"Let me in!" she yelled into the intercom.

The door opened, revealing the captain sitting at her desk, her expression characteristically stony, an eyebrow raised. "Ms Ellis. I see you finally read your notice."

"You're not killing them," Carys seethed. "You'll have to kill *me* first."

"Please sit down."

"I'm fine as I am, thanks. I just came here to tell you—"

"You will be seated and you will listen to what I have to say, or I will have you escorted to the brig and you will remain there until you have calmed down. Is that clear?"

Carys ground her teeth. With a supreme effort of self-control, she drew out a chair and sat on it, arms folded, glaring at the captain.

Bujold knitted her fingers. "I must explain several things to you, and I ask that you do not interrupt. Firstly, you knew from the beginning of our journey the reasons the *Bres* has an aviary. As well as providing a distraction and entertainment for the colonists during what was expected to be a long voyage, the intention was to release the birds on the new planet. This plan came with several expectations. It was known that some birds might not survive, that the ones who did survive might not reproduce, and that genetic diversity would be too limited for any species to become self-sustaining. I have to say, in my estimation the approach taken by Ua Talman's team in this matter was extremely unscientific."

The captain continued, "You are not stupid, Carys, and you are certainly not ignorant regarding birds. You must have been aware that, even if Prime had been suited to supporting avian life, the chances of your birds establishing breeding colonies were non-existent. You must have known from the beginning that taking birds to the new planet was a fool's errand. Am I correct?"

Carys looked down, muttering, "I would have looked after them."

"I'm sure you would have done your best." A softer note had crept into Bujold's tone that made Carys look up.

The captain's steely expression had turned pitying. Carys swallowed and focused on her lap again, her fury melting into discomfort that twisted her guts. Pitying looks reminded her of the faces of her rescuers in the Australian desert years back.

"What you have to accept," Bujold continued, business-like, "is that the *Bres*'s supply of bird food is finite. You know this. You are in charge of the stocks. There is also no guarantee that we will ever be able to replenish them. As I understand it, most bird species' diets are highly specialised. It makes no sense to devote precious time and resources to sustaining what are essentially useless animals."

"They're not..." Carys snapped, but the captain lifted a hand, signalling her continued command of silence. Carys pressed her lips together.

"The aviary has already outlived its intended lifespan. It should have been emptied and closed at Prime. My decision for a stay of execution was in recognition of your efforts in the mission to the planet's surface. But this situation cannot continue forever. It must come to an end sooner or later, and for everyone's sake I believe putting an end to it as soon as possible is the kinder option all around. I'm sure you would not like your birds to starve to death, and nor would you wish to witness it."

Watching her carefully, Bujold went on, "Naturally, this doesn't apply to your pet. I believe he eats meat, so there should be no problem with supplying the small amount of food he requires. And don't forget that your birds may be able to survive on the planet we are about to visit."

"What happens then?" Carys challenged. Screw Bujold and her demand to be heard uninterrupted. They were talking about the lives of hundreds of living animals. Hundreds of animals who would be put to death, based on the poor judgement and whims of the bunch of idiots who founded the Fleet. "What happens if you transfer all the birds to the surface? Do I go with them?"

The captain exhaled heavily. "You knew the score when you signed up. You're the bird keeper. The plan was always that you would care for the birds, whether on the ship or off it."

"And if you murder them all, then I have nothing to do, right? Like them, I'm excess weight, taking up resources. If the birds can't leave the ship because there's nowhere suitable for them to live they'll be killed, but either way, *I'm* leaving. Right?" Carys leaned forward in her seat and gripped the armrests.

"There are many factors to consider. We don't know what we'll find when we—"

"You can't seriously be contemplating abandoning me on an alien planet."

"*If* you were required to disembark at our destination, you wouldn't be alone. The Fleet is currently home to several uninvited guests and passengers with no defined role. For our onward journey when we leave Polaris, only essential crew will remain."

"If you always wanted to strand us, you should have done it on Prime. At least there we would have been able to live in whole communities of humans."

"Perhaps, but everyone made their choice, for better or worse. As I recall, you seemed happy to continue the voyage."

Carys's shoulders slumped.

"Now you understand the situation," said Bujold, "there's nothing further to discuss. I'm very busy with other matters."

Carys held the captain's frank gaze for several moments before finally accepting the hint and rising to her feet. Still, she hesitated. Surely there was something she could say, some argument she could make that would guarantee the lives of her birds and give her some control over her own future?

Nothing sprang to mind.

With heavy steps, she left the captain's office.

Before she'd gone far she encountered a familiar figure. Sheldrake was heading towards her, his head down.

But then he spotted her and halted. "What's up?"

The ex-corporal rarely acknowledged her these days. Her face had to be betraying her feelings.

"Bad news."

"Personal, or something to do with the ship? I don't know much about what's going on. Don't like to go on the 'net in case I get picked up."

"Both, I suppose. It might be bad news for you too, depending on your perspective. I wouldn't worry about getting picked up. Soon, all your worries will be moot."

"What do you mean?"

"Let's have a drink. I'll tell you all about it."

Five

"Beer?" Carys had never known Sheldrake to drink anything else, except for that one time on Prime when they had all drunk Miriam's smuggled tequila.

"Sure." Sheldrake's gaze roved the bar.

Carys input his order and hers. The ex-corporal had suggested they visit one of the most basic drinking establishments which, in the first stage of the voyage, even the lowest passenger class could patronise. Orders were anonymous, sent via keyboard rather than comm'd. He'd insisted they sat in a corner booth, which gave a good vantage point.

The place was otherwise empty—unsurprisingly considering the *Bres* was down about ninety percent of its original complement of passengers and crew. The bar smelled faintly of alcohol and sweat. The sanobot crisis apparently wasn't over.

Seemingly satisfied no one was about to leap out and drag him off to the brig, Sheldrake relaxed and rested an arm along the back of the bench seat.

"I don't know what you're so worried about," Carys said. "Bujold wasn't born yesterday. If she'd wanted you off the ship you wouldn't be here."

"I guess so." He didn't seem convinced. "It doesn't hurt to take precautions." He'd maintained his military crew cut and he was clean shaven. Even his civvies were soldierly in style, simple, plain, clean and crease-free. "How are you doing? Birds okay?"

"Uhh, yeah, they're good." *For now.*

The slot on the tabletop opened and a beer and gin and tonic rose up. She pushed Sheldrake's drink to him and took her own, glad of the short reprieve. She was regretting speaking to him in the passageway. She'd been in shock from her meeting with the captain. It wasn't her business to give the man a heads up about his future on the ship. His life was hard enough as it was after losing the profession he clearly loved so much. She didn't know how to tell him life was about to get even harder.

He took a sip of beer. "What about the others? I don't know what's been happening with them. Hanging out with you guys is a little risky."

"They're fine. Except for Waylis."

"The elf?"

She chuckled and put down her glass. "Don't let Setia hear you calling her that."

"She doesn't like it?"

"She thinks it's rude."

"I guess it is, but the resemblance..." He shook his head. "Warning noted. I don't want to get on the wrong side of Setia. She's scarier than Bujold. You were going to explain why I don't have to worry anymore?"

"That isn't what I said." *Damn.* He'd misunderstood. "I said your worries were moot, as in, they don't matter."

His frown encouraged further explanation.

"I was on my way back from a meeting with Bujold. She knows about you, or at least I think she does. She said there are several stowaways aboard and..." Carys took a breath "...she plans on getting rid of you all at our next stop."

His expression relaxed. "Is that it? I don't think it's going to happen."

"Huh? Why?"

"I bumped into an army friend just before I saw you. I've been keeping a low profile, but occasionally an old buddy will slip me some scuttlebutt. He said the latest word is the planet can't possibly be inhabited. It's too close to the massive twin star, making it too unstable for life to have evolved."

"Your friend said that?" Carys took the lemon slice from her drink and sucked on it.

"That's what he said."

She put the lemon down. "Wait. How can the science team know so much? Can we scan normal space from the Red Zone?"

Red Zone was the informal name given to the paths through ordinary spacetime the Fleet travelled, dwarfing the distances between star systems.

"We aren't in the Red Zone."

"You're kidding! We've arrived? Bujold didn't say a thing."

"There was an announcement this morning. Even I got *that* news."

"Shit." Not turning on your comm had its downsides, apparently. "Anyway, even if the scientists are right, Bujold could still put us off at Polaris B."

"Us? You're on the captain's list too?"

After taking another heavy breath, she told him about the rest of her meeting.

"Shit. I'm sorry." He put a hand on her shoulder.

She attempted a nonchalant shrug. In truth she was barely holding herself together. She appreciated his gesture, even though it nearly tipped her over the edge into a shameful display of excess emotion. He meant something to her, and that made his sympathy more affecting. During their long, non-stop march from the forest to the fledgling settlement on Prime, as they tried to get help for Miriam and Setia, she and the corporal had grown... not exactly close, but closer.

Shared hardship did that to people. She was bonded in a similar way to her adoptive siblings, Patrin and Kayla. They'd been Displaced Children, too, in the same secret Crusader camp in Australia, enduring terrible conditions, abuse and deprivation.

Memories of people she would never see again invaded her mind. She picked up her drink and downed it. "I suppose it had to happen sooner or later."

"We'll figure something out." Sheldrake patted her shoulder. "We can't let your birds die. That's cruel. It's wrong."

"I know, but even I have to admit Bujold does have a point. Some of those birds still have years of natural lifespan, and I can't conjure their feed out of nothing." Lifting her empty glass she asked, "Another one?"

"I'll order this time. The same?"

"A double."

"I can see we're going to be here a while."

Moving around the *Bres* was like wandering through a honeycomb. The Fleet's ships were broadly structurally identical: blocks comprising rooms of a range of dimensions slotted together around the central propulsion system. The purpose of the rooms varied according to section. In some places the largest rooms were family suites. In others they were cafeterias, their dividing walls removed. Elsewhere they were gyms. The equivalent of Setia's former tiny cabin was a public restroom in certain parts of the ship, a single-person sim amenity in others. Carys's aviary, towering three decks high, was a rock-climbing facility, a ship's hold, a rainforest habitat, and she didn't know what else in other locations.

The bar she and Sheldrake had been drinking at formed part of the fifth, uppermost deck. Low and wide, these places were also storage facilities, and—she vaguely recalled in her inebriated state—one of them was Mapper Robins's office. Maybe he needed the space to see his skeins.

The repetitiveness of the ship's structure, once you grasped it, made it hard to get lost. As soon as you recognised which area of a block you were in, you could navigate to where you wanted to go fairly easily.

Nevertheless, Carys and her drinking companion were struggling to find their way home. She'd lost count of how many gin and tonics she'd drunk, and Sheldrake had poured enough beer down his throat to sink a battleship before, unusually for him, moving onto shots.

They stepped into a lift, and she slumped against the wall.

"Which floor?" Sheldrake asked, swaying.

"Dunno." She thrust the heels of her hands into her eyes to clear the blurriness in her vision. The lift lurched, or perhaps she did. Either way, she found she was suddenly on the floor.

Deck, she reminded herself.

Or was it a floor?

"Which floor?" Sheldrake repeated in the same tone, as if he'd forgotten he'd already asked the question.

Now she was really confused. "I think it's a deck."

"Huh?" Sheldrake swung around and unbalanced himself. His legs twisted and he dropped to her side before putting his head on her shoulder. After a pause, he asked, "Where are we going?"

"Home."

"Back to Earth?"

"No. Cabin. Your cabin and mine. Where's your cabin?"

"Huh?"

"Which section?"

"Pretty sure this is F."

"No, which section for your cabin?"

"Can't remember."

"Me neither."

She rested against the wall. Sheldrake was a big, loose lummox leaning on her, but it didn't matter. She was sandwiched between him and the corner, which took both their weight.

"Guess we can sleep here," Sheldrake said.

She mumbled agreement, her eyes closing.

"No funny business, though."

"Whaa...?"

"No trying somethin' 'cause I can't defend myself."

"'kay. I wasn't thinking about it. But okay."

Sheldrake sat bolt upright and waved his arms around. "Have to fight them off... All th' time."

His sudden movement jerked her back to consciousness. "Fight what?"

"Women. All th' women." He sank onto her again. "All th' time."

"Right."

She had almost passed out once more when he spoke again. "That stuff I said. Y' know, what we talked about..."

She opened one eye. "Yeah?"

"'s jus' between you an' me, right?"

"'Course." She couldn't remember what he'd said, or what she had said, for that matter. "I won't repeat a word."

"Thanks." His hand rose into the air, loosely clenched.

It took her a moment to realise what he wanted. With great effort and concentration, she fist-bumped him. "'Night, Sheldrake."

"'Night, Ellis."

Six

Somehow, Carys had made it back to her cabin. She had no recollection of the journey. All she knew was she was in her bunk and she felt like shit. The last thing she remembered was sitting in the bar reminiscing with Sheldrake about their time on Prime, laughing about the moment a fountain of water had erupted from a tree and hit him in the face.

After that, the only image in her mind of last night was of a lift door repeatedly trying to close on the foot of her outstretched leg. That, and the sensation of something soft and heavy pressed into her side.

??

She shook her head, instantly regretting it. The clapper of an enormous bell seemed to swing from side to side within her skull, clanging against the bone. Reverberations passed through her and landed in her stomach. Its contents objected to the assault.

She leapt up, hand clamped over her mouth, and flew to her shower room. As she vomited into the toilet, she thanked the stars that she hadn't commandeered one of the luxury suites. Her cabin's head was only a few paces from where she slept. She would never have made it if she'd had farther to run. And Lineton would never have allowed her to borrow one of the few working sanobots to clean up the mess.

Exhausted and head throbbing, she crossed her arms over the

bowl and rested her forehead on them. The automatic flush sucked the puke out of sight and replaced it with a lemon scent. She dragged herself to the washbasin, stuck her face under the tap and gulped a couple of mouthfuls of water. As she straightened up, she avoided looking in the mirror. Yet she couldn't help spotting two beady eyes in the reflection.

Loki's perch stood beyond the open door.

Judgement was written all over his face.

He was probably only hungry, but she couldn't help feeling he deeply disapproved of her behaviour.

"All right, all right," she muttered. "I learned my lesson. No more getting off my face."

He didn't seem to believe her. He shuffled restlessly before lifting into flight. From beyond her view came the metallic scrape of talons on the refrigerator.

After staggering to the kitchenette, Carys gagged as she gave Loki his breakfast. She chucked two headache tablets down her throat, followed them with more water, and returned to bed. The aviary could wait a couple of hours until she began to feel human again.

But worries invaded her mind—the same worries that had driven her to drown her sorrows.

What would happen to her birds?

What would happen to her?

Guilt at leaving her adoptive family without even a goodbye note, let alone an explanation, also nagged.

She couldn't sleep.

To take her mind off things, she picked up the book lying face downward next to her bunk and scanned the pages. She must have read this book five or six times already, yet it didn't lose its appeal. If anything, the familiarity of the story made it more of a comforting escape. She'd often wished she could live in the book's world. It would be so much better than reality.

Her bed seemed to suddenly dip. Her empty stomach protested and she retched. Her cabin appeared to swim before her eyes, as if she were on a plane experiencing turbulence. Shutting them tightly, she prayed for the tablets she'd swallowed to work faster. She should be starting to feel better but she felt worse.

The sensation eased and she tried to re-focus on her book. It was no good. She was reading the same sentences over and over. Nothing was going in. She gave up and put the book down. As she turned onto her side, hoping to at least doze a little, her door chime sounded.

She ignored it.

If she pretended she wasn't here, whoever wanted to see her would go and look in the aviary and perhaps other areas of the ship. It would buy her some time before she had to live up to her responsibilities. After all, if she was going to be abandoned at Polaris and all her birds were going to be killed, what was the point of anything anymore?

"Umm," said a voice through the intercom, "Ms Ellis? I know you're in there."

Carys was silent. How did he know? She peered into the room's corners. Were there hidden cameras?

"The captain insists that you come with me to the briefing room immediately. I have permission to override your door security if you refuse."

"Bloody hell! Wait a minute." Carys threw back her covers. *Dammit. Damn Bujold and her bloody heavy-handed tactics. What did she want now?*

Carys hastily sought out her uniform. The jacket lay crumpled on a chair. She had no idea where the trousers were.

"Sod it," she seethed. If Bujold was in such a hurry, she could bloody well see her bird keeper in her pyjamas. She slammed the door release.

A young soldier waited in the passageway. His eyes popped as he took in her state. "Er, do you want a minute to, er...?"

"I'm fine, thanks. Let's go!"

Bare-footed and wild-haired, Carys marched alongside the young man. The route leading to the briefing room was mostly empty, but the few passersby they did encounter took a second and third look at the strange pair, gawping and sometimes chuckling.

Carys's irritation and resolve began to waver. She was cold, she felt sick, and her eyes were sore. Maybe defying Bujold by arriving in an unkempt state wasn't such a good idea. Carys began to feel like she'd scored an own goal.

When she reached the briefing room, the feeling intensified tenfold. The soldier had only mentioned the captain. He hadn't said anything about anyone else. Yet, now Carys thought it through, she realised that if Captain Bujold wanted to see her alone she would have requested her presence at the captain's office. The location of the briefing room implied...

Carys took in the four officials sitting around the table. If the passersby had gawped, the only way to describe the attendees' expressions was utter and profound amazement.

"Ms Ellis," Bujold said icily, "thank you for joining us. We seem to have interrupted your well-earned rest, for which I can only apologise. Please take a seat."

The officials' gazes followed her as she slunk to a chair. A jug of water sat at the centre of the table. She reached out, grabbed it, and poured herself a glass. "I don't feel well. Will this take long?"

"You must already know Purser Lineton," said Bujold.

The purser was looking daggers at her.

The captain continued, "I don't know if you've met Lieutenant-Colonel Broz or Ambassador Barbier."

Carys had heard about Broz. He'd taken over from the late Lieutenant-Colonel Markham. Barbier was news to her. "I didn't know we had an ambassador."

Bujold explained, "The presence of ambassadors was classified until after the first phase of the Fleet's mission. Each ship carries a diplomatic representative to lead negotiations with other intelligent species about joining the Galactic Federation."

Purser Lineton might have been angry about Carys's appearance, but Barbier looked apoplectic. His almost-black eyes burned as he glared at her and a flush suffused his olive skin. His thick, black hair seemed to echo his fury, shaped by a razor into jagged peaks.

"I see." Carys tore her gaze from the ambassador. "And you wanted to see me because...?"

"As you must have noticed," Bujold replied, "the *Bres* was recently attacked."

"It was?! I mean, she was? I mean..." Carys swallowed "... someone fired at us? Why?"

"Of course someone fired at the ship," Barbier snapped. "Didn't you feel the impact?"

"I thought that was my hang... I thought..." Carys's words dried as she took in the news. When she'd signed up to the Fleet, no one had mentioned the possibility of space battles.

The ambassador threw her a withering glance. He asked Bujold,

"Are you sure this person has something to offer? She barely seems able to function as an adult, let alone as a member of the crew. Least of all as a consultant regarding the situation we face."

"Hey!" Carys protested. But she saw his point. She took another drink of water. "If you don't need me, I'd like to go and lie down."

"Stay right where you are," Bujold retorted. "Ellis, listen. The *Bres* was fired upon by a ship we believe originated from the Polaris Ab system. As a result, we've returned to the Red Zone for the time being, but I don't want to give up the attempt to make contact. Clearly, an intelligent species inhabits the system. While they're obviously antagonistic, that doesn't necessarily mean they're unfit to join the Federation. Not so long ago, 'fire first, ask questions later' would have been humanity's answer to the arrival of aliens."

"Uh huh." Carys remained confused about what this all had to do with her.

The captain closed her eyes, took a deep breath and exhaled slowly between pursed lips. With a tone of infinite patience, she went on, "Before we were attacked, we managed to run some close scans of the life-supporting planet. Its surface is mainly water. The only landmasses are the peaks of mountain ranges, protruding from the oceans. What appear to be metropolises—if that's what they are—are air-born."

Carys blinked.

"Initial impressions indicate the dominant species, which has built starships capable of space warfare, is aerial."

"They're..." Carys recalled the information on the planet in the captain's notice, in particular its low gravity. "They're birds?"

Barbier snapped, "Of course they're not birds, you fool! Really, this is completely ridiculous."

"Ellis," Bujold said, ignoring the ambassador, "we've caught you at a bad time. Return to your cabin. On your way, take a detour to a sick bay, where I've heard they have an effective cure for your *illness*. Take it. Lie down for a couple of hours, and then come back here. In the meantime, if you're feeling up to it, think on the implications of what you've just learnt. It may be that your specialist knowledge means you have significant insights to offer. I certainly hope so."

Barbier looked away in disgust. Lieutenant-Colonel Broz stared without sympathy. A mocking smile garnished Lineton's lips.

Carys got to her feet and padded to the door, her shoulders sagging.
Her escort had disappeared.
Her feet were cold.
Significant insights to offer?
What a joke.

Seven

Bujold, Barbier and Broz.
 Carys smiled. They sounded like characters in a kids' comedy show.

"Is something funny?" Barbier snapped. The three had been deep in discussion, but apparently he was keeping a close eye on her.

She forced a serious expression but didn't bother answering. Scowling, the ambassador returned his attention to the captain and Lieutenant-Colonel. The triumvirate in the briefing room were clutching at straws. Did they know it? Maybe. Yet, even so, they were unaware of the depth of their ignorance.

She could have refused to 'consult' on the aliens of Polaris Ab, but what would have been the point? As soon as word got out she would be a pariah. Who in their right mind would withhold specialised knowledge in the current circumstances? The success of the mission could depend on it. Everyone's lives could depend on it.

But imagining she knew anything relevant to the situation was insane. Just because the aliens were aerial, it didn't mean she could predict their behaviour, culture, or even their anatomy. She might know a lot about birds, but bats, insects and plenty of other Earth organisms were aerial too. There were flying squirrels, flying fish and flying snakes. Some species of spiders also flew, casting out their silk to catch on the wind. She didn't know a helluva lot about any of them. She certainly knew f-all about creatures who evolved on a system hundreds of light years from Earth, who just happened to locomote via the atmosphere.

The hangover cure from the sick bay Bujold recommended had been effective. Carys's pounding headache had quickly vanished, her stomach didn't feel like it had been scoured with wire wool, and her mouth had lost its guano-depository taste. Before returning to the meeting, she'd put on her uniform, only noticing too late that it was crumpled and grubby and—she suspected—carried more than a whiff of the aviary. Barbier's laser gaze had travelled from her boots to her head when she'd reappeared.

Now it focused on her again. "Do you have anything to add, Ms *Expert*?"

The three officials had been talking for so long she'd lost track of their discussion. "To what? You've covered a lot of ground."

"To the subject of communication, of course. It stands to reason that if we're to get anywhere in our endeavour, we and the target species must understand each other."

"Well..." She considered the question. Birds' communication was primarily aural and visual—though the latter was mostly for sexual signalling, particularly male birds' colour and feather displays. There was also some utilisation of body language, again often for the purpose of selecting a mate or pair bonding. She guessed similar principles might apply to the species in the Polaris Ab system, but she wasn't sure how—

"This is a complete waste of time," said the ambassador tersely. "While we're waiting for her to answer, we could be actually *doing* something."

"Give her a minute," Bujold said.

"No," Carys replied, "he's right. I don't have any suggestions."

The captain frowned, dissatisfied.

Broz said, "I say we try transmitting their own radio broadcasts at them. Then, they'll know that, a) we're listening in to what they're saying, b) we're another intelligent species—"

"They'll know *that* from our massive starship," Barbier interjected.

One of Broz's eyes twitched. With no other reaction, he continued, "and, c) that we're attempting to make contact. Naturally, anything else we might send will be entirely incomprehensible to them."

An idea popped in Carys's head but she didn't voice it.

"Ellis?" Bujold asked.

"Nothing."

The captain said, "I can't help feeling we're missing something, but for the moment I don't have any other suggestions. So we're agreed? We shift into normal space much farther from the system this time, and approach slowly. I can see how a large, strange starship appearing from nowhere could provoke a hostile reaction. That may be the reason our first attempt to make contact failed. Hopefully, this new tactic will demonstrate we mean no harm."

"Hopefully," Barbier concurred.

Broz said, "It's a shame there's no galaxy-wide, mutually agreed sign of peace."

"That's the kind of thing we're striving for," said Bujold. "Perhaps one day we'll achieve it. In the meantime, baby steps. We'll learn as we go along. Eventually, we will establish effective protocols. Ellis, come with us to the bridge."

Carys couldn't fail to catch the quiet tut from the ambassador.

She'd never been on the *Bres*'s bridge. She couldn't decide if she was surprised or not about how closely it resembled the bridges of starships on drama vids. There was the pilot, sitting in the centre, watching a ghostly 3D holo of the ship suspended in front of her. The man sitting at her side had to be the co-pilot, present in case of an emergency.

Ship's officers sat at consoles ranged in a semi-circle. She didn't know exactly what each was doing. Reading scan data? Monitoring comms? Overseeing operations? Were weapons officers here too? Everyone seemed very intent on their jobs, though she'd noticed their gazes snap to their screens the moment the captain had appeared.

"Sit over there, Ellis," Bujold ordered, nodding at a vacant seat.

Carys took it, gripping the armrests nervously, feeling surplus to requirements. What was Bujold thinking, inviting her here? Her birds needed feeding. She hadn't been to the aviary since she'd woken up. She would be more useful there than on the bridge. She half-rose to her feet. "Maybe I should...?"

"Stay right where you are, Ellis," said Bujold.

She slumped into her seat.

To ease her anxiety, she scanned the room. When her gaze alighted on the pilot again, she noticed the woman had no controls. What was more, she and her co-pilot were the only people in the place wearing helmets. The pilot's gaze was riveted to the holo of the ship and her hands rested in her lap.

She had to be piloting via a direct brain/ship interface. Carys had heard of such things but never seen them in real life. What if something startled the pilot? Would the *Bres* wobble, throwing everyone off balance? Carys restrained a nervous giggle.

"Pilot, transition to normal space..." Bujold ordered, following with a distance measurement Carys didn't understand. She presumed it was farther out from the target planet than the *Bres* had appeared the first time around.

The pilot replied, "Copy, Captain."

"Comms," Bujold continued, "select one minute of the single-stream radio broadcasts we've been picking up, and prepare to transmit it at its original frequency to the planet surface."

"Aye, aye, Captain." The comms officer bent over his console.

Ambassador Barbier and Lieutenant-Colonel Broz sat at the rear of the captain in apparently designated seats. They ignored Carys, but the bridge crew were giving her sidelong glances, clearly wondering who she was and what she was doing here. She squirmed with discomfort, asking herself the same questions.

The pilot said, "Manoeuvre complete, Captain."

Carys hadn't felt a thing, and without an external view there was no indication the ship had transitioned to normal space except for the pilot's announcement.

"Comms," Bujold said, "transmit."

The officer stated his compliance.

Though no one moved or spoke, the atmosphere on the bridge altered. Silence stretched thin.

Nothing happened.

How long would it take for the aliens to react?

Perhaps they wouldn't even notice the transmission, given that it was in their own language.

Barbier asked, "How far out are we exactly, timewise?"

"We'll reach high orbit in around an hour," Bujold replied. "Ops?"

"Nothing to worry us yet, ma'am," the officer replied. "Scan data indicate three starships moving in orbital patterns, including the one that attacked us previously, plenty of satellites, and the same surface transmissions we were picking up before."

Broz said, "Seems odd to have starships simply circling the planet. I guess they could be cargo or research ships, but at least one has military capabilities. I wonder why."

"Exactly," Barbier commented. "They couldn't have been expecting us, yet they have defensive weaponry ready and waiting."

"It isn't so strange," Bujold replied. "Not so long ago, Earth had plenty of military starships."

"That was during the Crusader Wars," Broz countered. "Things have been scaled back considerably since then. Though it's true the Britannic Alliance have kept a few ships active in case of a surprise attack from outer space. That could be what's going on here."

Bujold drummed her fingers. "It's possible they're simply vigilant, or there could be a civil conflict going on and we just happened to arrive in the middle of it. Comms, repeat the same transmission."

A few moments later, the Operations Officer said, "Uhh, that got a reaction. All three starships have altered course."

"Let me guess," said Bujold. "They're heading in our direction."

"You got it, ma'am."

"Pilot, prepare to return us to the Red Zone at my order."

"Copy."

How long would it take for the alien ships to reach firing range? Carys was dying to know but she didn't dare ask. What was *she* even doing on the bridge? The Three Monkeys were carrying out their plan. She was merely a spectator. She would rather be in her cabin with Loki. He was probably wondering what had happened to her.

"Now," said Bujold, "we wait."

EIGHT

Half an hour had passed, and nothing had happened. There was nothing for Carys to do, and the only things to watch were the bridge crew performing unknown tasks and the holo of the *Bres* hanging in front of the pilot. The ship didn't even seem to change position as far as Carys could tell. Perhaps that was unsurprising. In the vastness of space there was nothing to steer around, and they were flying straight and true, heading for the aliens' vessels coming out to meet them.

She mulled over the idea she'd had earlier on how to communicate with the aliens. As nothing important seemed to be going on, she decided to give it a shot. "Captain, I was wondering—"

Bujold shot her a glance to freeze lava.

"Uhh... Permission to speak?"

Returning her attention to the screen on her armrest, Bujold growled, "Permission granted."

"I was wondering if, rather than transmitting the aliens' broadcast back at them, we might try using a universal language."

"*Universal* language?" Barbier scoffed. "Don't you mean galactic? Anyway, there are none. That's one of the points of the mission: to develop mutually comprehensible methods of communication."

Without looking up, Bujold said, "Continue, Ellis."

"I mean, I was thinking, even though birds don't respond to

other bird species' songs, they do react to their alarm calls. There are some sounds other birds make that most birds understand."

"Are you suggesting we tweet at them?" asked Barbier sarcastically.

"No, but..."

"For goodness sake," Bujold snapped, "spit it out."

"I was thinking... What about music? Humans who don't speak the same language can understand when a piece of music is sad or when it's happy and joyful."

Barbier snorted with derision.

"Or if not music then..." Carys faltered.

The captain regarded her with a raised eyebrow.

"We want to show them we don't mean any harm, right? We want to show our intention is to communicate with them. They have starships and can travel in space. One thing they must know about is maths. Is there a way we can transmit mathematical equations to them? Maybe they'll take it as a sign we want to share our knowledge."

Bujold turned her raised eyebrow to the comms officer. "*Is* there a way to transmit mathematical equations?"

The man frowned. "Possibly, Captain. Which ones did you have in mind?"

Barbier said, "I don't think there's a lot of point, even if it were possible. The essence of diplomacy is reaching common understanding and mutual accord. A jumble of numbers is meaningless and will only confuse matters. I believe Lieutenant-Colonel Broz has the right idea. If the aliens hear us repeat their own messages, they will know we're interested in them, in what they have to say, and that we're prepared to meet them at their level as a starting point."

Bujold drummed her fingers.

"Incoming message," the comms officer announced.

Backs straightened and all gazes focused on him.

"Oh, it's identical to the comm we sent. They're playing it back to us."

"Excellent," said Barbier. "We're already making progress."

"Please air it on the bridge," Bujold said. "I'm curious to hear what they sound like."

The comms officer replied, "It's audio, and it's outside normal human hearing range, ma'am. Too low. I can raise it if you like."

"Please do."

The man bent over his panel, and a few seconds later a shriek pierced Carys's ears. She winced. She was reminded of the screech of a barn owl, but this was louder and far more unnerving.

"Oops," said the comms officer. "I'll lower it."

The series of sounds that followed were somewhat like tweets but oddly discordant.

"That's enough," Bujold said. The noise stopped. "Re-transmit the same message."

While the officer obeyed, Carys pondered the aliens' speech. It tied in with their aerial environment. Low-pitched calls would carry long distances.

"One of their ships fired!" someone yelled. "Two seconds to impact."

"Pilot," Bujold snapped, "return us to the Red Zone."

Shit.

Would the *Bres* make it to safety before she was hit? The transition took longer than a couple of seconds. The ship had suffered damage the last time around.

The back of the pilot's neck was rigid as she focused on her holo guide.

"We should return fire," said Broz.

"No," Bujold replied.

A jolt jerked Carys's seat and ran through her body.

Bujold requested a damage report. Deck four maintenance level had been hit, casualties as yet unknown.

"More fire incoming," an officer announced.

"Captain...?" Broz pleaded.

"No," Bujold repeated. "We've been over this. I will not jeopardise this mission by engaging in an armed conflict. Pilot?"

The woman's head swivelled to face another of the bridge crew, who was staring hopelessly at his console. "Waiting for Catchpole, ma'am."

"Navigator?" Bujold demanded.

"Captain, I... I don't believe it."

"Navigator!"

The pilot seemed to need coordinates to enter the Red Zone.

"Ma'am," the navigator said helplessly, "our navigation system is down. And I have no points of reference, no gravitational data. All I know is the time and our velocity."

A second jolt hit.

"We must fire back!" Broz urged.

Barbier had paled and his eyes were wide.

"Pilot," Bujold said, "turn onto a reciprocal heading, maximum speed. Navigator, re-boot your system."

While the navigator vigorously jabbed at his console, a heavy force pushed Carys to one side. She clung to the armrests. The holo of the *Bres* had angled left. Then Carys was forced backward into her seat. What level of swing and acceleration was the pilot making for the compensators to be unable to cope?

"Fire incoming."

The gap between the announcement and the jolt was shorter. Their enemies were drawing nearer. The distance between the ships would have closed as the *Bres* about-faced.

Bujold requested a damage report. The officer barely had time to make it before Broz urged, "We must return fire. At this rate they'll shoot us to bits."

"Captain," said Barbier, "while I admire your resolve, our mission is not more important than the lives of our personnel."

"We will *not* return fire," Bujold declared.

"But if we run away like a dog with its tail between its legs," the ambassador countered, "it sends entirely the wrong message. We must maintain our dignity, our reputation, our status as a—"

"You will not question my authority!" the captain thundered. "Navigator?"

"The re-boot didn't work. Everything's dead. I'd have a better idea of where we are if I looked outside."

"They're firing again."

A crushing pressure stuck Carys to her seat. The jolt ran through her like she'd been kicked by a horse. Even she began to question Bujold's response to the attack. What weapons did the *Bres* carry? Heck, up until now Carys hadn't known the ship *had* weapons. But if she did, maybe shooting back wasn't such a bad idea. After all, the aliens had fired first. Humanity had come to them in peace. They were the aggressive ones.

If the *Bres* didn't return fire, could she outrun her attackers? If not, Bujold would have to change her mind or everyone would die.

How long would the captain's resolve last?

Broz was shaking his head. Carys lip-read the words 'shameful' and 'foolhardy'. If the ship survived, would Bujold survive as her commander?

"The enemy vessels are slowing down," an officer announced.

Silence reigned.

The man who had spoken gazed at his screen. "They're turning. Heading back to their planet."

A collective breath exhaled.

The navigator spluttered, "My system's working again. They must have been jamming it."

"It seems so," said Bujold. "Pilot, take us into the Red Zone at the earliest opportunity."

"Yes, ma'am."

Nine

There was no rarebit. Carys went back to the other end of the breakfast buffet and checked again, lifting the lids on the heated containers.

Where was the rarebit?

She needed it. Of all times, she needed it now.

Loki's talons bit uncomfortably into her shoulder.

"All right, I'm just looking, okay?"

She wished he hadn't come with her. Loki always attracted stares, and if there was one thing she hated it was attention. But he'd been unsettled lately, and that made him clingy. He was probably picking up on her mood. He'd always been sensitive.

The shadow of a figure crossed the staff area on the other side of the buffet.

"Hey!" she called.

It was unusual to see a human server. She wasn't going to let this rare opportunity go to waste. Not when it came to the availability of rarebit.

A man in a white ship's uniform stepped out, his expression a mixture of suspicion and annoyance. "Can I help you?"

"There's no rarebit. There's always rarebit at breakfast. Why isn't there any? Can you make me some?"

The man's eyebrows rose. "No...?"

"Why not? Isn't that your job?" A small part of her cringed at her rudeness. A very small and quiet part who didn't dare stand up to Disgruntled Carys.

The server smiled simperingly. "You misunderstand. I wasn't refusing. I don't know what you mean." Before she could answer, he continued, his gaze roaming the buffet, "Oh, cheese on toast?"

"Yes. Rarebit."

In truth, the *Bres*'s rarebit wasn't all that tasty. Despite the best efforts of the food technologists, none of them had ever been able to re-create the authentic taste of real cheese. Especially not tangy Caerphilly, melted and bubbling with a light brown crust on freshly toasted bread. But there was nothing else that reminded her so well of home and, with a little help from something with a taste that vaguely resembled rarebit, she could pretend.

"Cheese on toast is off the menu for the foreseeable future, I'm sorry to say." He didn't look remotely sorry.

"What? But... Why?!"

"The machine broke, and until it's fixed, there won't be any more of that particular breakfast dish. We have many more foods for you to choose from." He spread a hand expansively. "Sausages, bacon, eggs, congee, pickles, cereal—"

"I want rarebit! Wait. You have a machine just for rarebit?"

"Not only for cheese on toast. All toasted items. We've put in a ticket, but the mechanics are busy at the moment with the sanobots."

Carys clenched her fists impotently. Everything seemed to be breaking down. It was as if the manufacturers who had supplied the Fleet had only built the equipment to last as long as the voyage to Talman Prime. She felt like she was breaking down too. Pressure was building up inside her head. Her life had gone to shit. She needed her comfort food, but of all the thousands of dishes the *Bres* had to offer, rarebit was the one thing she couldn't get.

And there was something about the server's moustache that was deeply annoying.

"I'll leave you to make your selection," he said, retreating hastily.

She glared at the breakfast selection. Everything looked unappetising. Yet she had to eat something. She'd walked all the way to the refectory after a sleepless night replaying yesterday's attempted first contact farce over and over again in her head. She was full of anxiety and despair. If she went to work without eating she would be anxious, despairing *and* hungry.

"What's it to be, huh?" she murmured to Loki.

The refectory was filling up. Her ploy of arriving early to avoid other people had been defeated by the absence of rarebit and her own indecision.

Loki bobbed his head in the direction of the tray of bacon.

"Yeah, I bet you'd love some. It's far too salty for you, and you know it. Besides, you already ate."

"Is that bird sanitary?!" Another crew member had appeared beside her. The woman was so tall Carys could see right up her capacious nose.

Not dignifying the query with an answer, Carys grabbed the spoon for the scrambled eggs and piled them on her plate.

The woman's gaze followed her as she walked quickly to an empty table in the corner. Carys felt the stare burning into her back the entire journey. As she sat down she stared back, her expression defying the hawk-nosed bitch to report Loki's presence.

The woman turned her considerable organ upwards, and then focused on the breakfast items.

Carys ate fast. Loki was not, in fact, supposed to be here, and she didn't want either of them to get in trouble, considering her tenuous position on the ship. Her only way of—possibly—raising her status was by advising on how to deal with aerial aliens. That was going badly wrong. As well as having little to no idea on what to suggest, it looked like they would never even get the opportunity to make contact with the beings. They were too busy chasing the *Bres* away.

A shadow blocked the light.

Carys swallowed her final mouthful of scrambled egg and looked up. "Oh. Hi."

Her day hadn't gone well so far. She doubted the arrival of Mapper Robins was going to make it any better.

"Good morning," Robins said. "May I sit?"

"It's a free ship. You can sit anywhere. And you can have the table to yourself because I have to go and—"

"I don't eat breakfast," he interrupted as he took the opposite seat. "I want to speak to you. I was passing by and saw you sitting here alone, so I thought I would seize the moment."

She was about to make a lame excuse, but tiredness and a sense of defeat hit her hard. No words came out.

He took her silence as permission to carry on talking. "I'll get straight to the point. I have a proposal to make."

She groaned. "Not another one."

"I'm sorry? Oh, I see. You think I want to send you on a mission again. It's nothing like that."

"I wasn't even thinking you wanted to send me on a mission. Everyone seems to be proposing I do this, that, and the other these days. But I can't do any of it. I just wish you would all leave me alone with my birds. That, and rarebit. That's all I want. Literally all I want. It isn't too much to ask, is it?"

"That doesn't seem a lot," Robins replied warily. "However, if you would hear me out, you may be interested in what I have to say."

Carys pushed her plate to one side and let her arm flop heavily onto the tabletop. "I'm all ears."

"I'm looking for an apprentice and have been for quite some time. Mapping is a skilled profession. As well as a considerable practice, it requires certain rare personality traits. I believe you may fit the bill, and I'm not getting any younger. I need to begin training someone up or face the risk of leaving the ship without a fully trained Mapper. What do you think?"

She had only been half-listening, deep in her misery. The last of his words finally filtered through. She blinked. "You want me to be your apprentice?"

He lifted his hands. "Not exactly. I could show you some things. You could try casting a simple skein. See how you get on. Then we can both see how we feel about continuing."

"Me? Become a Mapper?"

"That isn't exactly what I said."

"I don't know. Birds are really my thing."

"Carys, you don't seem to be hearing me very well. Is something wrong?"

She shrugged. "I suppose I could give it a go. I mean, it beats being abandoned on an alien planet, right? Or being expected to offer advice on life forms you've never met. Or tending to animals that you know will never live out their natural lives." She rubbed her eye with the heel of her hand. "Can Loki come too?"

"I see no reason your bird cannot remain with you while you're at work But—"

"All right. I'll do it. When do I start?"

Ten

Before she could meet with Robins in his office, Carys had to feed her birds. At least they were living in a huge aviary rather than cages, so she didn't need to muck them out too. Guano was powerful stuff in concentration. Among the trees and undergrowth with insects, bacteria, and other small organisms, bird excrement just about disappeared by itself. Visitors might occasionally get hit by an off-white splat, but that was more entertaining than worrying.

But the aviary's days of being open to visitors were over, thanks to Purser Lineton. And, according to Captain Bujold, the days of the birds themselves were numbered.

With a heavy sigh, Carys took a sectioned tray from a shelf. Below the shelf stood a row of hessian sacks containing various grains, seeds, and nuts as well as specially formulated pellets of many kinds. When stocks ran low, it would be the pellets that would be hardest to replace. Other types of food humans also ate and could—theoretically—be taken from the ship's stores.

But Bujold would never allow it. She would never risk the crew's supplies for the sake of, as she had put it, useless animals.

Carys had always considered birds equally important as people, but she had to admit her opinion was in the minority.

She thrust a scoop into a sack and transferred the contents to a section of a tray. Later, she would go to the growing rooms to beg for green leafy vegetables, fruit scraps, and whatever else the growers could spare. Some birds only ate fresh food, which might be the first thing denied to them if things got tight.

She gave a long sniff, wiped her nose with her sleeve, and scooped grains into another section of the tray.

Faint tweets, squawks and screeches permeated the feed room from the aviary. The birds were hungry, and they'd seen her on her way in. They knew feeding time was imminent.

A short while later, she was ready to begin. As she left the office, she was almost mobbed as birds descended to eat from the tray even before she made it to the feeders. Others might have been intimidated, but she didn't mind the batting wings, questing beaks or grasping, scaled feet. The birds didn't want to eat *her*.

She filled the feeders and tossed the remainder of the food into the undergrowth, where certain species would have fun foraging. In the noise and bustle of concentrated eating, she watched her feathered friends, wondering what would become of them.

The truth was plainly evident: there had never been a proper plan for them when the Fleet set out. The birds had been brought along purely for entertainment purposes, to keep the rich passengers amused during their voyage, and nothing else.

Another realisation hit, and she blinked back tears. She'd become what she hated. She'd gone from rescuing and rehabilitating vulnerable creatures to being an agent of their destruction. She might as well have taken a position in an abattoir.

Robins beckoned when Carys walked into his office, inviting her to sit down beside him.

"This is the first time I've ever tried to teach someone my craft," he explained, "so it'll be a learning experience for both of us."

She settled uncomfortably into the seat. "You never had to tutor anyone before? I thought you were an expert. Don't the good Mappers get saddled with teaching duties?"

"The subject was broached, but in the end the higher-ups decided my time was best spent actually mapping. Then, after I signed up to the Fleet, the focus was even more on predictions, not passing on my knowledge. So..." he knitted his fingers and gazed intently into her eyes "...how are you feeling?"

She was about to answer *like absolute fucking shit* but then the oddness of his question struck. "Why? Does it matter?"

"It does indeed. Very much so. In the refectory you seemed... distracted. Casting a skein requires concentration, but that is only a small part of the process. In order to interpret the results accurately one must have a clear mind, uncluttered by personal concerns or heightened emotions. When we were speaking earlier you indicated you had rather a lot on your plate at the moment. And, if you don't mind me saying, you appear to be rather agitated and unhappy."

"Agitated and unhappy?" That was one way of putting it. But Robins's plan to train her up might provide a way out of some of her problems. She didn't want to put him off by admitting she wasn't in the best state right now. As a Mapper, she might have some control of her future. In fact... She frowned as the germ of an idea began to form. "I'm fine. I mean, some things are bothering me. But isn't that true for everyone? We're attempting to make contact with a species that wants to blow us out of the sky. Wouldn't that make the calmest person agitated and unhappy?"

"Fair point. The crew is definitely experiencing a dip in morale. However, if you were to become a Mapper, you would have to learn to put personal concerns aside. You see, mapping is as much an art as a science, and as such it's deeply susceptible to prejudices, biases, and other subjective influences. I thought you might make a suitable apprentice because you are level-headed, rational and intelligent, and you tend to keep to yourself. Close relationships are generally unwise in this profession. They can complicate matters exceedingly. It's a solitary calling."

As he'd been talking, his intense gaze hadn't wavered. When he broke eye contact Carys felt a sense of relief, as if she was a fly that had broken free from a spider's web. "Well, I prefer spending time by myself. As long as I have Loki and my books, I'm pretty happy."

Those penetrating eyes swept towards her face again. "You read books? The paper kind?"

"I do. I like the... the..." She swallowed, feeling stupid. Had she jeopardised what might be her only chance for a viable future?

"It's the feeling of turning the pages, and their smell, right?"

She nodded. "Something like that."

"Better and better," Robins murmured. "Now then," he went on in a business-like tone, "to work!"

He swept the wide desktop with his fingertips, and it sparked to life. Hundreds of buttons covered it. When she peered closer, she saw each button was marked by a tiny name. She recognised a few. All of them were aboard the *Bres*. But there were many names she didn't recognise. "Who are these people?"

"Some are crew on the *Balor* and *Banba*. Some are former passengers of the *Bres*. Some are people we left behind on Earth. A few are deceased." He pointed at a button.

Carys read *Lieutenant-Colonel Markham*. "Why do you include people who aren't even around anymore?"

"I don't always. But the repercussions of lives lived echo down the years, do they not? Markham's unfortunate decisions will impact what happens within the Fleet for a long time to come. We have hopefully learned from his mistakes. However, selecting who to include and who to leave out is part of the process. I will be honest with you, Carys, mapping is insanely complicated. To learn how to do it will require an enormous commitment. If you feel you aren't up to the task you should tell me now. I have other potential candidates I can approach."

"I want to do it." She had to do it. Was she coming across as overconfident? "I mean, I want to try." She noticed an anomaly on the console. "Whose is the red button?" It was too far away for her to read the name.

"That's me."

"Is it red so you make sure you always include yourself?"

"It's to make sure I *exclude* myself."

"Huh? But isn't what you do integral to what happens? Aren't you advising Bujold and the other captains about possible outcomes?"

"I am. But you must understand that what I do is predictive. And one of the easiest aspects of a skein to read is the sign of a probable demise."

"Ohhh. So you knew what would happen to Markham?"

"I knew that many futures included his death, yes. Naturally, I didn't inform him."

"Because he was an arsehole?"

Robins smiled. "Because it would have almost certainly triggered a chain of events leading to even more deaths. Markham was the type to go to great lengths to continue to live, sacrificing others in the hope of avoiding his fate. Almost certainly to no avail."

Her attention returned to the red button. "But you're not like that. You exclude yourself because you don't want to know when you might die."

He relaxed in his chair and folded his hands on his lap. "Have you heard of the tale of the traveller who tried to defeat Death?"

She shook her head.

"He was at the beginning of a long journey and on his first night, he stopped at a tavern. After eating his evening meal, he went to his room to sleep. But on his way there, to his great surprise he encountered Death in the corridor, scythe, hooded cloak and all. Death appeared equally surprised to see him and froze. The man saw his chance to get away and flew out of the tavern, abandoning his journey and his belongings, leapt onto his horse, and rode overnight back to his home town. Arriving at sunrise, he returned to his house, relieved to have evaded Death. He congratulated himself on his quick thinking and opened his front door, only to discover Death awaiting him.

"But," he stammered, "what are you doing here? I have ridden thirty miles to escape you!"

"Ah," Death replied, "that explains why I saw you at the tavern last night."

Carys softly snorted and said, "By trying to avoid dying he ran right into Death's arms."

"Exactly. It's an old story, but one with extreme significance for Mappers. When it comes to oneself, it's best for one's mental health to let things take their natural course. Which reminds me..." He sought out a button and held a finger on it, causing it to turn red. "That's you. I would strongly advise excluding yourself as you learn how to cast skeins."

"Noted."

"Let's begin with some earlier castings." He swiped the desktop again and a simple time and date display appeared. "The system is set to ship time here on the *Bres*. Anything else complicates matters exponentially. As the Fleet voyages through the galaxy and Red Zone, time passes differently elsewhere, including aboard the *Balor* and *Banba*." He set the date to several months ago. "That was when we were orbiting Talman Prime. Now we pick some names." Returning to the main screen, he selected several buttons. "And now we cast."

The room's lights dimmed and a set of fluorescent green dots appeared in the darkness, interconnected by very thick green lines. "Can you guess who the dots represent?"

"Not me or you," Carys joked. "Umm... Markham, Bujold, Purser Lineton, Coordinator Wulandri—"

"Captain Bujold and Markham are there, but think again. Whose actions were instrumental in the outcome of events back then?"

Her eyebrows shot up. "It's Setia, Miriam, Sheldrake, Waylis and...?"

"And a few others. Not Waylis. No Primians were programmed into the system at the time. I've added her since. See the connections? Try to focus on them while I add the entire ship's complement."

An array of thousands of dots and crossing lines of varying lengths and thickness shone brilliantly. Dazzled, Carys lifted a hand to her eyes. "How the hell do you interpret anything from that? It looks like utter chaos."

"It does, but it isn't. Look deeper, if you can. Can you still spot Setia and the others' connections now?"

She squinted as she searched the mess of filaments. After some moments, she replied, "I think so." She wasn't really sure, but she didn't want Robins to think she was too stupid to be a Mapper.

"It becomes easier with practice."

The skein vanished and the room's lights resumed their usual brightness.

"That's it?" Carys asked.

"That's far from *it*. But it's a beginning. There's a reason we don't use computers to interpret skeins. Even now, with their vast processing capacities, they cannot function like a human mind. When I read a skein, I am doing it with the knowledge of what has gone before, somewhat of an understanding of individual personalities and experiences, the potentialities of future events, my own correct or incorrect interpretations of previous skeins, and a host of other factors. If I were to be whimsical, I might say there's an element of necromancy about mapping, an otherness that's hard to put into words. Some Mappers go so far as to state they *feel* their way through a skein, allowing understanding to filter through from their subconscious. Certainly, I find it helpful to enter a trance-like state when attempting an interpretation."

Her shoulders slumped. It all sounded like gobbledegook. How could she ever hope to grasp the process? For a short while she'd forgotten her problems, distracted by curiosity about skein-mapping. But this was just as pie-in-the-sky as Bujold's proposal that she should advise on how to deal with the aerial aliens. It was hopeless. She was useless and all her birds were going to die.

Robins patted her back. "Perhaps that's enough for today. You don't need to decide now whether to enter apprenticeship. Go away and think about it. If you want to know more before coming to a decision, ask me. But once you begin, I would prefer that you don't back out. I must demand your complete commitment, nothing less."

"All right. I'll think about it."

Carys left Robins's office with a heavy heart.

Eleven

Days had passed since the second failed attempt to contact the aliens in the Polaris Ab system. Tensions had mounted aboard the *Bres*. Everyone had discovered how close the ship had come to being destroyed, and no one seemed to know what might happen next. Even Carys, in her role as consultant on the aerial species, was in the dark. She assumed more discussions had gone on within the Holy Trinity but she hadn't received an invitation to join them.

In the meantime, she'd taken Robins up on his offer to become a Mapper's apprentice. Her understanding of what mapping entailed was very much in its early stages, consisting mostly of a lot of nodding and of a growing appreciation of the massive task she'd undertaken. Between sessions with the Mapper and caring for her doomed birds, she had little free time. Nevertheless, Miriam had roped her into spending some of it with Waylis.

It wasn't that she disliked the Primian. In fact, she liked her quite a lot, preferring her to many humans she knew. It was just...

Unable to define the source of her discomfort, she squared her shoulders and pressed Waylis's door chime.

After settling her with a seat and a drink, the Denisovan had plenty of questions lined up for her, mostly relating to Earth and its history. She'd clearly been anticipating Carys's arrival. Carys answered the first few as well as she could, but then she said, "You know you can find out all this stuff by searching the ship's database? I'm pretty sure everything you want to know is in there."

"I know, but it's different hearing it from you. I don't know if I can explain, but when I read the history files it's just dry information. Hearing it from a person brings it to life, makes it more meaningful. Does that make sense?"

"I suppose so." Carys pretended to smooth back her hair, surreptitiously tapping her ear comm for a time check. She'd only been here ten minutes. Fifty minutes to go. "What else do you want to know?"

"Something that definitely isn't on the database. I'm curious about that." Waylis pointed at the insignia on Carys's uniform: a symbol depicting three hares running in a circle, joined at the centre by three ears.

Carys touched the badge. "I remember you saying the same symbol appears on Prime."

"It does. It's carved into rocks in several places, but no one understands where it comes from or what it means. What's its significance on Earth?"

"Well, the animals are hares, a smallish animal. And the symbol is a visual puzzle. Hares have two ears, but though these appear to have two ears they only share three ears between them. The symbol is old on Earth too, and it appears in a range of places—places that historians don't think were connected when the symbols were carved, so that's another puzzle. In some countries the hares are thought to represent peace and tranquillity. In my country it's said they represent three versions of the Christian god. Christianity is a religion."

"Thank you." Waylis was making notes. "That gives me a lot to think about, and your mention of religion reminds me of something else, I'm also interested in the Crusader Wars. You must have been a child while they were going on. Do you remember much?"

Carys stiffened. "Not really. Like you said, I was only a kid."

Waylis peered at her. "Did I say something wrong?"

"It's fine, but I don't know a lot about the war."

"Right... I thought you came from the West Britannic Isles. Wasn't your country invaded?"

"I don't know anything about the war!" Carys snapped. "Ask me about something else."

"Okay," Waylis replied hesitantly. "In that case—"

The door chime sounded.

Carys relaxed.

Setia and Miriam had arrived, but Carys was confused. Were they early for their babysitting shift?

"Carys," Setia said, "you're here too. What a coincidence."

Damn Setia and her sarcastic humour. "Yeah, big coincidence. Look, if you guys don't mind, I'll go. I'm really busy." Carys rose to her feet.

"Busy organising the Fleet's next attempt at contact?" Setia had lifted one eyebrow, giving her maddening know-it-all look. She'd also sidled closer to the door, as if to block Carys's exit.

"What are you talking about?"

Miriam said gently, "We know you've been involved in the planning, and we'd like to know what's going on. The captain has the ship on an information diet. In your position, you must know something. You can tell us. We won't pass it on."

Setia, Miriam and Waylis regarded her expectantly.

It was a set-up.

"You and Setia came here now on purpose, didn't you?" Carys accused. "Planning to interrogate me."

"You *are* rather hard to talk to," said Miriam.

"And while you're at it," Setia said, "why have you been spending so much time with Robins? Is that something to do with the plan?"

"There is no plan! Or if there is, I don't know anything about it. What makes you think I know so much? I'm just a flipping bird keeper." The cheek! She'd come to keep Waylis company when she could barely spare the time, only to find herself under cross-examination. "And if I did know anything, why the hell would I tell *you* about it?"

"Because we're your friends," Miriam murmured reproachfully.

"I don't know anything," she reiterated, her jaw clenched.

Setia sat down on a sofa, crossed her legs and examined the fingernails of her right hand. "You're being economical with the truth. Don't deny it. Not so long ago, after I dragged your drunken arse back to your cabin, you were spotted going to a meeting with the captain, the new lieutenant-colonel and some other guy." Her eyebrow lifted again. "In your pyjamas. And you were on the bridge when we dropped into normal space and got attacked for the second time. You've been in the thick of it right from the start, and, honestly, it's a complete mystery as to why you're keeping quiet about it all." She tilted her head, fixing Carys with a glare.

"That was you?"

"That was me what?"

"You're the reason I woke up in my cabin after I..."

"After you got shit-faced? Yes, it was me. After I found you passed out in a lift, I carried you to your new place and tucked you into bed. No need to thank me."

Setia's story made sense. She was certainly strong enough to carry someone her own weight across the ship, and it explained Carys waking up in her bunk. "What about Sheldrake? Did you take him home too?" She hadn't seen the ex-corporal since their drinking session.

"Sheldrake was with you? He must have left before I got there."

"How's he doing?" Miriam asked.

But before she answered, another realisation sunk in. Carys asked, "You know about the meeting with the captain?"

"The entire ship knows about it," Setia retorted. "Your forced march in your jammies was hot gossip. Don't forget that no one around here has anything better to do with their time than talk about everyone else. We want you to fill us in on what happened, explain what you've been doing with Robins and tell us what Bujold has planned. Is the ship going to rejoin the rest of the Fleet? Is the captain going to give up on Polaris Ab?"

"I don't know!"

Setia regarded her from under hooded eyes. "I think you do."

With a sense of defeat, Carys slumped once more into her seat and sank her face into her hands, muttering, "All right. I'll tell you what I know."

She'd been avoiding telling her friends about what Bujold had said. She'd delivered the news about the imminent expulsion of unwanted passengers to Sheldrake, and that hadn't gone well. She didn't want to tell Setia, Miriam and Waylis that the captain most likely intended to oust them too. Setia had sympathised—as far as she was capable of sympathising—when Carys had complained about her precarious position on the ship. Neither of them had known at the time that Setia was in the same insecure state.

Now, not only was she supposed to convey the bad news, she also had to tell them she'd probably secured her own future by becoming

Robins's apprentice. Bujold might expel the aviary keeper and her useless avians. She would not expel a trainee Mapper.

Carys looked from Setia to Miriam to Waylis. She opened her mouth to speak.

"Ms Ellis, report to the bridge immediately."

Carys started in shock. The captain's command had arrived via her ear comm, bursting through the words forming in her mind. She'd forgotten she was wearing the device, against her usual habit. Bujold also apparently had the ability to override the comm request function. If the captain wanted to speak to you, there was no formality of accepting the communication.

"Yes?" Setia asked. "You were going to say...?"

"I'm sorry. I have to go." Carys jumped up.

"What?! You can't just leave," Setia protested. "Why are you in such a hurry? What's going on?"

"I can't tell you. Or maybe I can, but it'll have to wait until later." She hurried out.

If there *was* another time. It seemed the captain and her cronies had come up with a fresh strategy for approaching the intelligent aliens of Polaris Ab. Carys hoped it was a good one.

Twelve

The captain's orders for all non-active personnel to move to the ship's interior echoed through the passageways. Stepping onto the bridge, Carys felt as though she was walking through treacle. All heads were down save four: the pilot—forced by her job to look forward—and Lieutenant-Colonel Broz and Ambassador Barbier, stiff-backed with tension. Broz's features twisted with barely suppressed fury. Barbier was pale and his skin softly gleamed with sweat. His knuckles were white as he gripped his armrests.

Only Captain Bujold was calm. She seemed almost serene, in fact, as if entirely in her element. Her gaze flicked to Carys. "Resume your former seat, Ellis. We are about to make a third attempt at contact."

"Third time lucky," Barbier commented in a strangled tone. "Captain, I still think, if you don't mind me saying—"

"I do mind. Please be silent. Ellis?"

Carys had halted midway to the place she'd sat before, fascinated by the exchange between Bujold and the ambassador. What was going on? What was different this time around? Were they about to be blown to pieces? She dropped into her seat, wondering if she was about to live out the final few hours of her life. So much for her plan to become indispensable as a Mapper.

If the *Bres* dropped into normal space near the aliens' planet, wouldn't they jam the navigation system again and attack? Only this time they might not give up their pursuit.

Bujold was insane.

"Pilot," the captain said, "return us to normal space at the same coordinates as our first entry to the system."

"Copy, Captain."

The first attempt had put them up close to the planet. There would be no waiting around this time.

"Ellis," Bujold said, "we recently received intelligence that has thrown a new light on things. The *Balor* comm'd to let us know they're in communication with the target species inhabiting the Polaris B system. It turns out the life forms of Polaris B and Polaris Ab are aware of the other's existence. Neither species has invented interstellar travel, so they have not visited each other, which is probably just as well. It turns out their attitudes are mutually hostile. They've been sending messages of hatred and belligerent intent for decades."

"*Ohhh!*"

"I see you understand what has happened."

Carys said, "The broadcasts we picked up?"

"Exactly."

"So the recording we played back to them was a declaration of war or something?"

"Who knows? But from their reaction it does seem likely."

"No wonder they came after us."

"No wonder indeed. So I have decided that this time we will go along with your suggestion of sending them mathematical equations. We'll see. It may do the trick."

"Hold on," Carys spluttered, alarmed. "It was only a thought. I mean, I don't have any idea—"

"No one will hold you responsible if the attempt fails."

Broz muttered, "Assuming anyone is left alive."

"Wait," Carys said. "If we know the aliens we're trying to contact have been sending antagonistic messages to the ones at Polaris B, can't we ask them to help us translate their language? I mean, they must understand it."

"The *Balor* informed us they do understand it, but they refuse to offer us any help with—I quote—*the evil freaks*."

"Entering normal space," the pilot announced.

"Comms, begin transmission," Bujold ordered. "Repeat it until I tell you otherwise."

"Aye aye, Captain."

What equations were being sent out?

$E = mc^2$?

The Law of Gravity?

Schrodinger's Equation?

Maths wasn't Carys's strong suit. Biology was more her thing. She couldn't begin to guess what formulas the captain might have selected or for what reason.

"Alien ships heading our way," Ops reported.

Broz glared at the back of Bujold's head. "It didn't take long to get their attention."

If the captain heard him or felt his eyes boring into her skull, she didn't react. She told the pilot to prepare to return the ship to the Red Zone.

Carys wasn't sure what the point was. The aliens would surely kill the *Bres*'s navigation systems again, leaving them sitting ducks. Unless Bujold intended to retaliate if the ship was attacked again?

"Fire incoming!" an officer blurted.

"Dammit!" Broz yelled. "It isn't working!"

"Hold your tongue, Lieutenant-Colonel," Bujold retorted, "or I will have you removed from the bridge."

The threat appeared to send him into a rage. He turned puce and he bared his teeth. Yet he remained silent.

Barbier's olive skin had faded to almost white.

A blow buffeted the ship. Carys rocked in her seat. A secondary shock ran through her: her nerves thrilling at the nearness of her death.

"More fire!"

"I insist we fire back!" Broz yelled, leaping to his feet.

"Sit down," the captain snapped.

"I will not. You're mad! You're going to get us all killed!"

Bujold's lips moved as she spoke softly via comm.

The *Bres* jerked once more, as if flicked by a gigantic finger. Carys held on grimly. On the one hand, the captain's determination to fulfil her mission was admirable. On the other, Carys had a feeling Broz was right.

"Hull breach, deck three," an officer reported.

Bujold dispatched a team to deal with it.

"Please, Captain," Barbier whined, "listen to reason. Don't sacrifice us all on the altar of your stubbornness. If you won't return fire, at least consider leaving orbit. That will show them we mean no harm. They may give up the chase as they did before."

"Wasn't it you who said we shouldn't run like a dog with its tail between its legs?" Bujold asked sardonically. Throughout the last few minutes she'd betrayed no emotions, appearing as tranquil as a lake on a windless day.

The bridge doors opened and three guards appeared.

Without any warning, the ship received a third hit. The impact shuddered through the bridge. Terrified glances passed between the officers as they gripped their consoles. Carys's heart was in her mouth. All her worries about her birds and her future were stripped away. Her life and all the decisions she'd made, right or wrong, had concentrated down to this moment.

Broz's mouth gaped as he realised the guards were here for him. "How dare you! I will not—" His next words were cut short as he was seized. "Let me go! I order you to release me!"

An undignified tussle ensued. The guards might have exerted control over their superior officer more quickly, but they appeared reluctant to manhandle him.

"I'll have you stripped of your position, Bujold!" Broz screamed. "I'll have you courtmartialed and executed!"

The captain turned away from the fight and asked for an update on the positions of the aliens' ships.

"They're basically surrounding us," came the reply.

A report of depressurisation on deck five came in.

"Don't do this," Barbier sobbed. "Please, we must defend ourselves or leave, and soon, before they hit the engines."

"Lift!" Carys exclaimed, the word leaving her lips almost before she understood what she was saying.

Bujold's attention pivoted to her. "What?"

"They fly, right? Send them the formula to calculate lift. Oh, what is it?" Carys flicked her hands in frustration.

The captain asked the bridge, "Does anyone know the mathematical formula to calculate lift in flight?"

Blank stares greeted her.

"Bernoulli's equation!" The phrase exited Carys's mouth like ejected vomit. "I don't know what it is, but you could look it up."

Every single officer frantically consulted their interfaces. The first to find it shouted out his discovery, and the comms officer hastily converted the information into a message.

While this was going on, the *Bres* received her fifth hit. Barbier slid from his seat and fell to his knees. The guards had subdued Broz and the lieutenant-colonel was on his way out of the bridge, slumped between his captors, head hanging in defeat. His short tenure leading the ship's military was over.

But no one was paying much attention to the disgraced officer or pathetic ambassador. A pregnant pause swelled as everyone awaited the results of the most recent transmission.

The pause stretched out tight as piano wire.

Carys began to feel faint. She realised she'd been holding her breath. She purposefully exhaled.

Still, no answer came.

Yet the firing had stopped. The new equation had had an effect. What that effect might be remained unknown as seconds and then minutes passed.

Barbier seemed to come to his senses. He got to his feet, adjusted his clothing and resumed his seat, acting as though he hadn't fallen to the deck in terror just moments ago.

Bujold gave Carys a look that spoke of gratitude and approval.

Carys's attitude towards the captain warmed, but then she remembered this was the woman who wanted to kill all the aviary birds. Carys looked away.

"Something's emerging from one of the ships," an officer announced. "It's heading right for us."

"A missile?" the captain asked.

"No, it's travelling too slowly. I think... I think it might be a shuttle."

"They're sending out a delegation," said Barbier. "Excellent. I will prepare to meet them." He stood up. "Your plan appears to have worked, Captain. Congratulations. I have to confess, I had my doubts for a short while."

Bujold threw him a derogatory glance. "Sit down, Ambassador. It will take some time before the shuttle arrives, and then several checks and procedures must be completed before alien life forms may come aboard. You have a long wait before you can meet our visitors."

Deflated, Barbier sank into his seat.

Thirteen

Sensing that Bujold would want to involve her in interactions with the aliens, Carys waited to make her move. A while later, when the captain was facing away, deep in conversation with Barbier, she rose to her feet and strolled casually in the direction of the exit.

"Return to your seat, Ellis," Bujold said calmly.

She hadn't even looked around!

Did the captain have a brain/net interface like the pilot, and a visual feed from the ship's security cameras? Carys slunk back. Disconsolate, she twiddled her thumbs. Loki was calling to her again. She hadn't seen him for ages and he was probably lonely as well as hungry.

Bujold concluded her chat with the ambassador, who left, and then she walked to Carys's side. Looking down she said, without rancour, "Until I dismiss you, assume your presence is required. Is that clear?"

Carys nodded.

"Good. You may not be one of the ship's military, but you are nevertheless a crew member and under my command at all times."

"I get it."

Bujold's eyebrows lifted.

"I understand, Captain."

"The suggestion you made earlier may have been integral to the success of the first stage of our mission. That was quick thinking. My estimation that you had a unique insight to offer was correct, but..."

Here it is.

"...your involvement is far from over. I'm guessing you were trying to sneak away just now because you don't want to help me. Is that it?"

The discussion was becoming far too close to the knuckle for Carys's liking. She glanced around the bridge. The officers were pretending they were very busy and couldn't hear a word of what was being said.

Sod it.

If Bujold wanted a frank answer she was going to get it. "Why should I help someone who wants to kill my birds?"

"Ah, that's it." The captain's features cleared. "I did explain the situation—"

"Yeah, very well, thanks."

"I see you continue to struggle to accept the inevitability of their fate."

Carys scowled, repeating the captain's words in her head in a mocking tone.

"Never mind," Bujold continued brusquely. "I'm sure you will understand eventually. In the meantime, I expect you to take a lead role in communications with the aliens. Ambassador Barbier will be your immediate superior. You must advise him as he establishes a relationship. Naturally, exactly what bumps he may hit on the road are nebulous as yet. I have instructed him to pay careful attention to what you say. If you believe he is acting contrary to your advice, you must..."

The captain's words faded as Carys's mind drifted to Loki and then the aviary birds. How much time would her new role as Barbier's advisor take up? Though she was curious to meet the flying aliens, the thought of spending long periods in the ambassador's company set her teeth on edge. More importantly, it would take her away from caring for her birds. No one else had the knowledge or expertise to fill in for a long period, and there was no time to train anyone.

A realisation hit. "I can't help you," she blurted. "Robins is teaching me to be a Mapper."

This got the attention of the bridge crew. They stopped pretending and all heads turned to her and the captain.

"Is he indeed?" Bujold asked, a crease of annoyance forming between her eyebrows. "This is the first I've heard of it."

"He selected me for personal qualities he said he couldn't find in anyone else. I'm indispensable, I'm afraid, so I can't—"

"Hmpf." Bujold's expression transformed to one of amusement. "Nice try, Ellis. I will speak to Mapper Robins. Wait here while I..." Her gaze became distant as she apparently listened to a comm. "Really?" she commented to the unknown speaker. "I see. Interesting. Standby for further orders."

Her attention returned to Carys. "There's been a strange turn of events. The shuttle appears to be empty."

"Oh, well, that's great. You don't need me after all."

"On the contrary, I need you more than ever. But before I decide what to do with you, I want to discover what's in the vessel's interior. That will take me a while. You have half an hour to complete any urgent tasks, then you must go to the shuttle bay. I will meet you and the ambassador there."

The *Bres*'s engineers had rigged up an umbilicus from the shuttle bay airlock, joining the ship with the aliens' vessel. Carys was impressed at the speed with which they'd completed the task. Then she realised they must have prepared for exactly this eventuality. Shuttles built by other life forms wouldn't necessarily be able to enter a human-made shuttle bay. Either their dimensions could be wrong or—

"It's too big," Barbier commented, noticing her appraising the umbilicus entrance. "The shuttle is vast. Lord knows what size the creatures are."

"Have you seen what's in it?"

Bujold was busy talking with a group of seven or eight soldiers. She hadn't mentioned anything about the shuttle.

"Surprisingly," the ambassador replied, "the area open to inspection is comparatively small, considering the overall size of the thing. Most of the volume must be taken up by the engine. Unless the drones missed something."

"Drones?"

"Military surveillance drones were used for the initial search. There's very little to see. Just empty, metal-walled spaces. Readings indicate the atmosphere is breathable, but there's no a-grav."

Bujold approached. "Ellis, I was planning on sending you in with armed support to see if you could glean anything not apparent from the drone footage, but I've changed my mind. It occurred to me there's only one reason the aliens would send an empty shuttle, and that's in order to transport some of us to them."

"Whoa," Carys murmured.

"I'm convinced the moment anyone steps aboard that thing it will seal its hatch and depart. Therefore I must think carefully on how to proceed. Ambassador, it wouldn't be wise for you to be present for first contact with this species. They jumped immediately to a hostile response as soon as our ship appeared. That was somewhat understandable, given the state of affairs with their nearest neighbour. I imagine they thought we were from the Polaris B system and about to attack. Nevertheless, they're clearly capable of deadly aggression. Therefore I would prefer not to risk my only highly experienced diplomat until a reliably friendly relationship has been established."

Carys had a strong feeling about where Bujold's reasoning was heading, and she didn't like it.

The captain faced her.

"But you're fine with risking *me*, right?"

Bujold's features hardened. "Insubordination won't get you anywhere, Ellis, and it certainly won't prolong the lives of your precious birds. I appreciated your input on the bridge earlier, but my gratitude has its bounds. Your guess that I want you to meet these creatures is correct. However, I won't be sending you in alone. As well as the military team here, I want to include some civilians. You may select one person to go with you. Think on it. I will take your suggestion into strong consideration, though I retain final say on who it should be. You have one hour."

"You want me to pick a friend to take into danger with me?"

"Some people would consider meeting a new intelligent life form an honour and a privilege."

"Some people are very stupid."

The captain gave a sardonic snort. "I will tell them *I* chose them for the mission. You won't have to take the blame."

"*Thanks.*"

As Bujold left, Carys considered who to nominate, if anyone. It didn't seem fair to drag someone else into the dicey venture. On the other hand, she might need all the help she could get. And a familiar face would be a comfort in a strange environment. One thing was for sure, she wouldn't be taking Loki with her this time. Not after what happened on Talman Prime.

How long would the mission take? She had no idea, and neither did Bujold by all appearances.

"Lucky you," Barbier remarked, drawing her from her thoughts.

"Really?"

"Of course. I would love to be in your place. I'm dying to meet these aliens."

Carys stared at him. She was reminded of Lieutenant-Colonel Markham prior to the first foray to Prime, expressing his regret that he wasn't coming along. His words had rung as hollow then as Barbier's did now.

"Let's hope it doesn't come to that." She had an hour to pack essentials, organise temporary care for her birds, and choose someone to accompany her. As she exited the bay, an idea popped into her head. She opened a comm.

"Carys," Robins replied. "Exciting news. It looks as though the citizens of Polaris Ab may be the second members of the Galactic Federation."

"You heard, huh? I suppose you also know Bujold wants me to be one of the team to make first contact."

"I had guessed you might be favoured."

"Yeah, big favour. Look, the captain wants me to pick a companion, and I was wondering if you could cast a skein to see who would be best."

"I can try," he replied doubtfully. "However, my skeins are all over the place at the moment. It seems the number of variable factors is huge. But..." he paused before continuing "...do you need me to tell you? Isn't it obvious who would be most suitable?"

She understood, and her brisk walk transformed into a trudge. "You're right. *Damn.*"

Fourteen

"I don't believe it." Setia dumped her backpack on the shuttle bay deck. "Bujold has a whole shipful of personnel to choose from. Why me? Didn't I do enough on Prime?" She inspected the pulse rifle she'd been allocated.

"Why wouldn't she pick you?" Carys countered. "You're super strong and you're trained in combat."

Setia gestured at the military contingent, running through equipment checks. "Uhhh...?"

"Okay, but I don't think any of them are as strong as you. Sheldrake certainly didn't seem to think so."

"I heard their armour had a power boost. Besides, my strength isn't important. If we end up on that low-grav planet, everyone will be strong. Even you won't be weak."

"What do you mean, *even me*?"

"Come on. You have to admit you won't be winning a weightlifting contest any time soon."

Carys gritted her teeth as she shoved rations into her pack, already regretting her choice of companion. Setia would be handy to have around if it came to a fight, but she had the diplomacy of a bull elephant in musth. Yet she also seemed to have a thing for protecting people she thought were vulnerable, like Waylis. Carys straightened up. "Yeah, now I think about it, you have a point. I'm utterly helpless."

"Was this Robins's idea?" Setia asked. "You two have spent a lot of time together lately, which you never got around to explaining. What have you been doing? Am I here because he saw something on his skeins?"

"The skeins are unpredictable right now, as you already know. You told me so when Bujold made her announcement about the Fleet's mission, remember? Now stop bloody interrogating me. I don't want to do this any more than you."

The captain entered the bay and headed for the military contingent.

Setia commented, "It's a shame she didn't pick Sheldrake."

"Sheldrake? Why? I mean, he's okay, but—"

"Not because he would be good for this trip. He would, but I meant for his own sake. This could have been his chance to prove himself and get back into Bujold's good books. Then he wouldn't have to sneak around all the time."

Carys bit her lip. "You're right. I didn't think of that."

Bujold had reached the military group. She addressed a burly, bull necked man. "Major Torres, I don't think I've introduced you to Carys Ellis and Setia Zees. They're veterans of the mission to Talman Prime."

Torres gave them a curt nod.

"Ellis, Zees, you'll be under the major's command for the duration of the assignment. You'll also be working with Dr Moody." The man she indicated was tall and thin and had the face of a twelve year old. A heavy fringe of white-blond hair didn't help the resemblance.

"You've received your briefings, gentlemen," the captain continued to Torres and Moody. Then she turned to the group as a whole. "The first objective is to thoroughly examine the shuttle's interior. If—as we guess—the vessel disengages and flies to one of the alien ships or the planet surface, your second objective is to establish peaceful contact. You are all armed, but you may only discharge your weapons when under immediate threat of physical harm. You will find the latest scan data of the planet on your interfaces. Naturally, you will be able to comm the ship at all times as well as each other."

Her eyes momentarily flicked upward. "You will enter the shuttle in eleven minutes and thirty-eight seconds. I'm clearing the bay in case of depressurisation. Good luck, everyone."

Depressurisation?

Setia gave Carys a worried look. She apparently had the same concern. What was Bujold expecting might happen? Could the shuttle be booby-trapped? Might it not be a shuttle at all?

"Hey, Captain!" Carys called out.

Bujold halted and turned.

Carys hurried over. Was she doing the right thing? She'd already put Setia in danger. She had only a second to decide. She blurted, "I want Corporal Sheldrake to come along too."

What was the man's first name? She was surprised to realise she didn't know.

"*Former* Corporal Sheldrake? I thought he disembarked at Talman Prime." There was the slightest hint of amusement in the captain's eyes. Bujold was playing with her.

"Well, he didn't." *As you know perfectly well.* "Can he join the team? It's very important," Carys added uncertainly, wracking her brain for something to back up her assertion.

"Because...?" The captain's left eyebrow lifted.

"Because... That's what the skeins say."

"Really." Disbelief leadened Bujold's words.

"Really. Robins comm'd me just now. You know I'm his apprentice. He tells me everything. I'm sure you'll hear from him in a minute."

Shaking her head, Bujold walked away.

Carys's heart sank. Setia had been right. This could have been Sheldrake's opportunity to redeem himself. If only she'd realised it in time. On the other hand, if the mission went south she might have saved his life.

"You can have him," the captain called over her shoulder, "if he can get here in the next ten minutes."

Sheldrake made it just in time, bursting through the shuttle bay entrance a few seconds before the door was due to be locked, clutching a duffel bag. He looked unusually dishevelled. Had he been drinking again, drowning his sorrows now he'd discovered the rumours were wrong, that the target planet was not only habitable but inhabited, and he might be permanently put off the ship after all?

His features displayed a mixture of gratitude and fear, as if he were already regretting his last-minute decision to come along. Then his face disappeared. The silver, liquid metal alloy of his EVA suit had slid over his body, up his neck and over his head, creating a dark visor. His suit was a civilian's like Carys, Setia and Moody's.

"My team will go in first," Major Torres announced over comm. "No one else is to take a step closer to the umbilicus until I give the all clear. Is that understood?"

Carys's murmur of assent joined the others.

The military men and women, also suited up, filed into the airlock. With a sense of leaden finality the hatch shut and heavy bolts slid home.

"We might end up not going anywhere," Setia commented. "That thing could depart as soon as Torres and his grunts board."

"I certainly hope not," Moody replied. "How extremely disappointing."

"Or it might explode," Setia continued sourly.

"I thought the same," Carys said, "that the aliens might have sent it here to blow a massive hole in the hull, but if they want to destroy our ship they don't need to go to so much trouble. Before they stopped firing we were taking a beating, and the *Bres* couldn't disappear to the Red Zone. The aliens jammed our navigation like the last time we were here. The captain took a huge risk to try to make contact again."

"But we could have fired back, right?" said Setia.

Carys shrugged. "I don't know the *Bres*'s military capabilities, and the only person who might be able to tell us is in there." She nodded at the closed hatch.

"The ship has pulse emitters," said Sheldrake. "She can defend herself if attacked, but I don't know much more than that."

While they'd been talking Moody had crossed to the umbilicus entrance. "What's taking so long?" He peered into the tiny window.

"I wouldn't stand so close if I were you," Setia warned.

"If the alien ship blows," Sheldrake said, "it won't make a helluva lot of difference where we're standing."

"I can't see a thing," Moody complained, "just the—"

"All clear," Torres announced over comm.

A beat later, the hatch locks gave metallic clunks and it opened.

"At last!" Moody exclaimed. The military team had only been gone a minute or so. The scientist stepped through the opening.

"I suppose it's our turn." Carys followed, holdall on one shoulder and pulse rifle on the other.

A couple of metres into the umbilicus her feet left the floor and she floated into mid-air. She grabbed one of the metal bars on the wall and began hauling herself along in Moody's wake. Her luggage and weapon became encumbrances in the zero-g, alternately bumping her and the umbilicus.

A tremor ran through the handholds. Torres must have remotely shut the shuttle bay hatch. They were sealed inside, the portal to the alien ship their only exit.

Setia passed opposite Carys, moving effortlessly from bar to bar. *Show off.*

Carys traversed a wide curve and a dark hole came into sight, lit by the beams from the soldiers' helmets. Moody disappeared into it. Setia was waiting outside, holding a bar lightly. She tapped her visor.

Carys couldn't figure out why so she ignored her.

Setia tapped her visor again. "Check your HUD."

Carys hadn't been paying attention to the figures displayed in a corner of her vision. The percentages of atmospheric gases were changing. The level of oxygen was increasing and the amount of CO_2 was dropping.

"The air on their planet must be different," Setia said.

"But still breathable."

"Let's hope so."

"We might not even go there."

Carys floated past Setia into the aliens' shuttle, entering a simple metal box a few metres square and crowded with bodies. Here, there was nothing to hold onto. She collided with someone.

"Hey, watch where you're going!" her victim complained.

Carys hadn't mastered the art of comming strangers and she didn't feel like apologising anyway.

Sheldrake cursed. "This place is tiny." His form blocked the light from the umbilicus.

"Everyone move inside," Torres ordered.

There was a general jumble as bodies bumped and jostled. Absent of gravity, it was free season on locations in the small chamber.

"There's something in here," Moody announced.

All movement ceased.

Carys spotted the lanky form of the scientist in a corner. He was holding a portable scanning device.

"What kind of something, Doctor?" Torres asked tetchily.

"It's organic, but that's as much as I know. The constituents don't match anything on the database. That may be why the drones didn't pick it up."

"Is it alive?"

"Impossible to say, sorry."

"Why can't we see it?"

"Perhaps because the light is too low? My scanner has detected its presence, but I don't know exactly where it is. I mean, if we looked around a little..."

"Everyone out," Torres snapped. "Now."

As the first person to obey floated towards the exit it slid shut, cutting off the light from the umbilicus.

The alien ship juddered and moved. Acceleration pushed its human occupants against the metal wall.

Carys had a vision of the shuttle tearing away from the *Bres*. The Fleet's ship, her home and the aviary shrank into the distance.

Fifteen

Someone's boot pressed into Carys's backside. She wriggled free, only for another boot to plant itself on her visor. She shoved the attached offending leg away from her face.

"Ugh!" she muttered. "Haven't those creatures heard of inertia dampeners?"

Wedged tightly in a mass of bodies squeezed against a bulkhead, complaining was her sole outlet. The rest of her team also squirmed, their personal space not just invaded but beaten into submission and utterly vanquished. Luckily, their EVA suits prevented even closer contact. Nevertheless, Carys drew her elbows into her stomach and closed her fists under her chin.

The bodies she was far too near wouldn't stop moving. Knees were thrust into her back and shoulders scraped against her side. As they adjusted their positions, she silently resented them.

"Is that you, Carys?" Setia's voice sounded tinny and weird, not like it should if she'd spoken over comm.

"Yeah, where are you?"

A knock resounded through Carys's head.

"Our helmets are touching," Setia explained. "I thought I would try an experiment."

"I'm glad this situation is working for you."

"Helps to pass the time."

Several minutes had gone by as the aliens' shuttle conveyed them to their unknown destination. The only words Major Torres had uttered was to advise everyone to stay calm and take care not to accidentally deactivate their weapons' safeties. The second piece of advice had introduced a potential scenario of which—up until then—Carys had been blissfully ignorant.

How long would the journey last?

Where were they going?

Would they ever be able to look each other in the eyes again?

"Once we get out of this human pancake," said Setia, "and if we get the opportunity, what do you say to you, me and Sheldrake splitting off from the others?"

"I say, firstly, please talk to me the normal way and, secondly, no way am I parting company with our military friends. What are you *thinking*? If the aliens attack I'd rather be behind a bunch of armed, trained men and women than off alone somewhere."

"Maybe, but don't you think we're more likely to be attacked if we're seen as a threat?" Setia maddeningly continued to talk via their helmets. She went on, "Don't forget this is first contact. Both sides are gonna be jumpy, wondering if the other is out to kill them. I'd rather not be with the hoo-ra guys in that situation. You know what they're like. When Markham wanted to commit genocide they were right behind him."

Carys wasn't sure that was a fair assessment of the ship's military. She guessed that, if asked, most would say they were only following orders, and, generally, she would feel a whole lot safer with Torres and his grunts. Yet Setia had years of experience working security for the great Elek. Maybe she did have a point. "Have you asked Sheldrake? He'll want to stick with his mates, won't he?."

"I asked him before I asked you. He's on board. It turns out feelings among his former buddies about him disobeying Markham are mixed. Only a few friends have stayed loyal. And he says Torres in particular hates his guts. If Sheldrake had known the major was in charge he might not have come on the mission."

So Setia had a helmet conversation with the former corporal too.

"I don't know," Carys replied. "I'll think about it." She might have argued they could be reliant on their team to get back to the *Bres*, but it was clear there was no way back without the aliens' help. The humans were entirely in the creatures' hands. Or wings. Or things.

As time dragged by Torres gave regular pep talks, telling everyone to keep their minds fixed on their goal. But the prolonged discomfort had made Carys hazy on what their goal was, except maybe one day to be able to freely move their arms and legs.

"I found it!" Moody announced.

"What have you found, Doctor?" Torres asked, forced evenness in his tone.

"The organic substance. Or, I *believe* I've found it. I've found *something*."

The misery of the circumstances had driven the scientist's earlier discovery from Carys's mind. Somehow, she'd forgotten about the imminent threat of an invisible alien being.

"Could you expand on that?" Torres asked.

"I can do even better than expand on it. If you'll give me a moment, I just need to figure out how to..."

A beat later, a vid played on Carys's HUD. It was a visor view partly obscured by a dark substance. Beyond the smear was the close-up of what seemed to be someone's groin. Mercifully, due to the extremely close proximity, Carys wasn't sure if her assessment was accurate, or if the person was male or female.

Torres said, "You're referring to the mark on your visor rather than the...?"

"Oh yes," Moody replied. "Not *that*. That."

A gloved finger appeared on the vid and traced a line through the substance.

"I've been wondering all this time what it might be," Moody explained. "I originally thought someone's EVA suit must be dirty. But I don't think that's possible, is it?"

"It isn't," Torres confirmed. "You're right. That stuff must be from inside the shuttle."

"Uhh," said an unknown voice Carys guessed belonged to one of the soldiers. "that shit's on my visor too."

"I don't believe it's excrement," Moody countered.

"Just a turn of phrase, Doctor," said Torres. "Switching to one-to-one."

Whatever conversation went on between the scientist and the major Carys didn't hear.

Eventually, Torres announced, "The organic material in here

with us is probably harmless. It might be left over from a cargo shipment."

His conclusion made sense. The aliens wouldn't have a shuttle ready and waiting to transport unexpected arrivals from another planet. They were using an ordinary hauler.

The journey continued on in cramped, awkward silence. The seconds and minutes displayed on Carys's HUD increased at a crawling pace, as if time dilation were playing out before her eyes.

She began to worry about Loki and her other birds. She'd given Miriam thorough instructions, but the woman knew next to nothing about caring for avian life. She was a beginner and good intentions could only take you so far.

If only she could comm her.

She *could* comm her!

Bujold had said they would be able to maintain comm contact with the ship.

Just as Carys was about to try, the alien vessel gave a sudden jerk and the passengers were flung across the chamber violently. Carys smashed into someone and her head knocked against the inside of her helmet. Torres repeated his command for everyone to stay calm and asked if anyone had been seriously injured.

Whether anyone had Carys didn't immediately find out. A scraping noise sounded from her external comm and a soft glow lit up the chamber.

The hatch had opened.

Sixteen

"All civilians remain here until I say you can exit," Torres ordered, adding, "That includes you, Sheldrake."

As far as Carys knew it was the first time the major had spoken directly to the former corporal. The disgust in his tone was evident. Once more, she debated the wisdom of inviting Sheldrake onto the team. But what was done was done.

The soldiers floated through the hatch in single file, rifles at the ready. Nothing seemed to be happening to them outside, but she couldn't be sure. Not being able to see more than the backs of their EVA suits or hear any dialogue between them and Torres was maddening. All she could make out was an ethereal glow and nothing else, no indication of the nature of the place they'd arrived at or what was here to greet them. At least there was no flash of weapon fire.

The atmosphere readings on her HUD had altered but only marginally, and the lack of gravity implied they remained in space, but that was as much as she could tell.

The last grunt had left, and Major Torres, waiting next to the hatch, swung around to launch himself through the opening.

It slammed shut.

The door had passed within a millimetre of the major's visor. He reared backwards as the portal closed, narrowly avoiding a horrible accident. The impetus of his movement carried him across the chamber and into Dr Moody, who cradled him like a child. Torres wriggled free and roughly pushed the doctor away.

Sudden acceleration pushed all the remaining passengers into a bulkhead.

The shuttle was on the move again.

"Just when I thought our trip was over," Setia said sardonically.

"Shut it, Zees," Torres snapped.

"I wonder why they split us up?" Moody mused.

"Makes us easier to control," Sheldrake replied.

"Keep quiet, everyone," Torres ordered. "I'm trying to comm my team."

Carys hung suspended by acceleration force against the side of the aliens' shuttle, consoling herself that at least this time she was sharing the confined space with fewer bodies. On the other hand, what had happened to Torres's men and women? They'd disappeared into the soft illumination outside the hatch. Thinking about it, the image was disconcertingly like stepping into heaven.

Torres suddenly jerked around and slammed his fist into the bulkhead. If he made a sound it wasn't broadcast over comm. His blow left a shallow dent.

Moody asked with concern, "Major? Has something happened?"

Torres's reply was strangled with suppressed emotion. "I can't reach them. All their comms are dead."

"Shit," Setia whispered.

Then silence pressed in. Carys recalled the soldiers in the *Bres*'s bay calmly checking their equipment. She remembered their young, serious faces, intent on their jobs.

"I'll request further orders," Torres announced, his voice businesslike again.

Carys became aware of her breathing, which had sped up, and she could hear the rushing of her blood. Surely the aliens intended to kill her and the others, the same as they had the soldiers. But if that was so, why hadn't they killed them all at once? Why split them up? And why go to the trouble of targeting just a few humans when they could have destroyed all of them on the *Bres*?

Nothing made any sense.

The silence continued as Torres presumably talked to Bujold. Carys hung in position, frozen with apprehension, going over her life choices of the last few years and regretting every one.

"We seem to be en route to a second alien vessel," Torres announced.

"How do you know?" Setia asked. But before the major could answer she said, "Trackers in our EVA suits, right?"

"Of course," was Torres's terse reply.

Naturally, the captain wanted to keep tabs on them.

"Well, I don't know about anyone else," said Setia, "but I'm not going down without a fight."

"We are not to discharge our weapons unless directly attacked," Torres said. "Captain's orders."

"Screw that. If we let them get the first shot in—"

"You're still under my command, Zees."

"We're a long way from the *Bres*, and the way things are going it doesn't look like we'll make it back. I'll look after number one, thanks."

Torres reached around and grabbed Setia's rifle. She pulled it back. Their tug of war descended into a struggle and they fought, their movements hampered by the force pressing them into the bulkhead. Moody murmured gentle protestations. Sheldrake struggled to reach them, but his movements were hampered by the acceleration force. Carys only watched, bemused at the irony of the situation. The fighters faced almost certain, imminent murder by aliens. What was the point of trying to kill each other? She was also mildly curious about whether Setia's strength was greater than the major's powered armour.

The two seemed evenly matched. Then the major managed to get his weapon across Setia's throat, but she successfully held it off while also attempting to knee him in a vulnerable spot.

The acceleration pressure shifted. The ship had changed direction. Sheldrake launched himself at the struggling couple. Carys had a split second to wonder whose side he was on before he barrelled into the major, knocking him away from his opponent. Torres slammed into the closed hatch. He kicked hard and flew at Sheldrake. Moody hastily got out of the men's way. A second fight ensued, the men held against the side of the shuttle.

"Cut it out!" Setia yelled. "This is dumb." When the men ignored her, she thrust the butt of her rifle between them and attempted to lever them apart. Moody joined in, grabbing the major's shoulders. Carys half-heartedly grasped Sheldrake and pulled.

The shuttle appeared to have reached cruising speed. The tussling group floated free in the centre of the chamber.

"Stop it!" shouted Setia. "Stop fighting. We're going to—"

They shot across the space, and the impact of hitting the bulkhead broke them apart.

"Die soon anyway," Setia finished.

Plastered to the wall, no one seemed of a mind to resume the brawl.

Deceleration had begun, presumably bringing their fate nearer.

"I would like to point out," said Moody, "that you, Ms Zees, were an instigator of the altercation."

"Me? I didn't start anything. I'm just not going to let those bastards take me lying down."

"I repeat," Torres stated between his teeth, "you will follow my orders."

Setia didn't reply.

If the months of getting to know her were anything to go by, Carys felt confident that Setia would do whatever she damned well pleased.

As they approached their destination, dread grew in Carys's throat, tightening like a stricture, strangling her with fear of what was to come. The feeling spread across her body, freezing her to the spot. Even during her mission on Prime, death had not felt so present, so almost palpable.

A hand took hers and held it tightly. She turned to see Sheldrake's dark visor. Recalling Setia's trick, she leaned over so their helmets touched. "We had fun in the bar that night, remember?"

"Yeah, we did, though I don't remember most of it. Except I think I told you my deepest, darkest secrets."

"Don't worry. I forgot them all."

"Maybe you're just saying that to make me feel better."

"If I am, does it really matter?"

"I guess not."

The shuttle continued to slow. Sheldrake briefly squeezed her hand then released it to grasp his rifle. It looked like he planned on going down fighting too.

Carys didn't know what to do. She was not naturally feisty like

Setia. She liked to think things through before acting. But what was there to think about? The choice appeared to be simple: attack the aliens at the first chance, or allow whatever they had planned to happen. There would be no time to judge the situation.

Gingerly, she touched her weapon. Torres's head flicked towards her, but then he refocussed his attention on the hatch.

The shuttle came to an abrupt stop. Metallic clunks sounded. Torres motioned everyone to a position opposite the exit. As they waited, Setia lifted her rifle to her shoulder and Sheldrake did the same. Torres offered no objection. After a moment's hesitation he copied them. Carys followed suit. Lastly, even Moody prepared to fire.

When the hatch opened, the same ethereal glow as before shone in from the aliens' ship. This time, Torres gave no orders to exit. Carys squinted into the empty space, but she couldn't make anything out.

Seconds dragged past in an agony of waiting. She checked her HUD. Less than half a minute had gone by since the shuttle's portal had opened. She'd thought it was five minutes at least. Her gaze moved back to the glow, then to the time display.

The glow.

The time.

A minute had passed, and still nothing had happened.

Her eyes growing tired, Carys blinked.

And then they were upon them.

Creatures swarmed the hatch, flooding in too fast to even register their appearance. All she knew was that great numbers of dark things had arrived.

Pulse fire flashed.

She fired too, aiming randomly into the heaving mob. Whether her shots had any effect, she couldn't tell. She had a vague impression of things bursting apart. Bits exploded into air.

She was taken. The things had overrun her, gripping her arms, her legs, her torso. Something was on her visor and had wrapped around her head. Her rifle was torn from her hands.

She could not see, could not move.

Where were the others? What had happened to Setia, Sheldrake, Torres and Moody?

The things enclosed her like a shroud.

Seventeen

Agony lanced from Carys's ankle, and she screamed. The things had carried her from the shuttle as she struggled and fought. They had torn her weapon from her grasp easily, like a hawk ripping the head off a pigeon.

They covered her visor—they covered her whole body—and she was blinded. Rustling filled her external comm as the creatures swarmed over her.

If her companions were alive they were saying nothing.

She was saying nothing.

"Setia? Sheldrake?"

A groaning voice echoed in her helmet but then cut off.

"Setia? Is that you? Sheldrake? Where are you guys? Are you okay?"

She hoped that, since she remained alive, so did her friends.

The things were manipulating her, pulling her arms and her legs, turning her around and around, front to back, head to toe.

A second jab of pain arrived. She flinched, but the grip of the things meant she couldn't move a centimetre. They'd hurt her arm this time. She was confused. How were they getting through her suit? It wasn't military grade, but it was tough. Yet the attacks had felt like the thrusts of a knife.

Her head was gripped, hard. All she could see was an artificial surface, pale beige and rough-grained like sandpaper. Pressure emanated from her neck, as if something was sawing at it, as if—

They ripped off her helmet, and fresh air burst over her. She was slammed around. The things were on her face. Sharp prickles danced on her skin.

Moans and gasps sounded from everywhere.

And rustling.

So much rustling.

That was how they'd hurt her. They'd cut off her suit.

"Get..." She forced the word out through a clenched jaw. "Off..." Her muscles bunched as she made a monumental effort to writhe free. "Me!"

"Carys?" It was Setia.

But she couldn't answer. The body of one of the things had clamped itself over her mouth and nose. Something tugged at her hair so hard she feared she would be scalped. Her ankle and arm burned.

Then the creatures were gone.

As fast as the things had arrived they left, racing from her, pummelling her in their haste. The sudden freedom after long minutes of restriction was disorienting. She lazily spun, the aliens' parting prods lending her momentum.

Someone was puking.

A quarter turn brought Moody into view. Vomit erupted from his mouth, spreading out in a wide fountain unhampered by gravity. The scientist's clothes were torn and his hair was wild. His baby face glowed red.

"Gross," Setia muttered.

She entered Carys's field of vision. Setia was barefoot and blood oozed in globules from a cut on her thigh. As their gazes met, she said, "Some welcoming committee, right?" Then her eyes narrowed as she peered closer. "They got you too?"

Carys looked down. Except there was no longer any 'down'. Her ankle was masked by blood. She checked her arm. The wound on it seemed shallower.

Sheldrake drifted past, his head near her feet. "They seem to like Torres best."

"Huh?" Carys had spun nearly full circle. She caught sight of a heaving mass of the things, obscuring something within their midst. She assumed it was Major Torres.

The exit leading to the shuttle had passed her gaze early on. Another hatchway opened from the round-edged chamber. Things exited from it, crawling, hauling pieces of EVA suit. The weapons they'd taken were nowhere to be seen.

A blob of vomit sailed close by. She ducked and hunched, narrowly avoiding a collision.

The creatures suddenly departed Torres in a flood. Dark-shelled and many-legged, they zoomed purposefully away, ten or so heading for the exit, roughly the same number flying to a corner, where they huddled.

The major was in a bad state, leaking blood from numerous wounds, and he was unconscious. Perhaps he'd fought the hardest.

"Stars," said Setia, "this place is a mess."

The contents of Moody's stomach and blood from many of the companions' injuries spread wider and wider. Soon, it was going to be hard to evade an encounter with an undesirable liquid. Yet it was almost impossible to manoeuvre. Unable to reach a surface, Carys had to twist and turn vigorously to edge herself in any direction, the cuts on her arm and ankle painfully protesting. "At least we're alive. I really thought we'd had it."

"Alive *for now*," said Setia.

"I thought *I* was the pessimistic one."

Sheldrake had managed to arrive at a bulkhead. He halted his motion, resting a hand on the flat surface. "You're both as bad as each other."

Carys and Setia shared a questioning look.

The major groaned and his eyelids fluttered.

Vomit was floating on a clear trajectory to his face. Setia reached out with a toe and gave the major a gentle push, sending him out of danger and towards the opening to the rest of the ship.

In response, the things in the corner rose in a throng, grabbed the major and propelled him back to the centre of the room, right through some puke.

Setia shrugged. "I tried."

Major Torres fully wakened. His gaze darted around the chamber, resting on each companion in turn. He patted his abdomen. When his hands came away wet, he said wonderingly, "What the...?"

"Sorry," Moody said, "I've been rather unwell." The scientist's face had paled to a ghastly shade of green. He appeared to be fighting a second urge to upchuck.

Sheldrake said, "You're wounded, Major."

"I know." Torres grimaced as he assessed his cuts. "Only superficially, I think. Took a knock to my head when they removed my helmet." He squinted at the others. "SITREP? Anyone seriously hurt?"

"We all seem to be okay-ish," Setia replied, "apart from the doc."

Moody was gagging, a hand clamped over his mouth.

"Carys and Setia were cut too," said Sheldrake.

Torres nodded ruefully, eyeing them. "Our alien hosts weren't too careful with their slicing." His gaze moved to the things in the corner.

Moody shook his head vigorously and mumbled something, but his hand remained over his mouth, blocking his words.

"What's that, Doctor?" Torres asked.

"Maybe he's been hurt as well?" Carys offered.

Moody's head shook from side to side more vigorously as he denied her assertion. His hand moved a fraction. "They're not—" He slapped his hand back into place. His pallor deepened and his torso bucked.

"Might as well let it out," Torres said drily.

"No!" Setia was closest to the scientist. Her arms and legs windmilled as she tried to move away.

Moody let loose.

"Shit," Sheldrake commented, "I feel like I'm gonna see my breakfast again too."

"Don't you dare!" Setia had been hit but it was mostly bile.

Moody apologised, wiping his sleeve over his mouth. A sweaty sheen shone on his forehead. "So sorry. What I wanted to say was, our captors aren't aliens. I mean, I don't think they're alive. They're robots."

Carys swivelled to take another look at the creatures clustered in the corner. There *was* a metallic look to them she hadn't noticed before. And they were in complete control of their movements, not flailing around due to the lack of gravity. They had to have some mechanism for propelling themselves, though nothing was outwardly visible. Also, despite acting in unison, none had uttered a sound since grabbing the newcomers from the shuttle. Unless they were telepathic, they were communicating or being controlled electronically.

Setia asked, "So we haven't met the real aliens yet?"

"That's my guess," Moody replied. "They want to get the measure of us before meeting us face to face."

"Well, the rifles they took from us are going to make a great impression."

"Makes sense," Torres said. "They don't know why we're here or anything about us. They don't want to leave themselves vulnerable to attack."

"I wonder what conclusions they'll draw," Sheldrake speculated.

The crowd of bots in the corner jostled each other. Were they observing their human captives or guarding them?

"What now?" Carys asked. "Do we just wait for our assessment results and hope we passed?"

"The major should ask Captain Bujold what we're to do next," Moody suggested.

"Not possible," said Torres. "No helmet, so no helmet comm. My ear comm might have worked, but *they* took it out." He jerked his chin at the bots. "We're on our own."

"I see," said the doctor. "I wonder if we can leave this room, or must we remain here and wait for the aliens to come to us?"

"Only one way to find out," the major replied. "But first we treat our wounds."

It was easier said than done. When they returned to the shuttle to retrieve their packs they discovered they were gone, which meant they had no food or water let alone any medical supplies. They had nothing except the clothes they were wearing, sliced up by the bots' inaccurate cutting. The material their clothes was made from didn't tear easily into bandages and they had no scissors. When the major reached for the knife he'd worn strapped to his calf he discovered it had been taken.

They returned to the chamber. Carys had one sock left after the bots' assault. The other one had gone the same route as her boots, wherever they were. She pulled off the sock and tied it around the cut on her ankle. Her arm wound was shallower and the blood oozing from it had begun to congeal.

Sheldrake helped Torres, doing the best he could to staunch the major's blood loss. Torres accepted his help but neither met the other's gaze and their expressions were set and hard.

By the time everything possible had been done to treat their wounds, the chamber was a mess of beads of vomit and droplets of blood. The liquids would occasionally meet, the surface tension would break and larger, combined globules would form. All the while, the bots carefully followed the humans' movements, angling their metallic bodies and—presumably—cameras relaying images and audio to their masters.

No sound except those the humans or bots generated reached Carys's ears while the medical care went on. If the alien ship's engines were engaged they operated silently.

"Time to move out," Torres announced.

"If we're allowed," said Moody.

The major ordered everyone away from the exit leading to the rest of the ship. With some difficulty, they complied. The trick to moving in zero g, Carys had discovered, was to never be out of reach of a solid surface. It also helped to make only gentle movements to avoid the risk of zooming into empty space.

Most of the group had unconsciously agreed on which ways were up and down, and all except Moody floated on roughly similar axes. The doctor had ended up resting against the overhead.

"If the bots don't stop me as I go out," Torres continued, "check the passageway and then follow in single file."

"*How?*" Setia asked. "This isn't exactly easy."

"Do your best." With this unhelpful reply, the major touched a toe to the deck and slowly drifted towards the hatchway.

The bots turned, focussing their attention on him, but they didn't otherwise react. Torres disappeared through the opening.

"I suppose it's our turn," Carys said.

"I suppose it is," said Setia. "You first."

Eighteen

A sandpaper-like surface coated the passageway, giving some purchase for Carys's fingertips and toes as she eased herself along. Having companions was a definite bonus. If someone accidentally floated too far from a wall, someone else was usually within reach to haul them back.

It was like a game The Floor is Lava in reverse.

Torres moved slowly at the front of the group. Sheldrake brought up the rear. Carys, Setia and Moody muddled along in the middle. The place was barely lit, which didn't help matters. The atmosphere was evidently breathable but it smelled stale, and there didn't seem to be a circulation system. The faint sensation of air currents Carys had grown used to on the *Bres* was absent.

A rustling sound caught her attention, and she searched for its source.

"It's the bots," Setia said. "They've been following us for a while now."

Carys spotted them. A short distance beyond Sheldrake, dark, humped shapes filled the passageway. The bots were keeping pace almost out of sight.

"Are they waiting to attack, do you think?" she asked.

"Probably just observing. If they wanted to kill us they could have. All they had to do was cut deeper when they removed our suits."

Moody said, "They must be continuing to collect data, or perhaps they're here to prevent us from entering prohibited areas."

"That assumes we're supposed to be going somewhere in particular," Setia remarked.

The scientist shrugged.

"This way." Torres scooted into an opening above his head.

They had passed several similar exits. As she followed the major, Carys wondered what made this one different. Maybe it was only that Torres wanted to get off the main thoroughfare. Puzzlingly, the vessel had appeared to consist only of labyrinthine passageways so far. They hadn't encountered any hatches or doors that might lead to rooms. If openings into other areas existed they were invisible to human eyes.

The new passageway was narrower, which meant the wall was closer and easier to move along. Their progress sped up. The narrowness also made it more confined, however, the air seemed harder to breathe. To take her mind off the uncomfortable sensation, Carys asked, "Dr Moody, what's your subject? I take it you aren't a medical doctor."

"Ha, absolutely not. I'm a xenobiologist. My thesis was on the growth stages of *Riftia pachyptila*, the giant tube worm."

"But xenobiologists study aliens, don't they?" She'd heard of tube worms. They lived in oceans. Earth oceans.

"They do indeed, yet without aliens to study, one must make do. Giant tube worms live near hydrothermal vents, which are thought to be where life first evolved on Earth. I was interested in them because they have a fascinating process for generating energy. At a certain stage of development, they acquire symbiotic bacteria through a process somewhat akin to an infection. Then they—"

Setia gave a loud, fake yawn and patted her gaping mouth.

Moody took the hint and stopped speaking.

"Go on," said Carys. *She'd* been interested.

"Another time, perhaps."

Carys threw Setia a harsh look.

"Dead end." Torres backed up, forcing Moody to back up too. Everyone turned awkwardly in the narrow space, gently prodding the walls to reverse their direction.

Sheldrake began to move ahead, but Torres ordered him to wait, adding, "I'm leading this mission, soldier."

The major squeezed past his team members. The bots had halted, hovering in the dim space beyond Sheldrake like a swarm of dark, lazy bees. As Torres approached they moved erratically backward, as if trying to figure out what he was doing. The major floated into their midst, one hand reaching out in front. Undeterred by this gesture, the bots didn't react, and Torres had to push a few aside to make progress. They bumped into the others, rustling.

"Out of my way, machines," Torres grumbled.

"I don't think they understand English," Setia said.

Yet after the major's complaint the bots *did* move. They swept ahead, almost out of sight.

"Something's controlling them," said Carys. "They just received an order to let us through."

As they returned to the main passageway they caught up to the bots again. The devices hung motionless, their pincer-like legs drooping.

Sheldrake was first to spot why the bots had stopped. "The bulkhead's opening!"

To Torres's left, a rectangular line a couple of metres wide and a metre tall had appeared in the featureless, curved surface. One side of the rectangle had opened a slit and the gap was growing larger.

Torres moved to the opposite wall. The bots started into motion again, and their legs drew up into their carapaces. As the hole widened, the leading bot disappeared into darkness. The others quickly followed. Just as the last made it to the gap, Torres reached out. Whether he'd intended to grab it or do something else, Carys wasn't sure, but his hand must have made contact. A flash lit up the tunnel and a crack of discharged electricity sounded. Torres swore and snatched his hand away.

The opening snapped shut. All the bots were gone.

"Are you hurt, Major?" Moody asked.

"Not badly." Torres was holding his hand to his chest. Using his non-dominant one he pushed himself forward. "Let's go."

They headed farther down the long, curving passageway. The arterial route sprouted more side passages, some large enough to fit a human, others smaller. Torres elected to ignore them. No more bots arrived.

"This place reminds me of an ants' nest," Carys commented.

"What I don't understand is," said Setia, "where are the aliens?

And why aren't there any rooms? I mean, where's the bridge and the engine room? Even an alien ship would have those, wouldn't it?"

"I doubt we're in the main part of the ship," Moody said.

"Then where are we?" asked Setia.

Sheldrake replied, "I really hope we aren't in the waste disposal system."

"I don't have a clue where we are," said Carys, "but one thing gives me hope—the ship hasn't moved since we arrived. The engines seem to be turned off. That must mean the aliens have continued to suspend their attack on the *Bres*."

"We're here for a reason," Moody declared, "and the bots left us for a reason. We just have to figure it all out. Then we can make progress."

"The only progress we'll make is if our friendly jailers show themselves," said Setia. "If we ever get back to the *Bres*, someone remind me to ask Bujold why I was picked for this bullshit again."

"Bots are on our tail," Sheldrake announced. He managed to add, "Approaching fast" before the devices were upon them.

Something sharp pricked the sole of Carys's bare foot, causing her to yelp and jerk her knee up protectively. Bots had suddenly filled the immediate space. One jabbed her back. Another poked her wrist. The attacks weren't life threatening, only painful. It was like she'd disturbed a hornet's nest. She flailed, trying to get away. Gasps and curses came from her companions as they suffered the same assault.

"What are they doing?!" Setia exclaimed. "And why?!"

The onslaught Carys was suffering was targeted mostly on the lower half of her body. She flew forward and encountered Torres, who was punching and kicking the bots. Ducking a fist, she snapped, "You're in my way."

"Stay right where you are."

"Sod that." She started as another sting hit, then gave the man a push. "Ow!" A bot had pricked her thigh. "They want us to move forward."

"I said, stay right where you— Uhhh!"

She had shoved him into the wall, convinced the bots were only trying to force them to go faster in the direction they'd already been heading. Using Torres's chest as a springboard, she sailed forward. In the space beyond the group, there seemed to be fewer bots and they weren't attacking.

"Move faster," she told the others. "They want us to speed up."

Not waiting to discover if the others had heeded her words, she thrust against a wall and travelled in a long diagonal arc to the other side of the tunnel. Halting, she looked back. A cloud of bots punctuated by the occasional thrashing arm or leg floated in the passageway.

"I said," she bellowed, "they want us to hurry up!"

Moody was the first to emerge. Swooping through the confined space, he joined her. Blood trickled from a wound under his eye. Setia flew out next. Carys didn't wait for the rest. She set off again quickly, before the bots had a chance to catch up and deliver more enticements to move.

The sounds from behind told her Setia and Moody were keeping up. After a minute or so's progress, she risked a glance over her shoulder. Sheldrake was rapidly closing the distance between them, and Torres could be seen too, though bots continued to plague him.

"Uh oh," said Setia.

Carys turned forward.

Like a crowd of angry rioters, more bots filled the space ahead. There were so many they entirely obscured the rest of the passageway.

"Oh dear," Moody muttered. "What now?"

What now indeed.

Carys rested a hand on the wall, hesitating. What was the bots' plan? They were about to enclose the humans on both sides. Was it a scheme to finish them off? She couldn't imagine many worse ways to go than to be slowly stabbed to death by a million needle jabs.

"That way." Setia pointed at an opening that, in her anxious state, Carys hadn't noticed.

She flew towards it, barely registering the pain from her injured ankle. Before she could take in the new place, Setia had joined her. Then Moody came flying in, his blond hair a fuzzy halo.

"I'm getting a sense of déjà vu," Setia commented.

Sheldrake arrived, and Carys took in their new situation. "Well, great."

They were back at the shuttle entrance. Somehow, they'd travelled in a circle and arrived back where they'd started. The blood they'd shed here and Moody's stomach contents had amalgamated to large blobs.

She covered her mouth and nose.

Two bloody hands gripped the sides of the entrance portal, and Torres pulled himself in. The major looked a mess. He'd lost some of his improvised bandages, and his wounds continued to ooze blood. His remaining bandages were soaked. The bots had hurt him further. Red marks of needle pricks dotted his exposed skin.

Noticing they were all staring he growled, "We rest now."

"Are you okay, Major?" Moody tentatively asked.

The man's eyelids were drooping. He seemed about to pass out.

"We should get back in the shuttle," said Setia. "That's what they want, right? Or else why did they force us to come here?"

"Makes sense to me," said Sheldrake. "Major Torres, I'll help you."

But when he approached the major, Torres angrily slapped his hand away. In a weak voice he said, "The shuttle. Yeah. Everyone into the shuttle. Move it."

The moment the hatch shut, metallic clunks sounded. The vessel was disengaging from the main ship.

Carys floated free for a few heartbeats, then she was slammed into the bulkhead and bodies piled on top of her. With a great effort, she squirmed out from under them. The acceleration increased and soon the only movement she could make was to breathe. The force pinned her arms and legs and pressed down on her stomach and face.

"Are they sending us back express delivery?" Setia asked, her voice strangely muffled.

Carys was amazed anyone could speak. From the corners of her eyes she spied Setia. She was on her front, her face crushed at an angle.

"You should turn over," Carys managed to squeak.

"Good advice. Hard to follow."

Time dragged past. As each excruciating minute stretched into the next, Carys had to consciously expand her chest to draw in air. As she relaxed, pressure instantly pushed air out in a fast exhale.

Was this the last part? Were the aliens sending them back to the *Bres*? Was the mission nearly over?

She hoped so. She hoped the aliens had only wanted to get a closer look at this new species that had turned up on their doorstep, and now the examination was finished they were sending them home. Bujold could take over now. The captain could begin the task of establishing the civilisation of Polaris Ab as a member of the Galactic Council, or whatever the new organisation would be called.

Carys hoped her part was over.

Quiet murmurings came from her left. She strained to turn her head. Torres and Sheldrake lay close together, and the ex-corporal was speaking to the major, who looked entirely out of it. The man's skin was chalky and his lips were blue. Sheldrake appeared to be exhorting him to wake up, or stay conscious, or something like that, but his appeals were useless.

Grimacing with physical strain, Sheldrake slid a hand closer to Torres's shoulder and jiggled it. The movement didn't register in the rest of the major's leaden body.

Carys said, "There's no point. He won't come around while we're like this."

"I have to try. I think he's..."

Sheldrake's expression was stricken.

She peered closer at the major. Could he be dying? He'd certainly lost a lot of blood, and he'd said earlier he'd taken a hit to the head. In the best of circumstances his condition could be precarious. In this situation, where it took deliberate effort to breathe, he wouldn't be getting the oxygen he needed.

"Torres," she attempted to yell and snap the major awake, though the words came out barely louder than normal volume. She held Sheldrake's gaze for a moment but then looked away. There wasn't anything she could do to help, and there wasn't anything she could say to ease Sheldrake's distress.

No one could do anything until this terrible journey was over.

She took another breath and this time the effort seemed even harder. Was the pressure increasing? To her right, someone groaned.

"Can't..." Moody said "take...much...m..."

He was silent.

The edges of Carys's vision turned black. She strained to inhale.

"Carys?" said Setia. "Carys, you have to—"

She awoke.

How long had she been out? There was no telling. She'd been dreaming she was falling into a deep, black hole from which she knew she would never emerge.

She could breathe freely again! She drew in a couple of deep lungfuls, relief flooding her. The painful sensation of pressure was gone. Their journey was over, or at the very least the shuttle had stopped accelerating. She sat up, rejoicing in the freedom of movement.

Then she realised gravity had returned. They had to be back at the *Bres*.

Major Torres!

Sheldrake was hunched over him, an ear pressed to Torres's chest. He lifted a hand to the major's neck.

"How is he?" Moody asked.

Sheldrake didn't reply. With a look of despair, he put one of his hands on top of the other and began chest compressions.

Oh, shit.

Carys watched in shock as Sheldrake worked. She'd known the mission was dangerous from the outset, but she'd never imagined the most capable and experienced member of their team would be the one to—

The hatch opened, sending a tremor through the shuttle. Light flooded in.

It wasn't starship lighting. It was too intense and the colours were wrong.

But of course it wasn't starship lighting. They couldn't be on the *Bres*. The shuttle hadn't fitted into the bay. It had been linked by an umbilicus. The *Bres*'s gravity field didn't reach it.

So if they weren't on the *Bres*...

Setia stepped to the open portal and peered out.

"Burnap's balls!"

Nineteen

Carys tried to stand but she was too wobbly. She crawled to join Setia at the hatch. When she caught sight of the view, she sank onto her backside.

Blinking and squinting in the strong light, she could just make out rank upon rank of billowing, wispy white clouds below, spreading to the far distance. The sky was pale blue like midday on Earth yet with a glaring difference: two suns shone in the heavens. She could barely look at one of them. The other sat directly in front close to the horizon, small and yellow-tinged. A much larger sun hung overhead, a vast lake of unbearable luminosity, bigger and brighter but more diffuse than its modest fraternal twin.

For all the energy pouring from the suns, little seemed to be reaching the planet. The air was frosty and thin. Her lungs ached and her eyes smarted. Unable to endure the spectacle of the sky any longer, she looked down.

The shuttle sat on a curved platform of smooth, grey stone. At the edge it simply stopped, as far as she could tell. Misty nothingness lay beyond it, and there was no barrier to prevent the unwary from tumbling to their deaths.

"Ahh, Polaris Aa," Moody breathed.

Carys jumped. In her preoccupation, she hadn't registered the scientist's arrival.

His eyes were squeezed almost shut and he was shading them

with a hand as he peered up. "I always wondered what it would look like to the naked eye. Marvellous. Simply marvellous."

Polaris Aa. The supergiant. The big sister to little Polaris Ab.

"I wouldn't look at it too long if I were you." Setia took a step backwards into the shuttle's interior.

"Indeed," Moody concurred. "I appreciate the sight but I wouldn't like it seared on my retinas." He gazed in rapt wonder at their surroundings. "Goodness gracious. How high up are we? It must be thousands of metres. I wish I still had my interface. I can remember some information about this planet but not the details."

"Did we even have details?" Setia asked.

"Quite a few. The scan data told us a fair amount. I'm not surprised we appear to be on a mountainside. All the land masses are mountainous. Oceans comprise eighty-six percent of the surface." His brow furrowed. "Where are our alien friends? We seem to be alone. I'm going to take a look around."

"Be careful," Setia said.

Moody stepped out onto the platform.

Carys recalled Bujold telling her something similar about the planet to what the scientist had said. The captain had also mentioned that the aliens were aerial and their cities were airborne. Yet there was no sign of any metropolis in the sky or any of the planet's inhabitants. When would the beings running the show appear? She leaned out and looked to the left and right. Where had Moody gone? All she could see was the platform curving out of view and all she could hear was the wind.

No, there was another sound, a huffing, puffing noise coming from behind.

Torres!

In her wonder at the new world she'd forgotten about Sheldrake's efforts to save the major's life. After turning from the brilliance of the exterior it took a moment for her eyes to adjust. Major Torres lay in the same position and Sheldrake continued to pump his chest. Sweat gleamed on the ex-corporal's face.

Setia stood over him, her eyes full of concern as she watched with her hands on her hips.

Sheldrake stopped what he was doing in order to press an ear against Torres's sternum. Then he resumed the compressions. Setia turned to Carys with a pitying look.

"Sheldrake," Carys said.

He didn't seem to hear her.

"Sheldrake," she repeated, "I think he's gone."

If they had medical facilities, blood, a defibrillator... If they had *anything*, there might be a chance to save the major's life. But they were far from these things, far from help. Not even their alien captors seemed to be around.

Setia held Carys's gaze as if suggesting *she* should be the one to do something.

She stepped closer and put a hand on Sheldrake's shoulder. He didn't seem to notice her. His skin was hot and his shirt was soaked. His sweat dripped onto Torres's body.

"Stop," she said quietly.

Still, Sheldrake didn't react.

"He's gone. There's nothing you can do."

The ex-corporal worked on, gasps escaping his tightened lips.

"Sheldrake! He's dead." She felt bad about snapping at her friend but there seemed to be no other way to get through to him.

It worked.

His hands fell to his sides and he straightened up, though his shoulders slumped. His chest heaved as he fought his emotions. Abruptly, he rose to his feet and strode to the hatchway. Grabbing the frame with one hand he leaned out, his head hung low.

Torres's eyes and mouth were open. He appeared mildly surprised, as if he hadn't imagined his end would come so soon but, on the other hand, he'd kind of expected something like this would happen.

Moody reappeared. He joined them and looked down at the body sorrowfully. "I didn't realise he'd lost so much blood. Or perhaps it was that head trauma he suffered when the bots removed his helmet."

Setia said, "Whatever was wrong with him, the high gs probably finished him off. Stars, this is awful. Do we have anything to cover him?"

But unless one of them donated an item of clothing or they used the corpse's own, there was nothing to blanket the dead man's face.

"We could turn him over?" Carys suggested.

Setia grimaced. "Maybe, but—"

"Don't touch him!" Sheldrake had returned. He stood over

Torres protectively. "Don't put a finger on him, right? Leave him alone!"

"Okay, okay," Setia said. "It's not like I was looking forward to it."

Moody said, "I'm afraid we must leave him here."

"Leave him here?" Carys asked. "Are we going somewhere?"

"We must. There's no one outside. We're alone in this place. Our hosts haven't arrived, though they must know where we are. They brought us here after all. If they were planning on meeting us they would have done so by now. Therefore, we must leave."

"Because that's what they expect?" Setia had the defiant look she always wore when she suspected she was being pushed around.

"I have no idea what they expect," Moody retorted. "However, if we wish to eat and drink we must go and find food and water."

"We have to take the major with us," said Sheldrake, his voice cracking, "or those bastards will get him. They'll cut him up to take a look at his insides. He won't get the decent burial he deserves."

"He does deserve a decent burial," Moody concurred, "but, unfortunately, we cannot give it to him. And as to carrying him around, well, that just isn't sensible for obvious reasons."

A sombre silence fell.

Carys, who had been focussing on the floor next to Torres's head, turned her attention to his face once more. She hadn't liked the man. He'd been typical military, bossy and rigid-thinking. But, then again, she hadn't liked Sheldrake at first either, and for the same reasons. It wasn't until she'd grown to know him better she'd seen a different side to him, a side she could like. She realised she'd never really known Torres at all. She'd only ever seen him acting in his professional role. The man himself could have been very different. Now she would never know.

She said quietly, "We could bury him here."

"I'm not sure there's any point," Moody said. "The aliens will surely dig him up. As Sheldrake mentioned, they must be curious about our anatomy."

"Of course there's a point," snapped Sheldrake. "The man deserves honour for his sacrifice, even if we're the only ones who will ever know about it."

The scientist nodded thoughtfully. "I apologise. I was thinking in purely practical terms."

"Let's do it," said Carys. "And we can say a few words. Sheldrake, you must know the right stuff to say."

"I'll try to remember."

The major had been a large man and heavily muscled, but moving his body was surprisingly easy. Carys had forgotten about the low gravity on this world. After spending so long in zero g the new situation had made her feel like everything was back to normal. It wasn't. As Setia had said, even a weak human was strong on this planet.

She helped to carry Torres outside, half-expecting to discover a welcoming committee just beyond the shuttle's exit. But Moody was right. They were alone. All that greeted them was bare, rocky mountainside. The platform the shuttle sat on seemed to be the only manufactured object in the place. The wind was icy and took her breath away.

"There has to be something else besides this platform," Moody said, "some kind of construction. What possible reason could there be for a landing pad in the middle of nowhere?"

"We can't dig a grave in rocks," Setia said. "Let's put Torres down for a minute while we figure this out."

They laid the body gently on the platform.

For the first time, they could see the shuttle from the outside. It was oblong with smooth, rounded corners that would slip easily through an atmosphere. The grey hull was matt and scored with marks, some old with crusted edges.

Carys shoved her hands into her armpits in an attempt to warm them. The mountainside rose out of sight above, and below it disappeared into clouds. There wasn't anywhere suitable for a burial. It would have been hard enough to dig the hole in soil without a spade, but digging this surface was impossible.

"We have to do something," said Sheldrake. "We can't just dump him."

"I'm not sure we have a choice," Moody said.

"Then I'll stay here. You guys go and do your thing. I'm not leaving the major."

"That's dumb," Setia said. "What are you going to do when the aliens come for him? Bite them?"

"I'll do whatever I have to!"

Moody tried to reason with Sheldrake, but the ex-corporal cut him off. An argument ensued, Setia joining in.

Sheldrake was clearly going through something. He and Torres had fought not so long ago, so Sheldrake's reaction was odd.

The aliens didn't seem to be coming for them any time soon, so Carys decided to explore. "I'm going to take a look around."

The others didn't answer, too intent on their disagreement. She walked to the mountainside edge of the platform. The rocks and shale of the slopes wouldn't have looked out of place on Earth. If it weren't for the massive sun beating down and the other one disappearing below the horizon, she might have been on any typical mountain back home.

She climbed up, the loose stones slipping under her feet and hands. At thirty metres above the shuttle, she stopped and looked back. Setia, Moody and Sheldrake continued to bicker over Torres's body.

Her companions aside, the view reminded Carys of a once-familiar sight. In her work with raptors she'd often rescued orphaned chicks. She'd climbed the mountains of West BI to reach their nests, gathered the bundles of fluff and carried them to safety.

Jutting out from the mountainside, the platform where the shuttle stood looked exactly like an eyrie. For animals forced by gravity to lumber awkwardly over land, the shuttle pad was hard to reach. For aerial creatures it was an easy landing place.

There was nothing else because the aliens didn't need anything else here. Whatever the shuttle usually brought to the surface could be transported away again by air.

Her gaze drifted to the distance and the setting sun. The intensity of daylight was fading. A red-hued haze gilded the far cloudscape, though the light from the sun above remained intense.

Just as her attention alighted on a particularly tall peak of cumulus, something burst from it. Wide wings spread from a narrow body and the head angled downward like a hawk scanning for prey. The creature circled once, its wings riding the air, then it plummeted into the clouds and was gone.

Twenty

After some searching, Sheldrake had found a level area of ground on which to place Torres's body. They would have to transport the corpse fifty metres or so down the slope.

Carys was loath to touch it. The thing had lost its resemblance to a human being. It was a darkened, horrible facsimile of the major as he'd been when he was alive, and no doubt the aliens would come for him sooner or later anyway, so what was the point? She was tempted to suggest leaving him on the platform. But in the time they'd spent looking for somewhere to put the remains, Sheldrake's agitation and grief had only increased. She feared he might lose his mind entirely if they didn't give Torres some type of burial.

So she helped to pick up the body and, slowly, they carried it down.

While she'd been helping in the search for a resting place for the corpse, she'd also been scanning the skies, hoping for another sighting of the flying creature, but she'd seen nothing.

Had it been one of the intelligent aliens? That had been where her mind first jumped. Yet, considering the general topography of the world, many life forms would be aerial. It could have been just an ordinary native animal. And surely if it was one of the ruling species it would have flown closer, curious about the newcomers.

It was a puzzle, and no one else had spotted the animal so she had no other opinions to draw on. She wasn't even confident the others had believed her when she said she'd seen something.

"This is it." Sheldrake indicated a roughly horizontal patch of shale.

Setia was holding Torres's shoulders, and Carys and Moody had a leg each. They tried to lower the body onto the patch, but the space was too small. Sheldrake barked instructions to move it this way and that, but to no avail. Torres was a big man and simply wouldn't fit. In the end, they had to turn him onto his side and bend his knees so he was in a foetal position. Sheldrake also folded the major's arms to the front. Carys averted her gaze from the corpse's rigid, blackening, surprised face.

They had climbed down into the misty, upper cloud layer. Frost iced the ground, freezing her bare feet, and her breath condensed at every exhale.

"Find stones," said Sheldrake. "As many as you can."

If there was one thing they didn't lack, it was stones. As she was collecting some, Setia came up to her and said softly, "He'll calm down soon. He just needs to get it out of his system."

"Maybe. I hope so."

There was no doubt who Setia was talking about. Carys glanced at Sheldrake. He was working with maniacal effort, filling his arms with pebbles and rocks. As she watched, he carried them over to the body and placed them gently and with reverence upon it.

Carys added her stones to the pile and collected more. The others did the same. Eventually, they erected a cairn.

"That's enough, right?" said Setia. "He's well-covered now. We need to finish up here and move on before we all die of exposure."

Carys silently agreed. Her teeth were chattering with cold despite the exercise.

Sheldrake seemed to battle with himself before nodding. His voice cracking, he said, "I don't know what religion he was, and even if I did, I can't remember what's said at any of the burials."

Moody patted his shoulder. "I'm sure Major Torres wouldn't mind. Just thank him for his service. Setia is correct. It's time to go."

Sheldrake murmured a few words over the remains while everyone else stood in respectful silence.

The obvious direction for them to go next was to continue

downwards. They would find nothing to eat on these barren slopes and any water would be frozen. They began the descent.

The incline became so steep they were forced to face the mountainside as they lowered themselves, clinging to rocks. Carys took a final look at the lonely pile of stones they were leaving behind, already disappearing into the mist.

Had Torres been married? Had he any children? He'd known and accepted the risks of his job, yet it seemed cruel that he'd died so far from home.

She returned her attention to the rocks she was gripping, reminding herself that her fate might not be so different from the major's if she were not careful.

The mist grew thicker until she couldn't see much more than her hands and feet. She and her companions had to call out regularly to avoid becoming separated. Her extremities were gradually warming up as she toiled, either due to exertion or because the ambient temperature was rising. Better blood circulation brought the realisation that her feet and hands were sore—her feet in particular. The rough ground was taking its toll on her soft-skinned soles and toes.

She paused and lifted a foot to inspect it. Her skin was pink and chafed and pinpricks of blood dotted her heel and toes. There was nothing to be done about it. Her boots were long gone, carried away along with her EVA suit by the robots on the alien ship.

She resumed her descent, but at the same time an explosion of sliding, crashing stones came from her left, quickly muffled by the dead air. Moody's loud and vehement curses sounded out, followed by, "I took a tumble, but I'm fine. No broken bones."

"Take it easy, Doc," said Sheldrake.

He sounded calmer, Carys was relieved to note.

After Moody's accident, her descent took on a more careful, rhythmic pattern. She would reach down with her left foot, questing for a firm rock or patch of dusty soil. Then she would push the fingertips of her right hand into a crack and grip firmly. Next, she would lower her right foot, and then move her left hand downwards, grasping for something to hold onto. So, step by slow step, she moved through the cloud layer.

Her mind drifted. The events that had taken place since leaving the *Bres* took on a dreamlike quality, as if they might never have happened. She began to imagine she was back in West BI on a rescue mission, a pair of orphaned eagle chicks nestling in a pouch on her back. She half expected that when she emerged from the mist, she might see the green hills of her homeland stretching as far as the eye could see, glistening after recent rain.

There was a second cascade of stones, shattering her trance-like state.

No one called out as Moody had before to explain the source of the noise.

"Was that you again, Doc?" Sheldrake asked. "You okay?"

"I'm perfectly fine. I did not fall."

"Ellis?" asked Sheldrake.

"Not me."

Setia added, "Wasn't me either."

Carys halted, panting.

The ensuing silence from her companions grew more and more uncomfortable until Moody stated the obvious: "If it wasn't one of us, then who was—?"

Another sudden rush of tumbling shale cut off his words. This noise sounded farther off.

As it tailed away, Setia's muttered curses drifted through the mist.

"It could be nothing," Carys said. "The surface is probably slipping all the time."

"All the more reason to get off it as soon as we can," said Moody.

That seemed to be the general agreement. Carys resumed her steady descent. She wasn't going to hurry, not when a single misstep or loose rock could send her to their destination faster than she would like.

What *was* their destination? What lay below? They were leaving behind inhospitable land, but whatever they were heading towards might be worse.

The mist thinned during her musings until she spotted a small, dark figure a short distance away. The person had seen her too.

"Hey, Carys," Setia said. "It *is* you, right?"

Carys momentarily halted again to give Setia a brief wave. Some minutes later Moody also became visible and then she saw Sheldrake, too, farthest out.

While they'd been in the thickest area of cloud they'd moved far apart. Now they could see each other the group angled their movements to draw closer.

They were the only living, moving things as far as Carys could see. Whatever might have caused the anonymous rockfalls remained invisible. She guessed—hoped—it was natural erosion.

The strong wind at the upper levels had dropped as they'd entered the cloud layer, but the noise of another wind was rising. But was it wind, or was it—"

"I can see water," Moody announced excitedly.

Carys looked over her shoulder and down. Not only was grey-blue water visible, vegetation sprouted from the rocks leading to the ocean. Tough, smooth, spines radiating from central crowns dotted the mountain slopes.

"Thank the stars," said Moody. "We're nearly there. I wasn't sure how much more of this I could stand. My feet are killing me."

"Nearly there?" asked Setia. "Is that where we're going?"

"Naturally," Moody replied. "Where else?"

Carys scanned to her left and right. An expanse of nearly vertical rock face spread out to each side. The ocean did seem the obvious place to go. Yet the water was likely to be salty and undrinkable. Her mouth and throat were already parched.

Moody said, "We should descend to the waves."

Carys regarded the ocean again, doubtfully. The waves didn't seem high or dangerous, but something felt off. She couldn't put her finger on it, so she didn't say anything and continued to climb down.

The cloud cover that had shrouded them burned away. The rays of the gigantic sun seared them once more, though only half of the star remained above the horizon. Carys's exposed skin had turned pink, promising severe sunburn soon, but there was no shade anywhere. Moody was the palest of them all and would suffer the most, but if he realised his predicament he didn't mention it.

The scientist was almost bounding down the slopes. It was clear why he'd slipped before. He was overeager, acting like the kid of a mountain goat that hadn't quite found its feet. Carys was about to call out a warning and advise him to slow down, when the scene below distracted her. What was wrong with it? She'd seen plenty of seas and mountains in her time. Though the plants were different and the colossal orb in the sky was new, everything else should have looked about the same. It didn't.

Moody was a good fifteen metres below Sheldrake, who was closest to him. Setia wasn't far behind. Carys's slower pace had left her last of all.

A strong sense of foreboding hit.

"Stop!" she blurted. "Everyone, stop going down."

"Huh?" Setia squinted up, lip curled. "Why?"

Carys didn't want to look stupid by uttering the accurate answer: *I don't know*. So she said, "Just do it."

Moody either hadn't heard or was deliberately ignoring her. He'd continued his rapid descent.

"What's up, Ellis?" Sheldrake asked.

"It isn't safe." It was the best answer she had. "Dr Moody! You have to stop!"

"I don't see any cause for concern," Moody replied in a soothing tone. "The sooner we reach the water the sooner we can rest."

He was passing one of the spiky plants. A particularly large, thick-stemmed specimen, it was the lowest of them. Beneath it, in the zone Moody had just entered, no plants grew. The rocks were large, bare, and smooth.

"Sheldrake!" Carys yelled. "Get him! Bring him back!" She turned fearful eyes to the darkening half of the horizon. Sure enough, it was different. And in the brief second she watched, it altered. It was growing, rising.

The ex-corporal stared at her as if she were mad.

"Please!"

He didn't need further urging. He slipped down the rocks like a sailor sliding down a ship's ladder.

"I must protest," Moody complained as Sheldrake reached him.

"You've gotta do what Ellis says." Sheldrake grabbed the scientist's arm and dragged him upwards.

Moody's bare feet scrabbled at rocks and his free arm waved about, but he seemed to quickly give in to the stronger man's will. He allowed himself to be hauled higher.

Meanwhile, Carys continued to focus on the ocean, almost unable to believe what she was seeing.

Setia followed her gaze. The other woman's face screwed up as she tried to make out the source of Carys's fear. "Holy shit."

She'd seen it.

The *Bres*'s scientists had initially concluded this planet was uninhabitable due to its proximity to supergiant Polaris Aa.

They'd been wrong. It clearly was habitable. But they'd been right that the influence of a massive celestial body could be devastating to life.

Approaching them was a tidal surge larger than Carys could have imagined. That was what her subconscious mind had been trying to tell her. As soon as she'd seen the rock face denuded of all plant life she should have understood.

"Move it, Doc!" Sheldrake had seen it too.

The men raced up the stony slope much faster than they'd climbed down it.

The wave hit the farthest edge of the mountainside, where it curved out of sight. Though the rational part of Carys's brain told her she was in the safe zone, evidenced by plants and dust lying thick in the cracks between rocks, she ascended higher. She couldn't help it. The idea of being caught up in that monstrous swell filled her with horror.

The dark water occupied her entire vision. Now frozen, she clutched rocks so tightly her hands hurt. The immense setting sun, the creature she'd seen wheeling in the sky, Torres's death, the journey in the alien shuttle, the bots on the alien ship, all was forgotten. Only one thing was on her mind: the wave.

It had nearly reached them.

Her gaze snapped downwards.

Sheldrake and Moody were gripping the mountainside like their lives depended on it. Pressing their stomachs into the rocks, they watched the water with wide eyes.

It rose.

The crest skimmed the tips of Moody's toes in the gentlest of wet kisses. He flinched and jerked his knees up.

Then it was gone.

Twenty-One

They had found a hollow in the cliff face in which to spend the night. 'Hollow' was a generous way to describe the spot. It was the merest indentation in the stubborn verticality of the mountainside. Lying down was out of the question. The best the place offered was the opportunity to sit rather than cling to rocks to avoid falling.

Re-ascending to a higher point where the ground was flatter was out of the question. If they were not already exhausted, the temperature on the upper slopes was too low. No one would have lasted more than a few hours before succumbing to the cold.

Here, perched like puffins on a scrap of semi-level shale, they might see another day. However, along with their survival would come increased hunger, thirst and weariness. To Carys, the prospect felt better than death—for the time being. If things continued as they were she wasn't sure how long she would feel the same way.

"If we prop ourselves back to back," Moody suggested, "we may be able to get a little sleep. I don't know about you guys, but I could certainly use forty winks. It's fascinating how a brush with certain death takes it out of you."

"Fascinating," Setia said wryly. She went on, "Carys, how did you know that wave would hit? You started yelling before it even approached."

"I didn't know it would hit right then. And it wasn't a wave as such, it was the tide."

"The tide?" Setia shook her head. "When I was a kid I used to play in the storm outflow on the local beach. I remember tides. The sea would go out, then a few hours later it would come in again. That was no tide. That was a tsunami."

"No, tsunamis are caused by tectonic activity. Tides are caused by the gravitational pull of celestial bodies. You can't have a sun the size of Polaris Aa in the vicinity without a massive effect on the planet's water. When I saw no plants growing on the rocks below a certain line, I guessed it was because no plants *could* grow there. Plants are tough and resilient. You'll find them in all of Earth's tidal zones. For nothing to grow on the lower slopes of this mountain, the force of water regularly sweeping across them had to be tremendous. I would be surprised if any plants at all grow on the coastal sea floors."

Setia frowned. "I thought birds were your thing. How come you know so much?"

"How come you're so suspicious when I know something you don't? What can I say? I read a lot."

"It was an astute observation," Moody commented, "and I am extremely grateful for it. Going back to my proposal, Sheldrake, would you mind being my partner as we attempt to get some rest? We are fairly close in height."

"Sure," Sheldrake replied. "We could all use some shuteye. You go first. I'll wake you in an hour or so."

The two men turned back-to-back and shuffled sideways to prop themselves against the cliff. Moody relaxed and closed his eyes.

"Want to do the same?" Setia asked Carys.

"We can try."

They moved into the small remaining space next to the men. Carys ended up facing Sheldrake, their knees almost touching.

"You go to sleep, Carys," Setia said.

"I don't think I can." She was cold, hungry and dreadfully thirsty. She knew from childhood experiences that privation made her more alert, not less so.

"In that case..." Setia settled against her back, and in a few minutes Carys felt her go limp.

The night was not dark. Though Polaris Aa had sunk out of

sight, its rays continued to shine around the planet, turning the sky deep red and allowing the glimmer of only a few stars.

Was that why the aliens were so insular? They'd developed space travel yet they hadn't tried to venture beyond the confines of their star system. Or not as far as she knew. They'd made contact with the intelligent life forms in the Polaris B system but only declared hostilities. Was it because—to them—the universe consisted of few other suns? The arrival of the *Bres* must have been a huge surprise.

"Have you figured out what's going on?" Sheldrake whispered.

"With Setia? Don't worry. She's always like that."

"Not Zees. I mean what's happening here. What do you think the aliens are trying to do with us?"

"I don't know. I can't figure it out. If they want to kill us this is an elaborate way of going about it. But they're an extraterrestrial species, so who knows what they're trying to do? We have to survive as long as we can and hope it all becomes clear eventually."

"You're right. We don't have a choice, but..." Sheldrake's features turned pensive in the dim red glow of the night sky.

"What?"

"I really want this mission to succeed. I want to make sure these aliens join the Federation the Fleet is setting up. For me, it's about more than survival."

"Why?"

"It just is."

There was a conviction in his tone stronger than Carys had ever heard from him, not even on Prime when he'd been deep in his military mindset. Sheldrake had always been a principled kind of guy, but this was something else. Desperation seemed to underlie his words.

She replied, "First, we survive. Then we can tackle the whole Federation thing." She hoped his need to fulfil the mission's purpose wouldn't lead him into doing something stupid. He would risk all their lives.

His head had sunk low as he brooded.

"Sheldrake," Carys said. "I'm sorry."

His gaze met hers. "For what? None of this is your fault."

She heaved a heavy sigh. Setia began to slip sideways, heading for a nasty drop into the ocean. Carys reached around and pushed her against the rock face. Setia snorted and shifted, settling again.

"I'm the reason you're here," Carys explained. She told him how she'd asked for him to join the team in the mistaken belief she was helping him. "If it weren't for me, you would be safe on the *Bres*."

"Don't beat yourself up, Ellis. You didn't know this would happen. I appreciate the favour. Doesn't matter how it's turned out. Have you thought up a plan yet?"

"Uh, no. Not die? How about you?"

"Nope. Nothing. But we need to think of something before the others wake up."

"Do we? Maybe we should all decide on a plan together."

"It's better if one person takes the lead, makes the decisions. We lost Torres, so someone needs to step into his boots. It's better this way. Believe me."

"Is that what being in the military has taught you?"

"There's a reason it's set up like it is. In life-or-death situations you need a hierarchy of command. That's what works. Not democracy. We can't get mired in decision-making, second-guessing everything. It wastes time and we'll end up fighting amongst ourselves. Look, Zees is a loner at heart. She isn't a team player. It's not her fault, but that's how it is with her. If it comes down to it, she'll put herself first. Dr Moody's too much in his head. I don't think he even realises the trouble we're in yet. When he does, he might go to pieces. You and me, we're different. We're steady, and we look out for other people."

"Didn't Setia save your life on Prime when you fell into a fissure?"

"She did and I'm grateful. But she didn't have to put herself in danger to do it. She pulled me out of that hole like a magician pulling a rabbit out of a hat. It was easy for her. If things get tough..." He shrugged.

Carys thought he was underestimating Setia's capacity for caring for her fellow human beings. But he didn't know her very well. He hadn't spent much time around her after the *Bres* had departed Prime. "I don't have any ideas, but if you want to run something by me I'm happy to hear it."

"These aliens are like birds, right? Maybe you can guess how they might be thinking."

"Urgh, don't start. That's what Bujold thought too. But I know sod all about those creatures. I can't guess the first thing about how they might think."

"You said you saw one earlier. What did it look like?"

"I saw something flying. I don't even know if it was one of them."

"C'mon, Ellis. You've gotta try harder."

"How about *you* try harder?" She was seething. Why was he putting all the responsibility on her shoulders? Didn't she have enough to do just keeping herself alive?

"Calm down. I know you can do it. I have faith in you. And, don't worry, whatever plan you think up, I'll back you, one hundred per cent."

"Gee, thanks."

Silence fell between them, broken only by the sough of waves on the rocks far below. Despite rejecting Sheldrake's proposal that she become de facto leader of the team, she did think hard about what they should do. She cast her mind back to the glimpse of the creature in the sky, the single sign of life anyone had seen since they'd arrived on the planet. She delved once more into her memory of the sighting, and it occurred to her there had been something odd about the animal's appearance, but she didn't know exactly what.

As time passed while she waited to wake Setia, a second tide arrived, filling the air with a rushing sound. Then it was gone. The sky began to brighten. Sheldrake decided to wake up Moody, so Carys woke Setia too. The other woman started violently and Carys had to turn and grab her, nearly causing them both to slip to their deaths. Setia apologised and told Carys to go to sleep.

The stars had faded. Even the occasional satellite passing overhead had disappeared. Soon, Polaris Aa would emerge and irradiate them with its terrible rays. Carys closed her eyes, her mind remaining a blank about any future plans. As it was, she would be happy to survive the next few hours.

Twenty-Two

A deep, bass rumble shook Carys from her slumber. Her first realisation as she returned to consciousness was that Setia's back was rigid against her own, almost as hard and unyielding as the mountain slope. Her second realisation was a painful sensation emanating from her left cheek. Whilst deeply asleep, she had slumped onto a rocky protrusion. It felt as though it had bored a hole into her face.

Polaris Aa had risen. Half-visible around the curve of the mountainside, the sun hung fully above the horizon, taking up a vast amount of sky and casting Sheldrake and Moody's forms into shadow.

She lifted her head. "Wha...?"

"Stay still," Setia hissed.

Carys focused her blurry vision. Sheldrake still sat opposite, but he wasn't looking at her. He was looking at a spot to her rear, his expression grave and intense. Moody was awake too and peering over his shoulder, his gaze focused in the same spot as Sheldrake's. The scientist's eyes were round and his mouth slack.

Sheldrake's attention flicked to her before moving away again. He'd given no indication of what he was looking at or what she should do about it. He was frozen, his hands clasping his knees.

The rumble sounded again.

Carys hadn't been sure if she'd dreamt it and there might be some other reason for her companions' terror, but now there could be no doubt. The thing Sheldrake and Moody were looking at, the thing that Setia had warned her not to trigger with her movement, had to be the cause.

Her mind flew back to the *Bres*'s bridge and the sound recording the comms officer had played, piercing everyone's ears with screeching. The officer had explained he'd over-adjusted the pitch of the aliens' 'speech', which was below human hearing range. Yet she could clearly hear this thing she couldn't see. Or had she sensed vibrations in the air and rock? Maybe the creature was only a wild animal attracted by the sight of new, strange arrivals in its territory.

"We have a visitor?" she softly asked.

Sheldrake glared at her and gave an almost imperceptible shake of his head.

Somewhere behind her rocks scraped together. Some broke loose and bounced heavily down the cliff. Distant splashes sounded from below.

The thing had moved and, whatever it was, it was big. The mission team had scrambled over the nearly vertical slopes for hours yesterday without dislodging much more than small rocks and shale. Anything larger had already been weathered away—until this animal had happened along.

Carys's chest tightened over her hammering heart. Her companions' fear was infectious, regardless of the fact that she couldn't even see what was provoking it.

"Setia," she whispered, "you have to scare it off."

"Shh!"

"Don't shush me," she murmured. "That thing might think we're new, tasty prey that's suddenly appeared in its habitat. It might try its luck and attack. You have to frighten it away."

In truth, she wasn't sure she was giving good advice. All her knowledge was based on Earth species. The animals on this planet might behave entirely differently. But she had a hunch she was right. The thing had moved closer. It was interested in them and probably wouldn't leave until it had investigated further. Even if it didn't intentionally hurt them, something so big could easily prod or poke them from their precarious positions.

But Setia remained still.

There was another crunch and rattle as more rocks were scraped by the passage of a large animal.

"Setia!" Carys urged.

"If we don't move it might not think we're edible."

"Nice theory. That doesn't work for birds, so maybe not in this case either."

"All right, all right, Ms Know-It-All. What do I do?"

"Jump up—without falling off. Shout as loud as you can and wave your arms around."

Sheldrake said, "I'll do it."

"No, Setia has to. She's closest. If you scare it, it might decide to bite only the nearest, non-scary thing. In other words, her."

"Okay," Setia muttered, "here goes."

Carys braced herself against the cliff, stiffening with tension, terrified that she was wrong. A split second later, the support of Setia's body was gone. Her friend had leapt up. Carys turned. At first, all she could see was the back of Setia's legs, trousers cut to shreds by the aliens' bots, skin scraped and grazed by rocks.

Then she saw it.

The creature was even bigger than she'd imagined. Perched awkwardly on the steep slope, its higher leg was tightly bent, the lower one fully extended, both sporting huge, taloned feet. Small, smooth, dun-coloured feathers clothed the legs and extended up the bulbous body, washed pale by the intense sunlight. And the wings...

"Shout!" she yelled.

But Setia was silent.

Carys clambered upright, twisting to face the creature. She lifted her arms, though the movement felt slow and cumbersome.

Something about the alien wasn't right. Its body didn't conform with anything in her imagination. She registered limbs where there should be none—extra limbs?

She opened her mouth to scream, but her throat constricted and nothing came out. Feebly, she waved her arms. They felt weak and heavy and they sank to her sides.

A roar erupted from behind her. Sheldrake was up and shouting.

Expletives exploded from his mouth as he bellowed at the creature.

It didn't have any effect.

The monstrous head tilted one way then the other as the alien appeared to try to make sense of what it was seeing. It stepped forward. A stone broke loose beneath its foot, unbalancing it. The spreading, impossibly large wings beat as it briefly lifted from its position. The draught hit Carys.

"Back up!" Sheldrake ordered.

Was he talking to the alien, or did he mean *they* should back up? But she couldn't move and neither, it seemed, could Setia.

"Ellis! Zees! Move!" Sheldrake grabbed Carys's shoulders.

His touch snapped her from her trance. "Setia!" She took her friend's arm and shook it.

At the same time, the creature lunged and grabbed Setia around the waist.

It had hands!

How?

How did it have wings *and* hands?

Setia shrieked and punched upwards, her fist smacking into the bottom of the creature's throat. Unfazed, it raised her up, pulling Carys upwards too.

She tightened her grip on Setia's arm.

Setia punched again and again, her free fist hammering the animal's chest and neck. She viciously kicked it. Had it been an Earth creature, her blows might have killed it. But this thing seemed indestructible. Her reaction only seemed to fuel its curiosity as it lifted her higher and peered closer.

Carys was being lifted as well. Her feet left the rocks and she dangled, swinging free.

"Let go!" Setia called out, jiggling and jerking her arm to loosen Carys's grip. "Let go of me!"

"No!" Carys grunted as she clung on, fastening her other hand on Setia's wrist. "Hit it! Hit it with everything you have."

But Setia had to be already hitting the creature as hard as she could.

Carys felt a hand grasp her, sending a shudder of pain up her leg. Sheldrake had grabbed her wounded ankle.

"It's no good, Carys," Setia panted. "Let go of me, you idiot. Save yourself. Get away while it's distracted."

"No!"

A worse pain than the one from her ankle was building in

Carys's chest. Setia wasn't the best friend in the world, but there was no way she was going to give her up to this horrendous beast.

The great wings beat again and the creature rose into the air, taking Setia with it and, by extension, Carys too.

There was a sharp tug on her leg from Sheldrake, breaking her hold on Setia's arm. She fell onto rocks. Her knees smacked into them and she tumbled sideways. The fall to the ocean loomed, but something caught her shirt and she hung suspended, her arms windmilling before she was hauled backwards onto solid ground.

The creature was already metres away, flying out over the waves, Setia held tight to its stomach. She continued to fight, punching and kicking, squirming to break free.

Helpless, Carys watched. A knot thickened in her throat and her chest heaved.

The alien flew on. It was heading south, perpendicular to the rising sun, at an astonishing speed. Now she could see it at a distance, Carys knew this was one of the creatures she'd seen yesterday soaring at a high altitude. What would it do with Setia? Where was it taking her? Would aliens be along soon to get the rest of them?

"Oh my goodness!" Moody exclaimed.

What had he seen? Carys squinted for a better look at Setia and her captor, but nothing seemed to have changed.

"Ellis," said Sheldrake, "there's something you need to see."

He gently touched her shoulder.

Tearing her focus from her friend, Carys turned.

More aliens were approaching, but they were crawling across the cliff face from Moody's side of the mountain. Though they seemed to be the same species as the alien that had taken Setia, they were smaller, much smaller, only the size of an adult human. Perhaps they couldn't fly. They appeared to rely heavily on their hands to make their way across the rocks.

"We stand a better chance against these," Moody remarked, squaring his fists.

There were seven of them. Even with the additional strength conferred by low gravity, Carys doubted she and her companions could put up a good fight in their weakened state. At least two against one? It was unlikely they could avoid whatever the aliens intended.

They halted a few metres away. Their light golden eyes, bisected by vertical pupils, surveyed the beings from another world. The humans stared back.

Concern for Setia snapped Carys's attention back to the wide ocean. Her gaze returned to the distant flying creature. It continued to flap lazily, its burden loose in its grasp. Setia appeared to have given up fighting. Was she injured? Had it killed her? Or perhaps she'd wisely judged that this was not the moment to make her captor release her.

It did anyway.

Carys screamed.

Setia's tiny figure plummeted towards the water, turning over and over in the air.

She hit the surface of the ocean and disappeared.

Twenty-Three

Setia...

In her mind's eye Carys saw her friend stepping gingerly over spilled water in the *Bres*'s restroom, admonishing her for calling Waylis an elf. Carys saw Setia tossing Miriam over a stream on Talman Prime. She saw her sipping a Margarita in one of the *Bres*'s bars, chuckling over some joke.

The creature that had taken her friend continued to fly nonchalantly over the open waves, as if it had only discarded a piece of rubbish inadvertently picked up.

The place where Setia had vanished was already impossible to distinguish. The distance was too great. Had she risen to the surface of the water? Surely a fall from such a great height would have killed her.

Carys choked.

"What?" Sheldrake asked. "What's wrong? What were you screaming about? Did you see something?" He shaded his eyes as he peered out to sea.

Carys squeezed out, "It... It dropped her."

"Are you sure?"

She swallowed. "I'm sure."

"That creature must be two or three miles away," Moody said, "and the sunlight is extremely strong. You might be mistaken."

"I'm not mistaken!" Carys covered her mouth and breathed in

deeply. Then she let her hands fall to her sides. "I saw her hit the water."

"Then..." Sheldrake murmured.

Nothing further needed to be said. If Setia had been dropped into the ocean, even if she survived the impact, how could she swim all the way back to land? And if she managed the feat, how would she scale the cliffs and find them?

"I'm sorry," said Moody, "but there's nothing we can do to help her, and we have more pressing issues at hand."

The human-sized aliens remained clinging to the rocks a few metres away, watching with their strange, golden eyes. As soon as they saw they had the newcomers' attention once more, they crawled forward.

Carys backed up to the edge of the small hollow.

Now she was less distracted, she could take a good look at them. What had at first appeared to be extra limbs were, in fact, only their arms. The confusing thing about their anatomy was that their legs formed the framework for their wings. Coated in fine feathers, the wings were attached to the creatures' armpits, stretched out to their knees, then more wing material covered the space between half of their long, prehensile tails and the inner section of their lower legs.

It was the weirdest body form Carys had ever seen. No Earth animal had it as far as she was aware, not flying squirrels, sugar gliders, flying lizards nor any other non-avian aerial species. The advantage of the aliens' anatomy was obvious: these creatures could hold tools, and they could grip rocks to traverse the steep slopes of their planet's landmasses and yet also fly/glide across the oceans. If any form of life on this world could evolve high intelligence and become dominant, it was this one.

Had a similar species ever appeared in Earth's evolutionary history? Maybe it had, but one of the mass extinctions had wiped it out. Humankind had been fortunate to not encounter this competitor.

"What do you think they want?" Sheldrake asked.

"Who knows?" Moody replied.

The one at the front of the group spoke. The sound it made was like the rumble of its bigger cousin but higher-pitched.

"They seem to want to talk," Moody commented.

Carys blurted, "They can tell us how to save Setia! Maybe they have a boat or something." Even as the words left her mouth she knew how stupid she sounded. How could they possibly convey the idea of a boat to these aliens? What use would they have for boats?

The group simultaneously edged closer. Carys moved backwards and stumbled over the lip of the hollow.

Sheldrake grabbed her. "Take it easy."

Moody said, "I don't *think* these ones mean us any harm."

"You don't know that!" Carys exclaimed. "They might mean us a lot of harm, just different harm from the one that killed Setia." She gasped. She'd said it. She'd stated the fact that Setia was probably dead.

With perfect timing, all the aliens' heads simultaneously swung sideways and they gazed out over the ocean. Carys looked in the same direction, but all she could see was water and empty air, dazzling in the rays of Polaris Aa. The aliens chattered among themselves and the two at the rear crawled away. The remainder moved towards the humans. The leader arrived within touching distance of Moody and reached out, its bizarre monkey hand open.

Moody didn't flinch but neither did he touch the offered hand. "I believe it wants something."

"They're scared," said Sheldrake. "They've seen something out there."

Carys couldn't decide who was right. Maybe they both were. She couldn't think. Her head was filled with the image of a tiny figure spinning in the air, plummeting towards distant waves.

"What do you want?" Moody asked the creature. He performatively patted his ragged, dirty clothes. "I have nothing to give you."

The creature stretched further and gently stroked the scientist's arm. As if emboldened by Moody's non-reaction, it grasped his wrist.

"Oh!" Moody muttered. "I'm not sure..."

Another alien chattered loudly and flapped a hand while staring intently at the horizon.

The one holding Moody gave a firm pull on his arm.

"They want you to go with them," said Sheldrake, "and fast."

"Only me? All of us, I should think. Though I agree the matter seems urgent."

Carys could also feel the creatures' tension, though whatever was causing it remained beyond her sight.

"We should do what they want," said Moody. "I'm sure they mean to help us."

"You don't know that," Carys snapped. "Look what one of them did to Setia."

"But not one of these," the scientist countered. "These seem to be different."

"They're just younger, that's all. Anatomically, they're the same."

A shock ran through the creatures, and they chattered noisily. Moody's alien let go of him and ran back to the others. They appeared to come to a decision and they began to hastily crawl away, following the two who had already left.

Sheldrake said, "We should go with them. Some shit's going down. They were trying to protect us."

"You don't know that," said Carys. "We can't trust them."

"Maybe not, but I trust my gut."

Moody wasn't even arguing. He was already scrambling over the rocks on the tail of the departing aliens.

"We have to leave with them," Sheldrake urged.

"No!" Carys gazed out over the ocean. The alien that had taken Setia was out of sight. Where had she hit the water? "If we leave, how will Setia ever find us? We have to stay here."

"Stay here with no food, no water, and in this light? We won't survive another day."

Carys couldn't deny the truth of his words. They were all badly sunburned, and on the slopes there were no trees, no crevices, nowhere to escape the scorching beams.

But something kept her rooted to the spot.

"Ellis," said Sheldrake, "I know what you're thinking. But you're wrong. Zees wouldn't want you to wait for her. She would want you to save yourself."

The small aliens had vanished around the curve of the mountainside, Moody on their tail.

"C'mon!" Sheldrake urged.

Blinking away tears, she stepped towards him.

"That's it," he said. "Let's go."

They hurried after Moody, but by the time they reached the other side of the curve he'd disappeared.

"What?" Carys abruptly halted. "Where's he gone?"

The mountainside continued into the distance, featureless except for rocks dotted with spiny plants, already baking in the heat from Polaris Aa.

"He's gotta be here somewhere," Sheldrake peered downwards, as if Moody and the aliens might have descended to the waves.

An arm appeared from some rocks and waved.

"There he is!" yelled Carys.

As they neared the arm, Moody's head joined it. He was standing in a cleft between two boulders, one protruding over the other, hiding a gap in the slope. As they approached the scientist dipped inside, making room for them to enter.

Twenty-Four

The relief at being out of the sun was enormous. Carys halted, blinking, basking in the cool shade and moist air. She was standing in a large, bare chamber, its walls and ceiling patterned in brilliant shades.

"Who could have imagined it?" Moody remarked. "All that time we were struggling on the exposed mountainside *this* was beneath our feet."

Carys wasn't sure what *this* was yet. Circular openings, flattened at the bases, led from the room. Only four of the original aliens remained. Now they were indoors they held their wings close to their bodies. Rather than holding their tails aloft as they had outside, they allowed them to flop passively on the floor.

"Yeah," Sheldrake said. "Looks like that shuttle platform wasn't in the middle of nowhere after all."

Carys cast a glance at the cleft through which they'd entered. It was the only irregular shape in the place—a gash in the chamber wall. She stepped over to it and peered out.

This provoked immediate chattering among their alien hosts.

She glimpsed the distant form of another of the large beasts heading closer before she was dragged away by their hosts. "Hey!" She shrugged off the clinging hands. "Don't touch me."

Moody said, "They're trying to keep you safe. They're trying to keep us all safe. That's why they brought us here."

"You don't know that. You don't know anything about them."

For a scientist, Moody was jumping to an awful lot of conclusions from scant evidence. His excitement about meeting real aliens seemed to have gone to his head. Nothing else mattered. Not the loss of Setia or Torres, nor the fact that they were stranded with no way to contact the ship.

The two aliens she'd rebuffed remained too close for comfort. She moved away, but as she did so, one grabbed her shirt. It rubbed the cloth between its three fingers and opposing thumb.

"Let go of me!" With a shudder, she attempted to unfasten the fingers. The alien's hand felt bony, cool and slippery as silk.

It released her shirt but immediately transferred its touch to her face, prodding her cheek. She slapped the hand away. The alien backed off, chattering to its friend.

Moody began, "I believe they're only curi—"

"I don't care what you believe! What's wrong with you? Have you gone crazy? Why do you trust them?"

"It seems obvious they're curious about your clothes. They don't wear any, so they must be wondering what are our bodies and what are coverings."

The aliens moved to an opening and clustered there, watching the humans.

"I think they want us to go with them," said Moody.

"That doesn't mean we should." Carys looked wistfully at the gap in the external wall.

"You need to forget about Setia," Sheldrake said. "I know it's hard, but she's most likely dead, and if she is alive there's nothing we can do to help her."

They were led to another room. This one had furniture—of a kind. A low bar ran around the perimeter and a number of raised flat surfaces stood in front of it. Carys and her companions hesitated in the doorway. The aliens waited in the centre of the room and watched them expectantly.

"What are we supposed to do?" Sheldrake asked.

As if in answer, one of the creatures approached him and gently took his arm. He was guided to the low bar.

"Ohhh," said Carys as recognition struck.

Before she could explain, the alien with Sheldrake delicately climbed onto the bar and squatted on it, wings closely folded.

Carys said, "They want us to sit down."

"Sit?" Sheldrake asked, eyeing the bar. "On that thing?"

"Well, not exactly. They want us to perch. They can't sit like we do."

Sheldrake shrugged and then lowered himself onto the bar. His perplexed, uncomfortable look was so comical Carys almost chuckled, despite her sadness over the loss of Setia.

"I see," said Moody. "Makes absolute sense." He sat down next to Sheldrake. "I must say, however, it is rather uncomfortable."

The humans' actions provoked a great deal of discussion among the aliens. The one who had brought Sheldrake to the bar bent down to stare at the man's lower half.

Carys had no option except to join Sheldrake and Moody. The rounded surface was hard and unyielding, and she was forced to bend her knees up to her chest to squat on it.

More aliens appeared in the doorway, carrying wide bowls. They brought them in and placed them in front of the humans.

"Water!" Moody exclaimed. "At last. Thank goodness."

The central bowl contained what did seem to be water. Bowls on each side of it held different liquids. One was brown and opaque like river water filled with sediment. The other was pale green and steamed.

"I don't think we should drink anything except water," Carys said, "if that's what the middle one is. The others might be poisonous to us."

"Excellent point." Moody leaned over the central bowl and sniffed. "Can't smell anything." He dipped in a finger and cautiously touched it to the tip of his tongue. "I believe it *is* water. We're all dreadfully thirsty. In the circumstances, it would be reasonable for one of us to take the risk of drinking it. I'm willing to play guinea pig, but I'm not sure how."

It was clearly a problem. The bowl was wide and shallow. It wasn't too large to pick up, but he would probably slop water all over himself if he tried to drink from it. On the other hand, to bring his lips sufficiently near the surface to drink he would have to submerge his nose. He wasn't a cat or dog with a lapping tongue or an elephant with a handy trunk. As Moody tried to figure it out, the aliens continued to watch.

Then one stepped forwards and picked up the water bowl.

"No, no," Moody protested. "Don't take it away. We want it."

Carys ran her tongue over her dry lips. "You'll just have to try." She hoped that water wasn't a precious commodity around here. Whatever Moody did it seemed bound to result in spillage.

The scientist awkwardly lowered himself to the edge of the bowl and tipped it towards his waiting lips. Water dripped out on the table but he did a reasonable job of minimising it. He gasped, "Tastes wonderful. I'm sure it's fresh water. It would be wise to be cautious and only drink a little, but to hell with it." He tipped up the bowl again and drank long draughts as the liquid spilled out on each side of his mouth.

"Hey, buddy," said Sheldrake, tapping Moody's shoulder, "leave some for the rest of us."

The scientist sat up and wiped his lips. "I do apologise. I got carried away. Please, help yourselves."

"You first, Ellis," Sheldrake said.

"No, you're bigger than me. You must be thirstier."

It was testament to how thirsty Sheldrake was that he didn't need further urging. He drank deeply before raising his head. "If it isn't water, that's two of us poisoned."

Carys was similarly unable to resist the chance to slake her thirst. The water was cool and it tasted clean and sweet, as if from a mountain stream. By the time she'd finished the bowl was sitting in a puddle.

While she'd been drinking more bowl bearers had arrived. The drinks were removed and replaced with 'food'.

"Gross," Sheldrake commented.

He was probably referring to the inches-deep container of live maggots.

Other foods included raw grains, a green mess, and stems covered in tough, brown nodules.

"Can we risk eating this?" Carys poked the green stuff. It was cold and jellylike. Though she was hungry, her stomach churned with disgust. "Food from this planet could kill us."

"We have no choice," said Moody. "Yet everything is..." he appeared to struggle for words "...quite unappetising."

It was the understatement of the century.

"We can't eat this shit," said Sheldrake.

That was more like what Carys was thinking.

"We can't eat this," Sheldrake repeated, addressing the aliens.

"They don't understand." Moody pointed at the bowl of maggots and shook his head firmly. "No good for us, I'm afraid."

Carys said, "They won't understand you either."

"I know," the scientist replied, "but perhaps they'll guess my meaning."

"I doubt any of it is safe for us to eat anyway."

Moody countered, "We may be stuck here a long time. We must eat or we'll starve to death before rescue arrives, assuming we're ever rescued."

The prospect of never returning to the ship was appalling. Carys already missed Loki desperately, and she was concerned about the aviary birds. Miriam could do the basics but she couldn't tend to their long-term needs, and Bujold already had plans for their destruction. How long would the captain wait before giving up hope for the mission members' return? How much longer would she continue to allow the ship's resources to be 'wasted' on birds?

Even if the remaining members of the mission team eventually made it back to the *Bres*, it might be too late.

"I know what they'll understand." Sheldrake picked up some of the green slop between his fingertips, pretended to eat it, and then mimed vomiting.

"Uhh," Carys said, "I don't think that's going to work."

"Why not?" Moody asked. "It seems pretty clear to me. Well done, Sheldrake. Smart thinking."

The aliens immediately cleared the bowls, apparently concluding something from Sheldrake's actions.

"You see?" Moody said. "They do understand. They're going to bring us different foods that may be more palatable to us."

Carys agreed that the aliens would probably try other dishes, but Moody clearly didn't know much about the nutritional strategies of birds. The first foods the aliens had brought appeared to conform to Earth avians' diets, and though it would be wrong to assume the aliens were like birds in every way, there were similarities that were hard to ignore. She hoped she was wrong about what was coming next, but she feared she was right.

They waited several minutes.

"I can't wait to see more offerings," Moody commented. "I'm absolutely famished."

Carys shifted uncomfortably on the bar. The hard surface was digging into her buttocks.

More food arrived.

"At last," said Moody.

The aliens set the bowls down.

"What...?" Moody bent over them and his features twisted. "What the hell is this stuff? It looks absolutely disgusting."

New substances filled the dishes—liquid substances of a range of colours and textures. Bits and pieces of what might have once been other foods hung suspended in the fluids, and the odours given off were acidic and somewhat putrid.

Sheldrake wrinkled his nose. "Looks like someone already ate it."

"I think you've got it," Carys remarked.

"You mean this is...?" Moody's eyebrows rose to spectacular heights. "Surely not. Why would they...?" Understanding dawned on his face. "Of course. I was forgetting."

"You were forgetting what?" Sheldrake asked.

"It's a common habit among birds to feed their young with partially digested, regurgitated food."

"What?" Sheldrake turned green.

Carys said, "When you mimed puking up your guts, they assumed—"

He put a hand over his mouth and gagged.

Twenty-Five

No one seemed to know what to do about the food situation. More dishes were offered but nothing humans could eat. In the end, the aliens brought water again, which was gratefully received. The ache in Carys's stomach eased somewhat by filling it with liquid.

The light in the room was fading. There were no artificial lights in the ceiling or walls. Instead, rays shone from numerous slits. The beams had a natural, golden quality. Was it sunlight, reflecting through a series of mirrors to illuminate the habitation? The strength of a sun like Polaris Aa would allow for the possibility.

"What are they doing?" Moody asked.

The bowls of water were being removed and, along with them, the low tables.

"I guess feeding time's over," said Sheldrake. "They tried their best but we can't eat their food. We'll have to fend for ourselves somehow."

"We will," Moody agreed. "I wonder if they will allow us to leave this place."

"There's only one way to find out." Sheldrake got to his feet.

"Look," Carys said, "I don't know what's going on any better than you two, but I think we should rest. I'm exhausted after that night on the mountainside, and we don't seem to be in any danger. I know I was sceptical at first, but I think you were right, Moody. The attitude of these aliens is different from the one that took Setia. They want to help us, or at least protect us. We should figure out how to communicate with them and spend some time recovering."

Sheldrake replied, "It's early days. We shouldn't relax our guard yet. If we're gonna sleep, we should take turns keeping watch again."

"And if something happens," Moody said, "what could we possibly do about it? We're unarmed and outnumbered. We're utterly defenceless. We might as well do as Carys says and take the opportunity to fully rest ourselves. Who knows what tomorrow may bring?"

The tables were gone, the light had dimmed to twilight, and the aliens were watching expectantly once more.

Moody asked, "Will they bring us some bedding, do you think?"

"Probably not," Carys replied. "They most likely expect us to sleep on our perches."

"I see." The scientist lay down on the floor. "Well, this is going to be rather uncomfortable, but never mind."

Carys curled up in a corner of the room, resting her head on her arm. The aliens seemed to guess the humans wanted to sleep and left them alone. The room suddenly turned dark, as if someone had closed the apertures leading to the exterior.

In the anonymity of darkness, Carys silently wept. She wept for Loki and her birds, who would die if she couldn't make it back to the *Bres*, and she wept for Setia. It was only now her friend was gone that Carys realised how much the woman had meant to her. Their relationship had been candid. They hadn't spared each other's sensitivities. But their abrasiveness had been like that of siblings, confident to speak their minds, knowing the other wouldn't take offence. They'd had an understanding borne of mutual affinity.

She had brought Setia here.

And now her friend was dead.

———

When Carys awoke her arm was stiff and sore and her neck had a crick in it. The wound on her ankle was throbbing, too, but upon inspection it didn't look infected. Sheldrake was already awake and alone, perched on the bar.

With a groan, she sat up. "Where's—"

"He's gone to check the place out."

"He just left? No one stopped him?"

"The corridor's empty. No guards. Look for yourself if you don't believe me."

"I believe you." She rubbed her neck.

"Bad night?"

"You can tell? How about you?"

"I slept okay, but there's an empty, angry hole where my stomach used to be."

His words reminded her how long it had been since she'd eaten, and a sympathetic growl issued from her middle. She was ravenous. "Same here."

"We've gotta eat today. If we don't, we'll start to get weak and confused. Gotta keep our wits about us."

"Hmm." She stood and stretched, gingerly twisting her neck to one side and then the other. "I don't disagree, but we might have to overcome some squeamishness."

"I'm not eating maggots! We should look around on the mountainside and find our own food."

She walked to the door and peered up and down the empty corridor. "Assuming we aren't prevented from leaving this place, what do you think we'll find to eat? You saw what it's like out there. And it's dangerous. Another one of the big aliens might swoop down and..." She couldn't complete the sentence. The loss of Setia was still too raw.

"We'll have to take our chances. Besides, we have to try to contact the ship. Let them know we're alive. We'll never do it from in here."

She turned to face him. "How do you propose we do that?"

"The *Bres* will be scanning the planet. If we built something, like stones laid out to spell HELP, they might see it."

Carys wasn't confident the *Bres* still existed. With her navigation jammed she wouldn't be able to jump to the Red Zone, and the aliens had at least three ships with military capabilities. Even if Bujold changed her mind about firing back the *Bres* might not win the battle.

But voicing her doubts wouldn't help matters. "That's not a bad idea."

Footsteps sounded in the corridor. Moody was back. "Come with me, guys. I found something. You have to see it."

"What?" Sheldrake asked, getting to his feet.

But the scientist was already hurrying away. He said over his shoulder, "I want to show you and see if you agree with me about what it is. It's remarkable. Not at all what I was expecting."

He was heading in the opposite direction from the way they had arrived yesterday. The corridor curved, and an opening in the wall came into view. It was circular with a flat base.

"That's one of the vertical access points," Moody remarked, scurrying past it. "Useless to us."

Carys took a look through the portal. A wide tunnel ran straight upwards and downwards, with narrow ledges set into the wall at intervals. She leaned farther in to try to see the bottom but it disappeared into darkness.

A flurrying sound came from above. An alien was descending, gliding smoothly around and around. It lightly touched a toe to one of the ledges and then, as she watched, it flew past and descended into the tunnel's depths.

"Carys!" Moody had halted and was waiting, hands on hips. "We have to hurry. We don't know if our hosts might decide to restrict our freedom. They don't seem to know what to make of us at the moment, but who knows how long that state will continue?"

He took them farther along the corridor until they reached a smaller doorway. "These may be for aliens who haven't completely mastered flying yet."

Beyond him was a set of spiral stairs leading downwards. The treads were wide and the steps progressed at a shallow gradient. Beckoning, Moody raced down them.

Carys and her companions navigated six or seven turns until the stairway abruptly stopped at an exit. Like the other openings it was circular, but a smooth, featureless door sealed it.

"Don't worry," Moody announced. "It's fine. It isn't locked. Or, at least, it wasn't a moment ago." He pushed the door.

As it opened, noises from the other side leaked out. Mechanical noises. Hammering, clattering, and a faint, low hiss Carys was sure she'd heard before but she couldn't place it. There was also the chatter of alien voices.

The voices quietened and so did most of the mechanical sounds. Some noises continued: a regular *thump, thump, thump* and the jangle of something metallic falling.

They were in a workroom, or perhaps a factory. Rows of aliens—a hundred or more—perched on bars at low tables. They seemed to be making netting from a fibrous material. At the farther end of the room bright blue flames flared.

Acetylene torches?

Were they causing the familiar low hiss?

"What is this?" Sheldrake asked. "What's going on?"

Moody replied, "They seem to be making large, loose bags. The smaller workers create the main part by hand, and larger aliens attach metal chains."

"They weld them?" Carys asked.

"Only to join the chains to make a loop. I've no idea what the bags are for. I just thought this place was a remarkable find. This area we've been brought into is clearly for manufacturing, isn't it? It has to be. Raw materials are flown to the platform where our shuttle landed, and workers transform them into—"

"I think we're going to be okay," Carys blurted. "We'll be fine, for now, anyway."

"You mean the workers won't turn us in to their superiors?" Moody asked. "I'm not sure that's at all certain. If it is a manufacturing area, presumably there are supervisors, managers, and so on. Sooner or later, someone important is bound to discover our presence here. And then they will report to the authorities."

"No," said Carys. "I meant if they'll lend us a welding torch and one of those metal containers, we can eat."

Twenty-Six

Carys drew tiny circles in the dust on the floor of the chamber where she and her companions had slept, and then motioned towards her open mouth with her hand, fingers and thumb pressed together at the tips.

The alien looked at her.

What was it thinking?

What was going on behind those golden eyes?

What did it make of her?

Compared to the aliens' pointed saurian snouts, human faces had to seem strangely flat. And what did it make of her teeth? Its own were long and sharp, suited to tearing and cutting. Human dentition, particularly molar teeth, would be confusing. It had no need to grind up its food. If the aliens were anything like Earth birds, the grinding would take place in a crop, aided by grit and stones.

"It's grain," she said, frustrated. "Grain. You brought us some earlier."

Clearly, there was no point in speaking. The words coming out of her mouth were utterly meaningless to it. But surely the 'eating' gesture wasn't hard to understand.

She plucked at the circles in the dust once more, but this time she pretended to move the grains to the alien's mouth. As her hand neared its razor-sharp teeth, it pulled its head backwards sharply and moved away, shuffling on its taloned feet.

She sighed in frustration. Loki wouldn't have been this obtuse. Nor would most of the birds in the *Bres*'s aviary. If there was one thing bird life on Earth understood, it was the need to eat. Why was it so hard to communicate this simple message to a being from another world?

Carys sat on her haunches, ruminating.

"I'll try," said Moody. He patted his stomach and pointed at the circles Carys had drawn. "Mmmm. Nom nom. Delicious."

Chuckling, Carys said, "Thanks. That should do the trick."

"Something needs to do the trick," Sheldrake grumbled. "I'm starving."

In the end, no attempts to communicate the desire for the aliens to bring them grain again worked. They tried everything, but their hosts barely glanced at drawings in the dust, and though they studied the humans' mimes more intently, they obviously couldn't make head nor tail of them.

It was only later in the day, presumably 'dinner time', when the aliens brought a range of food again, that the humans could finally show what they meant.

Carys sprang upon the shallow bowl of raw grain. "This! We can eat this, but we need to prepare it first." She scooped up a handful and let it fall between her fingers. "What next, Moody? Sheldrake? Help me out here."

Moody grabbed a fist of grains and put them on the table. Then he proceeded to pretend to grind the pile with his still-closed fist.

The aliens watched.

"They'll never get it," Carys said. "We'll have to show them." She picked up the bowl. "Let's go back to the factory."

Work on the factory floor had stopped and the place was empty. Perhaps it was lunchtime. Carys and Moody pulled fibrous material used for making nets out of a metal container. The container was large, far larger than they needed for their requirements, but it would have to do.

Meanwhile, Sheldrake had set off in search of a welding torch. Half of the group of aliens followed him while the others stayed with

Carys and Moody. The watchers stood in a half circle, their gazes fixed on the humans.

"You know," Carys said as they worked, "something doesn't add up. Have you noticed their teeth? What are they doing eating the types of food they gave us?"

"I had noticed," Moody replied, "but I didn't want to say anything. It is odd that a creature with a predator's teeth would eat cereals, vegetation and small insect life. Very odd indeed. But I refrained from voicing my observation, for obvious reasons."

"You thought Sheldrake and I would assume we were on the menu?"

"Something like that. I thought it was unlikely, given our hosts' behaviour towards us so far, and what's the point in worrying about something you can't prevent?"

"We could have run away—escaped back to the mountainside."

"Our chances of survival out there would have been slimmer."

Carys turned the container upside down and shook it before carefully scooping out the threads that remained inside. "Well, if this works, we will have improved those chances quite a bit, though I doubt we'll ever get off this planet."

"One step at a time."

Sheldrake was back. "I found one, but I can't move it without detaching the gas supply. It's fed from a pipe that runs into the wall."

"Then the mountain must go to Mohammed," Moody announced.

Sheldrake gave Carys a puzzled look.

"He means we have to carry the container to the torch."

Before they picked it up, she poured half of the bowl of grains into it, creating a layer one grain deep on the bottom. Sheldrake brought the bowl while she and Moody carried the container between them.

The aliens followed like a crowd of locals fascinated by the strange antics of tourists.

The implement Sheldrake had found clearly was one of the torches they'd seen being used earlier, but they couldn't figure out how to make it work. They also had nothing to use as a cover for the container. Their shirts were all too small, as well as full of holes, and there was the risk of setting the cloth alight.

The plan seemed doomed to fail.

"It's no good," Sheldrake said. "It was a good idea, Ellis, but even if we manage to get this thing working..."

His features dropped into an expression full of despair, and Carys wondered how much he'd really come to terms with Torres's death and how much he'd only been putting on a brave face.

"We can do this," she said.

"We can," Moody agreed. "Fear not. We'll figure it out. We must."

Indeed, they had to. Carys's stomach was an angry monster demanding to be fed, and she was already feeling the weakness Sheldrake had foretold.

One of the aliens stepped forward and removed the torch from Sheldrake's grasp.

"He wants us to put it back," Moody said, "before we hurt ourselves."

The alien's demeanour—as far as Carys could interpret it—did seem to indicate the attitude of an adult taking a box of matches from a three-year-old.

But then the alien did something to the torch, and a blue flame spurted from its end. He returned it to Sheldrake and stepped away a few paces.

"I think they're fascinated to see what we're going to do next," Carys commented. "Okay, Sheldrake, you do the honours. Moody, help me lift this thing up."

Along with the scientist, she hoisted the container into the air, giving Sheldrake plenty of room to work. The ex-corporal leaned under the container's base, angling the torch at it.

Whatever metal the container was made from, it was highly conductive.

"Uhh," Moody said, "this is getting rather warm."

Carys felt the same, yet there were no tell-tale sounds coming from the interior indicating her plan had worked. "We have to hold it as long as we can."

Ow.

The heat was becoming unbearable.

"It's no good," Moody gasped. "I have to..."

They partly lowered, partly dropped the container to the floor. Sheldrake moved out of the way just in time. "Guys..."

"We couldn't help it." Carys shoved her burned fingers into her armpits.

Their actions had provoked intense interest among the aliens. A loud chatter arose, and several examined the container and its contents. One gingerly touched it with a taloned toe, pushing it across the floor before staring at the place it had landed.

Luckily, the surface didn't appear scorched.

"We have to try again." Carys took a peek inside the container. "I don't know how much longer they're going to let us mess around." She pulled her shirt down to cover a finger and prodded the grains. Some had changed colour to a deep brown. Her hope that she'd found a solution to the food problem began to slip away. If the grains only cooked they would be even less edible.

"We need the equivalent of oven gloves," Moody said. "That would do the trick."

Sheldrake said, "You can use my... Uhh, yeah, that'll work too."

An alien had appeared carrying a pile of the fibrous material. It helpfully pulled it in half and gave one load to Carys and the other to Moody.

As the humans started up their process again, their onlookers clustered so closely Carys feared someone would get singed. An unbearable amount of time seemed to pass, though in reality it was probably less than a minute. A cooking odour emanated from the suspended pot. Then she smelled the acrid scent of burning.

Damn.

It wasn't going to work.

She couldn't see Moody but she felt his side of the container sag. He appeared to be coming to a similar conclusion.

Pop!

A puffed grain flew out of the container. She barely registered it before she lost sight of it. She had no clue where it had landed.

"Ha!" Moody exclaimed.

He said something else, but his words were drowned out by a cacophony of pops. After nearly reaching burning point, the grains were finally bursting. The explosion of grains caused the container to rattle and shake, and numerous projectiles flew out, showering everyone present. Carys hoped some would remain inside. The aliens drew away in alarm.

"You can stop heating them," she told Sheldrake. "They're hot enough."

Moody was laughing.

Sheldrake grinned as he held the acetylene torch like a trophy. "You did it, Ellis. You goddamned did it. I knew you had it in you."

Carys's feelings were mixed. She was glad they would finally have something to eat, but her mind was back in Australia. Holding a billycan she huddled over a campfire, a starving Displaced Child popping grains spilled from the harvest, painstakingly gathered from the dirt.

Twenty-Seven

Many popped grains remained in the container. Many more were scattered all over the floor. Hunger prevented Carys from caring too much about eating dust on the tiny morsels she, Sheldrake and Moody gleaned after eating the clean ones.

At first, the aliens watched. Their silence seemed to indicate they were surprised by the humans' behaviour. There was no way of telling for sure, but even to other humans, people picking up dirty popped grains from the ground and eating them would have been surprising.

Then, the aliens began to help, finding grains in nooks and crannies and handing them over. Carys accepted them gracefully, but she couldn't help feeling like a pet goat being fed treats by children.

When no one could find any more grains, she and her companions prepared to pop the rest of the raw ones, but before they started one of the aliens ran up with a flimsy metal sheet.

"A lid," said Moody. "Excellent. I knew accepting help from these creatures was the right decision. We would have died of thirst or been picked off the mountainside by their older cousins if we hadn't."

"You think they're the same species?" Carys had come to the same conclusion.

"They may be different sizes but they're the same in every visible respect as far as I can tell. In fact, I would say there are more differences between human children and adults than I've observed in our hosts."

Sheldrake said, "Let's do some more popping. I don't know about you guys, but that handful of popcorn barely scratched my itch."

"It isn't corn," Moody corrected.

"I know, but I don't know what else to call it."

Moody continued, "You know, we may have fatally poisoned ourselves. We have no idea whether the alien grain is edible for humans."

"I'm pretty sure we already had this conversation," Sheldrake retorted. "If we don't eat, we're gonna starve." He waved the lighted acetylene torch. "Lift that thing up."

After suffering no immediate ill effects, they returned to their room somewhat less hungry than they'd been when they left it.

There had been a shift in mood. The aliens' attitude towards them had changed. How, exactly, Carys couldn't articulate, but she felt it nonetheless. She sensed a change in herself, Moody and Sheldrake, too. This change was easier to define. Prior to popping the grain, their prospects of living longer than a few weeks had been slim. Now, assuming the aliens' food could sustain them, they might live for years on this planet.

The dishes they'd rejected earlier remained on the tables along with bowls of water. The aliens rapidly cleared them away. Carys wondered if they might bring more grain. She hoped they would, but trying to ask them was probably hopeless. They hadn't understood her gestures before, and there was no grain left to use as a communication prop.

"I can smell something." Sheldrake drew himself up to his full height and sniffed the air. "What *is* that? It smells like..." His words petered out. He stepped to the doorway and leaned around it.

Carys also sniffed but the only odour she could detect was the musky fragrance the aliens emitted.

"Man, I'm still so hungry," Sheldrake commented, moving back into the room. "Maybe I'm imagining it, but I thought I smelled barbecue."

"Barbecue! Ha!" Moody chuckled and shook his head. "Chance would be a fine thing."

But Carys could smell it too. Except the scent wasn't quite like barbecue. Fishiness underlay it. "You're not imagining it, Sheldrake."

The aliens were chattering. Gently, they pushed Carys and the others to the seating. As they sat down, a new dish arrived. Several aliens carrying a long platter carefully manoeuvred into the room and placed the dish on the table.

"Is that..." Sheldrake gawped. "Is that a-a snake?"

"It's cooked!" Moody exclaimed. "Whatever it is, it's cooked. Perhaps they understood from us popping the grain that we can't eat raw food."

To Carys's eyes, the long, slim, roasted animal lying on the platter looked like an eel. The crisped skin had once been black, and the flesh appeared dense and meaty. The similarity to an eel disappeared when it came to the creature's head, comprising a third of its length and tapering to a point. The cooked eyes protruded from the skull in a grotesque caricature of the grain recently popped.

One of the waiting aliens stooped low and took a bite. Its pointed teeth sliced easily through the flesh. Watching the humans expectantly, it chewed.

"It's showing us how to eat it," said Moody.

Carys said, "Or maybe that it's safe to eat."

Except maybe it wasn't safe, not for humans.

Heaving a sigh, she dug her fingertips into the meat. It was hot but didn't burn. She worked a small piece loose and lifted it to her lips.

"Good luck," said Sheldrake.

She nibbled the edge of the morsel. It was sweet and salty, but that was as far as her assessment went. The food tasted like nothing she'd ever eaten.

"What's it like?" Moody asked.

"Not bad. It's hard to describe."

"Is there any bitterness? Do your lips feel numb?"

Carys shook her head. "Here goes." She put the whole thing in her mouth.

Moody said, "I'm not sure that's wise. It would be better to wait after consuming just a little and assess the effects."

She swallowed. "Some poisonous mushrooms take days to kill people. Even if I feel fine tomorrow, that doesn't mean this thing is edible. And we already ate the grain, so how would we tell which one made us sick?"

"Makes sense to me." Sheldrake plunged his fingers into the meat and tore off a large handful before doing his best to cram all of it in his mouth. He nearly succeeded. He said something that might have been *It's delicious* but it was hard to tell. After a few chews he finished what remained in his hand and tore more meat off the bones.

"Oh well," said Moody, "if you two are throwing caution to the wind, I suppose I should do the same."

Once they began to eat, the long days of deprivation sparked a gorging frenzy. Within fifteen minutes, there was little left of their meal and their hands and face were covered in grease. Carys felt uncomfortably full and nauseated. She also felt mildly embarrassed. Dinner etiquette had never been a big thing while she was growing up, but she'd crossed the line into acting like a complete pig. She wiped her sleeve over her mouth and across her cheeks.

Sheldrake leaned back against the wall and rubbed his stomach. "If we're all gonna die, that was a fabulous last meal."

Moody prodded the skeleton. "This seems to be cartilage. What do you think, Carys?"

She peered at the bones. They were translucent and, after picking one up, she discovered they were flexible. "Who knows? Maybe they're made from a substance we don't— *Oh!*"

A couple of aliens had snatched up the remains of the creature. They swiftly broke the skeleton into fragments and passed them out to the others. Even the head was dismantled. One of the eyes plopped to the floor but was swiftly retrieved.

They ate the leftovers, crunching them loudly with their strong jaws and sharp teeth.

"Waste not, want not, I guess," said Sheldrake.

The aliens seemed to relish eating the parts the humans could not, blinking rapidly as they chewed, nodding in apparent appreciation. Had they given their human guests a precious, hard-to-procure dish? Maybe eating meat—or fish—was rare. Carys felt touched and slightly guilty that their hosts were going to such lengths to help the strange beings who had appeared on their mountain.

Did they know she and her companions weren't from this planet? She hadn't seen any interfaces or anything similar. The aliens didn't even seem to use comms. How did they get their information?

"Guys," Sheldrake said, "now we're in better shape, we need to make moves. We should try to contact the ship and report on our situation."

"I'm not averse to the idea," said Moody, "but I'm at a loss as to how."

"It's simple. We go out onto the surface and create a big sign with rocks. The *Bres*'s scanners will detect it and Captain Bujold will know we're here. She can send down a shuttle to pick us up."

"Forgive me, but that sounds *rather* optimistic."

"Or she can start negotiations for our return. Whatever. Doesn't matter. The point is, we've gotta try. We're on a mission, remember? We have a job to do, and we're not done yet."

Twenty-Eight

The problem was, when they retraced their steps to the entrance chamber and tried to exit via the gap in the wall, the aliens wouldn't allow it. They stood in the way, backs to the exit, waving their arms. Some of them unfolded their wings too, as if to give extra weight to their meaning: the humans should not—or were not allowed to—leave.

"What now?" Moody asked.

"We force our way through," Sheldrake replied. "There's nothing else for it. We can't stay here forever."

"But they might bite us," Moody countered, "and I do *not* like the look of those teeth."

Carys said, "They've been kind so far and virtually let us have the run of the place. I don't think they'll bite." She stepped up to the crowd and gently eased herself into it. Their feathers were soft as eiderdown. Then two aliens grabbed her and pushed her away.

"I'm sorry, we have to leave," she said soothingly. She stepped forwards again. Up close, she could see networks of lines in the aliens' golden irises. Their pupils dilated as she approached. They were clearly feeling strong emotions about something.

"Maybe this isn't such a good idea," Moody said. "What if we manage to leave and they don't allow us to return?"

"We have to take that chance," Sheldrake retorted.

"We have to leave." Carys pushed with more effort into the crowd. When the aliens' strange, bony hands touched her again she disengaged their fingers and stood her ground. "We have to go."

She turned to Sheldrake and Moody. "You two, get over here. Don't make me do this all by myself."

"Shit, you're right." Sheldrake strode over and grabbed one of the aliens by its shoulders. It let out a shriek and gabbled to its fellows.

"Don't hurt them!" Carys protested.

"I wasn't going to." He released the creature, but his aggressiveness had done the trick. The ex-corporal stood taller than everyone and on this low-g planet he was much stronger. The aliens shrank away fearfully.

"Great," Moody muttered. "Now they definitely won't let us in again."

The path to the exit was clear. Carys walked the remaining steps and peered out. Morning cloud mercifully obscured Polaris Aa. The immediate area dropped steeply down to the ocean, which churned, battleship grey. In her short time within the mountain, she'd forgotten the steepness of the slope.

After quickly scanning the clouds, she climbed through the gap.

The coarse stones were rough under her feet. She'd also grown used to the smooth floors of the aliens' habitation. She climbed away from the cleft in the mountain and then straightened up.

Moody and Sheldrake emerged. The aliens didn't follow them out.

"We have to go high," said Sheldrake, "above the clouds. Or the scanners might not register our signal."

Carys was sceptical the scanners would pick up anything, clouds or not, or that the *Bres* was even scanning the planet, assuming the ship still existed. But she didn't have any better ideas.

If it hadn't been for her lighter weight, she didn't think she could have managed climbing back up the mountain. Within ten minutes she was puffing. Within half an hour she was gasping for breath. Months aboard a starship had taken its toll on her fitness.

They ascended through the mist to the chilly upper regions, staying close to avoid losing each other.

Moody remarked, "It's a shame our alien friends don't have clothes to lend us."

"Yeah," Sheldrake said, "I wouldn't mind a few feathers right now."

After an hour, unable to go any farther, Carys halted to catch her breath. She was feeling light-headed and, despite her exertion, the cold was really beginning to bite. Her feet and hands were freezing, and the rest of her wasn't much warmer. Feathers would certainly have helped. A thick layer of fluffy down was great insulation.

Moody and Sheldrake rested too, their exhalations steaming from their mouths. Sheldrake put his hands on his hips, one knee bent, the other locked as he propped himself on the precipitous incline. Looking downwards, he announced, "Cloud's cleared."

They had already entered the zone only relieved of Polaris Aa's burning beams during the red twilight that passed for night here. Now, the sun blazed across the entire landscape, fading the hues of the rocky mountainside and sparkling the distant ocean waves.

Carys was reminded of Setia plummeting from the skies, released from the clutches of the monstrous alien bird. A sudden sob caught in her throat. She swallowed it. "We should make the sign. I can't see any reason to go higher."

Sheldrake turned his attention to the upper slopes, squinting as he appraised them. "We ought to put it next to the shuttle platform. The *Bres* will have tracked all the vessels in orbit. They'll know the shuttle landed there." He jerked his chin at the protrusion a hundred metres or so higher.

"A distance like that isn't going to make a big difference," Carys countered, "not to starship scanners. We're already tired. If we carry on we'll exhaust ourselves for no reason. And I don't know about you guys, but I'm bloody freezing."

"Carys is right," Moody said. "Besides, the construction of the sign is more important than its position."

"Two against one?" Sheldrake shrugged. "Democracy wins."

"What exactly are we supposed to be making?" Moody asked.

"We make the word HELP with rocks. It's simple, short, and there's no mistaking that a human must have made it."

They set about looking for large stones noticeably darker than the others. It proved a hard task. Polaris Aa had baked the mountainside, washing all hues to a uniform pale grey. But they had the advantage of being able to move large rocks to access the ones sheltered from the planet's suns. Sheldrake and Moody would work at a boulder, twisting and hefting it, and Carys would reach into the hollow to lift out the unbaked stones.

Slowly, they gathered a pile of rocks of a darkish colour.

Carys placed another on the pile. "How many do we need?" She inspected her hands, which were beginning to chafe. Her toes were already numb.

"I'm guessing... fifty?" Sheldrake replied.

Her resolve faltered. There were only about twenty rocks in the pile.

"No need to guess," Moody said. "We can work it out. If we want to create a sign with letters, say, two metres high—"

"Not big enough," Sheldrake interrupted. "The scanners will never pick up anything that small."

"Actually, they will, especially if they've been programmed to look for signals such as the one you propose."

"I'm going to look for more rocks," Carys announced. The men would take a while to come to a decision.

Neither Sheldrake nor Moody seemed to notice as she wandered away. She spotted a small area of roughly level ground and headed for it, deciding to rest for a while and maybe rub some feeling back into her toes.

When she reached the area she cast a glance back at Moody and Sheldrake. They were still talking. With a sigh, she set about clearing the many loose stones strewn over the ground to create a smooth space. As she worked, she wondered how so many stones had ended up in this spot. Had they washed down in a rainstorm? That didn't seem to be the case. They were scattered all over the place, not in any particular shape indicating a natural cause.

Had something living brought them? She couldn't think why a native animal would put stones here, but then she didn't know anything about the creatures of this planet. The slopes seemed absent of any life forms except the bird-like aliens, and they would have no reason to...

She gasped and leapt upright. Her foot hit an unstable stone and her ankle bent sideways. Unbalanced, she fell. Sliding and tumbling down, she desperately flailed, seeking something to grasp to halt her progress. Her hand slapped a pointed protrusion and she managed to cling on with her fingertips.

Nose pressed to rock, she drew in deep lungfuls of air, relieved she'd stopped. She shifted her position and blindly sought with her other hand for something to hold. When she felt secure, she lifted her head.

She'd only fallen a short distance. Sheldrake and Moody were scrambling towards her.

"You okay?" Sheldrake called out.

She nodded. Her breathing had eased, but she didn't trust her voice. What she'd found had been a shock, but to Sheldrake her discovery would be devastating. Should she tell him? She would have to. It would take hours to complete their task, if they even managed to finish it today. Sheldrake was bound to figure out the meaning of many scattered stones on flat ground.

He helped her to her feet. "Are you hurt?"

She began to shake her head, but then she put her weight on her twisted ankle. Pain shot up her leg and she winced, grabbing his arm for support. The ankle was the same one the aliens' bots had sliced as they removed her EVA suit. It had been healing, and now it was fucked up again.

"You *are* hurt." Moody had reached them too. "It wouldn't be wise for you to continue working. Not here, where a false step could lead to a nasty accident. We'll help you to go back. Sheldrake and I can manage without you."

"Yeah," said Sheldrake, "we can do it between us. We've figured it all out."

Carys replied, "I'll find my own way back. I hate to leave you to it, but you're right. I'm no good to you like this. I just hope the aliens will let me in again. They might not like the fact that we forced our way out." She had something more important to say, but she didn't know how to put it.

"Only one way to find out," said Sheldrake.

"Wait," she said, "before I go..."

"What?"

"That place up there, where I fell from..."

He looked up the slope. "What about it?"

"I-I think…"

"Spit it out, Ellis. We haven't got all day."

"I think, when we predicted that the aliens would come for Torres's body, we were right."

Sheldrake's features drooped and his arms hung at his sides. His head low, he clambered off without another word.

Twenty-Nine

Carys's progress down the mountainside was slow and awkward. Her ankle was already swelling and whenever she accidentally put her full weight on it a sharp spike of pain shot up her leg.

She'd wanted to wait with Moody for Sheldrake to come back, but the scientist had assured her she might as well leave.

"He'll return soon," Moody had said. "He just needs a few minutes."

"Torres's death hit him so hard. I don't get it. He told me the major hated him for disobeying orders and standing up for Setia against Markham."

"I don't understand his reaction either, but he's a good man."

Carys couldn't help but agree, and she was in no fit state to be of any use to her companions, so she left. Making her way downwards, she mostly had to sit facing the ocean and use her hands and good leg to bump from rock to rock. Her palms and fingers were already sore and the new method of locomotion wasn't helping. She was often forced to stop and rest. Once, when she looked back up the slopes, she spotted Moody and Sheldrake working.

She made progress, and she grew warmer as she entered lower altitudes, though now the spiky plants made another obstacle to her efforts. When she'd reached the area of the entrance to the aliens' habitation, she rose gingerly to her feet. Propped on an outcrop, she peered to the left and right, seeking the gap between two large rocks.

It was nowhere to be seen.

She checked up the slope again, and then she looked down at the ocean. She'd thought she was in roughly the right place, but she had to be wrong. The problem was, everything looked the same: rocks, plants, ocean, sky, blazing sun and smaller sun.

No, not everything was the same. There had been a hollow where they'd spent the first night. Moody had disappeared around a curve when he'd followed the aliens. The cleft between two rocks had been beyond the curve.

Nothing like a hollow or curve was visible.

She'd come to the wrong place. Somehow, as she'd descended the mountainside, she must have gone off course.

Carys swore. She was thirsty and hungry and her ankle hurt like hell. Yet she had no choice except to wander to and fro, trying to find the entrance to the aliens' abode. Moody and Sheldrake were out of sight. Even if she'd been in a fit state to climb up to them, it wouldn't be fair to ask them to take a break and show her the right way back.

Wincing and muttering curses, she limped and hopped in what seemed the most likely direction, though really she had no idea. More monotonous rockscape appeared, apparently no different from the area she'd left. This had to be the wrong way. She turned and went back.

After another half an hour of scrambling, she no longer knew where she was. Had she passed the spot where she'd first stopped? Had she gone higher or lower? She hadn't seen the scoop in the mountainside where they'd rested or anything like two boulders marking the entrance to the aliens' abode.

She halted, exhausted.

Polaris Aa was burning her skin to a crisp, she had no clue where she was, and she couldn't contact Moody or Sheldrake. They might have finished creating the sign by now and could be looking for her. The two men would be tired out, and her stupidity in getting lost meant they had to expend more energy. She sank onto a rock, rested her elbows on her knees and put her head in her hands.

I'm an idiot. A useless waste of space. A liability.

What on Earth had Bujold been thinking? Why had she included the freaking aviary keeper in the mission team? The captain was a moron and everyone was paying the price.

She lifted her gaze to the endless ocean, feeling a temptation to jump.

At least her ordeal would be over. She'd screwed up long ago when she'd signed up to the Fleet, and the consequences of her dumb decision were playing out. She only wished she hadn't brought Loki along from Earth. But she'd had no choice. He was bonded. He would be missing her, up on the *Bres*, wondering what had happened to her.

That familiar umbilical tug emanated from somewhere inside. She could feel him. She could hear his *kee kee kee*. She could see his bright, intelligent eyes watching.

Dammit.

She couldn't give up. Giving up would be cowardly. It would be letting down Loki and the aviary birds, and it would be letting down Sheldrake and Moody.

With a great effort, she pushed herself upright. She would do her best to help her companions try to get back to the ship. She would find the gap in the rocks if it killed her.

She took a step, tripped, and fell.

Oughh!

Landing on her back, she slid down, gasping, buffeted by rocks, scratched by plant spikes. This time, it took long seconds for her to find a way to stop. She managed to shove her foot into a crevice. The shock reverberated up her good leg but the horrible sliding ended.

Thanking the stars she wasn't on Earth, where the higher gravity would have made her accidents and injuries so much worse, she took stock of her new surroundings. The ocean was close, the upper reaches of the mountain farther away, and she was just as lost.

Wearily, she turned onto her front. There was nothing for it. She would have to climb up again. Hating this world and everything in it, she reached for a rock to grip.

Something wasn't right.

Something odd had caught her eye, but she'd looked away again before realising it. She peered left and right, up and down.

What was it?

The landscape seemed different. Yet all she could see was the usual—

There.

A short distance below her, maybe eight or ten metres, lay a pile of rags. There wasn't anything remarkable about the remnants of clothing, except they shouldn't be here. The aliens of this world didn't wear clothes, and neither she, Sheldrake nor Moody had removed any of their cut and torn garments, which meant...

A shockwave of understanding hit.

The clothes were Setia's.

She'd made it back. She'd survived the fall into the ocean and she'd swum kilometres to reach the mountain—an impossible feat, yet she'd done it.

Carys had known about Setia's physical advantages, conferred on her by an alien on Earth, but she hadn't known her friend had *that* amount of strength and stamina.

They'd given her up for dead. They hadn't waited to see if she might make it back.

Carys slumped against the rocks, guilt and regret washing over her.

Setia must have been exhausted when she reached land, yet she'd climbed as far as she could, searching for her friends. Had she called out to them? Were they already inside the mountain by then and so didn't hear her?

No, no, no.

Somewhere in Carys's misery a question niggled: why had Setia taken off her clothes? That part of the story conjured from the evidence didn't make sense.

She eased herself downwards to take a closer look. Perhaps the clothes weren't Setia's. They could have belonged to Torres. The aliens might have discarded them after they collected his body. Though why they would have placed them in a pile was a mystery. As she drew closer to the forlorn heap she noticed it was a strange shape. It was too lumpy for simple textiles, as if something was filling them out.

As if...

The oddity of the shape resolved itself.

Carys gasped.

Setia!

It wasn't Setia's clothes, it was *her*. She was curled up, her head tucked under her arm, her knees drawn into her chest. Barely any of her skin or hair showed, and what was visible was almost the same colour as her garments. Her ordeal through the ocean and on her climb had caked her in dirt.

"Setia!" Carys screamed.

She slid down the slope faster, nearly falling in her haste.

"Setia! Wake up! It's me, Carys. You're going to be okay. Setia!"

Setia didn't react. Her body didn't move a millimetre in response to the shouts.

Was she even breathing?

Carys halted. She was on a protrusion overlooking the place where Setia lay. The immediate area beneath her curved inwards. With climbing equipment she might have attempted it, but without it there was a serious risk of falling. And if she fell and died or was injured, Sheldrake and Moody would never find her. They would never know Setia was back and needed help.

Carys leaned out. "Setia! Can you hear me? If you can, move something. Anything. Just so I know you're still alive."

No reaction.

Carys stifled a sob and whispered, "Setia, please."

Thirty

"She's right there! Just a little farther." Carys scurried down the mountain. This time, the route was embedded in her mind like a branding. As she'd scaled the slopes to find Sheldrake and Moody, ignoring the agony in her ankle, she'd been aware that if she forgot her way her friend would die. She couldn't allow that to happen.

"Slow down," Sheldrake called. "You'll have an accident."

"Hurry up!"

Setia could be on the verge of death. She must have exerted herself nearly beyond the point of exhaustion to swim back to shore. She'd been without water and food for days. She'd been exposed on the mountainside for two nights and under the beams of an immense sun for two days. She might only have a short while before her body would give out, and if that happened Carys could never forgive herself.

Her throat was raw from screaming for Sheldrake and Moody. Her ankle was a ball of fire. Her hands and feet were bleeding. None of it mattered. All that mattered was reaching Setia.

"I can see her," Moody announced. "My goodness. It's no wonder she didn't respond to your shouts. Are you sure she's still—"

"Don't say it!" Carys yelled, swinging around to glare at him. "Don't you dare say it."

"Take it easy," Sheldrake said. "We'll get her. Don't worry about it. We'll reach her. Whatever it takes."

But once they had assessed the situation, his confidence seemed mistaken.

The spot where Setia had finally given up her efforts, where she'd collapsed, unable to go on, happened to be one of the most inaccessible parts of the slope. There was no getting down to it without a rope, and to reach it from below would require descending a considerable distance and climbing up.

The effort might not have been impossible for Sheldrake—the only one among them with some strength left—but he would have to carry Setia back along the same route. That would require at least one hand, even if he slung her over his shoulder. Two hands were needed to complete the climb.

After discussing the possibilities, their words petered to silence.

Carys stared down at her friend, unable to accept the facts.

Setia was just a few metres away, but she might as well have been on the other side of the ocean.

"There has to be a way," Carys said. "There *has* to. What if...?"

An image popped into her head. Sheldrake could dangle her by a rope made from their clothes knotted together. He could lower her to Setia and then pull them both up.

But it wouldn't work. If they all stripped naked they didn't have enough textiles to make a rope the required length.

Could she jump down and try to wake Setia? If she were conscious, they might manage the climb together.

She was about to suggest the idea when Sheldrake whispered, "Shit."

His eyes were focused out to sea, squinting in the sun's glare. Carys followed his line of sight.

In the far distance, something was moving among wisps of cloud.

Something with wings.

No.

"We have to leave," Moody urged. "If we're fast, we'll make it inside the mountain before it arrives."

Carys retorted hotly, "You can do what you like, but I'm not going anywhere without Setia."

"There's no point," snapped Moody. "I hate to say it, but she's clearly dead. We were too late. And if we don't go now that thing will drop another one of us in the ocean." He began to ascend the slope.

"Fine! Go." She turned to Sheldrake. "You'll help me get her, won't you?"

He peered at the approaching alien. "I don't know, Ellis."

"We abandoned her once already. We can't do it again."

"I get it, but the mission's more important than any of us. You and me need to survive if we're gonna see it through."

"The mission! Who gives a shit about the mission anymore? We're screwed. The *Bres* probably no longer exists. We're on our own, and that makes each of us more important than anything."

Sheldrake was silent, his attention fixed out to sea.

"There has to be a way to reach Setia," Carys continued. "We just need to think of it. Maybe we can hide until the alien's gone. It might not even notice Setia. I didn't at first."

But there were no hiding spots for them on the steep, open slopes.

And their enemy was drawing nearer every wingbeat. It flew at an astonishing speed.

Despite what he'd said Sheldrake didn't leave. As he hesitated it soon became too late to get away. The alien was flying directly at them. It had clearly spotted them from afar.

Carys attempted to alert Setia one last time, but to no avail. The woman hadn't moved one iota from the time Carys had first found her. Moody could easily be right. Perhaps remaining near the body as the predator flew closer was a wasted sacrifice. But if they ran from it and saved themselves, what was the point of anything? What a miserable existence it would be to live in constant fear of discovery, always remaining out of sight.

The alien was flying on a direct heading like a rocket locked on them. Carys checked Setia again, hoping beyond hope to see a sign of life.

There was none.

But she noticed something. In this area of the mountain, not far above sea level, the slopes were dotted with stones. Weathered down from above, they had caught among the rocks on their slow progress to the ocean.

She stooped and picked one up. On Earth, it would have weighed at least three kilos. Here, she hefted it easily in one hand.

"Good idea," said Sheldrake, also picking up a stone.

The alien swooped down and landed near Setia, ignoring the healthy humans. Picking its way across the rocks it stepped closer, its strange head angled low, wings raised high for balance. Its arms hung loosely as if forgotten.

What did it want with Setia? Was it checking this was the same human it had dropped from the sky yesterday? Was it the same alien as before? It looked the same, but so did all the smaller aliens living in the mountain.

"Hey!" Carys called. "Leave her alone!"

The alien's head snapped to the side as it looked up.

"Ellis," Sheldrake murmured, "maybe that wasn't such a good idea."

"What do you suggest we do? Let it take her again and finish the job it set out to do last time?"

"I'm just saying..."

The alien returned its attention to Setia. When it reached her it bent low. With its wings spread, it was hard to see what it was doing. Setia's body shifted a little. Had it prodded her? Or was she finally coming around?

"Leave her alone!" Carys screamed, launching a stone at the creature's head.

The missile sailed over it and smacked into lower rocks.

She grabbed two more stones. At the same time, Sheldrake threw his. It glanced off the alien's outstretched wing.

"Damn!" he exclaimed. "That should have been an easy throw. Why's it so hard to hit?"

"Different gravity," Carys replied. "We aren't used to it."

The alien had turned to face them, golden eyes glaring. Setia lay between its feet. Stretching out its wings, it opened its razor-toothed mouth wide, as if to issue a deep-throated roar. Yet no sound came out. A deep shuddering sensation like thunder ran through Carys, but there was no thunder. The ground vibrated.

She threw again. This time, the stone flew so close the creature must have felt its passage. Another stone issued from Sheldrake's hand and whistled over the alien's shoulder.

Carys tossed the second stone into her right hand and hurled it. But the alien had simultaneously crouched to pick Setia up and the stone passed through empty air.

"No! Put her down!" Impotently, Carys clenched her fists before feverishly scanning the ground for more projectiles to launch. While she was looking, she heard the *whoosh* of two massive wings beating. The alien had taken to the air. It had picked up Setia. It was taking her away again.

Carys screamed her rage at the creature, incoherent with grief and fury. Why wouldn't it leave them alone? What use did it have for Setia? The creatures already had Torres. Why did they want her too?

The alien flew to Carys and Sheldrake's level and rose higher. Setia dangled, doll-like, from its grasp. Her head lolled and her face was ghastly white. The alien clasped her like a trophy. It was gloating. It was showing them that their efforts were useless, that it had what it had come for and there was nothing they could do about it.

Its wide mouth opened once more and its barrel chest expanded as it prepared to issue another silent, victorious roar.

A stone thunked into it right above its flared nostrils, jerking the head with the impact. A screech issued from its mouth. Blood poured from the wound. The majestic wings shivered, and Setia slipped from its grasp.

Sheldrake leaned way out over the precipice to snatch at the falling figure. His fingers closed around her shirt, but he was overbalanced and about to follow Setia down the mountain. Carys seized the waist of his trousers and yanked it.

He stumbled backwards, drawing Setia into his arms, gasping, "I got her."

The alien flew slowly away, its head hanging low, dripping blood.

Setia's head rested on Sheldrake's chest, her eyes closed and her features peaceful like a sleeping child.

Carys swallowed. "Let's get her to safety before it comes back with its mates. Good throw, by the way."

"Copy that, but it wasn't me who hit it."

"Huh?"

Someone was scrambling down the slope.

It was Moody. "Well done, Sheldrake. That was a nice save. How is she? Is she—"

Carys said, "You came back."

"I changed my mind. I decided it was wrong for me to leave. We're all in this together."

"You threw the stone that hit it?"

"I saw how your efforts were hampered by the lower gravity. I made a simple correction to allow for it."

Thirty-One

"*Bitch.*"

The word was a barely audible, breath of a whisper escaping Setia's lips, but to Carys it meant everything. She collapsed over her friend and wept with relief. "Thank the stars."

Setia was alive.

She was alive.

Somehow, she'd survived the fall into the ocean, a gruelling long-distance swim, and extreme dehydration, hunger, and exposure to Polaris Aa's merciless rays.

"You'd... er," Sheldrake murmured. "You'd better give her some room, Ellis."

His gentle chiding brought Carys back to reality, and she sat up. Her friend's body had felt painfully emaciated. She was also deeply sunburned, though her skin was cool to the touch. She lived, but she might be on the edge of death.

"Yes," Moody concurred, "our friends seem keen to take a look at her. Perhaps they might help."

Despite the humans' aggressive exit from the aliens' abode, no one and nothing prevented them from returning. Which was just as well. The shelter was the best chance any of them had at a continued existence.

Sheldrake had softly laid Setia down in the entrance chamber. Either the aliens' hearing was acute, the chamber was being watched, or they had some kind of alarm system, for a few seconds later the winged creatures had appeared.

As soon as Carys moved back from Setia, the aliens crowded in and peered at and poked her curiously.

"Be careful!" Carys exclaimed. "She's weak. She needs rest, but first she needs water. Please bring her water." Carys mimed drinking.

Whether or not the creatures understood, she couldn't tell. Four of them gathered Setia up from the ground.

"Hey!" Carys protested. "What are you doing?"

Naturally, they didn't reply. They began to carry Setia out.

"No, you can't take her. Leave her here. Leave her with us!" Carys tried to grab the aliens carrying Setia, but others prevented her.

"I wouldn't stop them if I were you," said Moody. "I'm sure they mean to help her."

"But they don't know what they're doing. We're the first humans they've ever met. They don't know anything about our anatomy or physical requirements. Their 'help' could kill her."

"There is something in what you say. Nevertheless, our hosts don't appear to be unintelligent, and they have a much better understanding of their environment and its toll on living beings. I feel confident they will give her the best care we can expect in the circumstances."

"Yeah," Sheldrake said, "the aliens are probably the best chance Zees has right now."

"Rubbish," Carys snapped. "I'm going too. I'm not leaving her alone with them. Who knows what they might do to her?" She hurried out, limping and cursing her twisted ankle.

The group carrying Setia had reached the end of the corridor. Carys trotted painfully after them to catch up. The aliens ignored her as they went along. She could only glimpse Setia's limp form within the huddle.

They reached the hole leading to the shaft and, before Carys could do anything, they stepped into it. The aliens swept aloft. Two held Setia outstretched between their grasping hands as their wings beat higher, their companions flying above them.

"No!" Carys leaned out, squinting upwards. The walls of the shaft were smooth save for jutting ledges spaced too far apart for her to climb between them. *Damn.*

She hobbled to the end of the corridor using the wall as a prop, and then went down another and another, seeking stairs to the upper levels. But she couldn't find any. She became lost, wandering the maze of passages until she was reduced to slowly hopping along. More by luck than design, she suddenly found herself looking into the room with the bar around the perimeter and low tables.

"Ellis," Sheldrake said, "where did you go? How's Setia doing?" He sat with Moody at one of the tables. The aliens had provided another barbecued eel, and the ex-corporal's face and hands shone with grease.

"They took her upstairs and I couldn't follow. I got lost." She slumped disconsolately down next to Sheldrake.

"You've been gone hours," said Moody. "Have you really been wandering all this time?"

Carys nodded unhappily.

"Did you see anything interesting on your travels?"

"Interesting? No. I was looking for a way to go up to the higher floors. I don't think there is one. Not if you don't have wings."

"Well, that seems perfectly understandable. Why build stairs when you can fly?"

"There are stairs leading down to that production plant we found earlier."

"True. I'm not sure—"

"Eat some of this, Ellis." Sheldrake held out a chunk of fish. "You must be half-starved."

The food looked tempting, but Carys had a greater need. She'd already locked onto the wide bowl of water on another table. "In a minute. I have to drink something before I shrivel to a crisp."

The water flowed like nectar down her parched throat. She took a moment to savour the sensation before taking another long drink, and then returning to Sheldrake's side. She took the lump of greasy flesh and bit into it hungrily.

Through a full mouth she asked, "Did you manage to make the signal?"

Moody replied, "We did complete it eventually. We were descending the slopes when we heard you calling."

"I still say we should have made it bigger," said Sheldrake. "The scanners will be looking at the whole planet."

"The landmasses only," Moody argued, "and there are precious few of them."

Carys tore another portion of fish from the bones. "And the aerial cities."

"Ah, yes. I'd forgotten about them. Regardless, the area of non-aqueous zones is a small fraction of the entire surface and, as someone said, the *Bres* will have tracked the movements of the shuttle that brought us here. There may be people examining this very spot as we speak. Our signal will stick out like a sore thumb."

"I certainly hope so." Sheldrake leaned his back against the wall and stretched. Then he frowned. "Aerial cities? What are they?"

"Places the aliens live, I suppose," Carys replied. "All I know about them is that they exist. Bujold mentioned them."

"Doctor?" Sheldrake asked.

Moody shrugged. "I don't know any more than Carys."

Sheldrake whistled. "Cities in the air. Who woulda thought?" He frowned again and then asked Carys, "What was it Zees said when we got back? I didn't catch it."

"Uhh... I didn't catch it either. I only knew she spoke."

Bitch.

Setia had said the word bitch, and Carys was pretty sure it was meant for her, though why exactly her friend had called her that she didn't know. Setia was the type of person who spoke her mind and worried about it—rarely, probably—later. Why did Setia suddenly hate her so much?

It didn't matter. Carys could live with being hated. The Crusaders who had kept her captive in the Australian desert had made their hatred of the kidnapped children clear on a daily basis. What she couldn't have lived with was the guilt of causing Setia's death.

Several aliens crowded into the room and gathered around the remains of the meal.

Moody said, "I think they want to—"

Carys barely had time to snatch the last handful of fish before the aliens descended on the dish. They polished off the bones, skin and head in no time. One of them upturned the plate and licked the grease with a long, blue tongue.

"Clear the table," Moody finished.

"They love that thing," Sheldrake commented. "It's cool they share it with us."

"It certainly is," Moody concurred.

While all this had been going on Carys had been thinking, and she'd come to a conclusion. "We have to find Setia. Who knows what's happening to her? They could be doing anything. They might even plan on giving her back to one of their bigger cousins."

"That's unlikely," Moody said, "but anyhow, what you propose is impossible. You said yourself we can't reach the upper levels where they've taken her without the benefit of wings."

"I thought of a way. We go back to the shuttle platform and search for another entrance to the mountain. There has to be one. The aliens have to get the materials to make... whatever it is they make... from somewhere. My guess is that shipments arrive by air and they carry them inside. There has to be a way to access the upper floors somewhere around there. We just didn't notice it. We thought the place was deserted so we didn't look."

"Hmm..." Moody put a finger to his sunburned lips. The man's formerly pale skin was the colour of a cooked lobster.

Carys guessed she didn't look much better, and going outside would mean subjecting them all to the devastating rays of Polaris Aa once more, but it couldn't be avoided. Not if they were going to find Setia.

"You're forgetting something." Sheldrake prodded her ankle.

Though his touch was gentle, she winced. The joint resembled a small, pink melon.

"*You* can't go anywhere till you're healed up," he continued, "not unless you want to do permanent damage. I'm no medic, but even I can tell you that."

"Also," said Moody, "you may not be correct. The production materials might arrive by boat."

"No way," Carys retorted. "Not with those tides. There's no shipping on this planet. I guarantee it." Yet she couldn't deny that Sheldrake had made a good point. No matter how much she might want to, she wasn't capable of scaling the mountain any time soon. It would be days before she could put any serious weight on her ankle. "Maybe tomorrow, you two could..."

A look passed between Sheldrake and Moody, and her words petered out. It was a lot to ask of the men, who were already exhausted from the day's labour and deeply sunburned.

"I would be happy to try," Moody said, "*if* I thought Setia was in danger of serious harm. But I'm sure that, wherever she is, she's receiving better care than we can provide in our current circumstances."

"You can't be sure of that. Even if the aliens are friendly, they know hardly anything about human anatomy. Besides," she added as another thought occurred "we're forgetting what happened today. You hit one of the big aliens with a stone. We hurt one of the rulers. It's obvious they're in charge on this planet, and the ones looking after us are their slaves or something. There are bound to be repercussions. It might not be safe for us or Setia to stay here any longer."

"Maybe so," said Sheldrake, "but the same applies. We have to take our chances. You're going nowhere with that busted ankle, and this place is our best option right now. So let's forget about leaving, okay? We sit tight and wait for the *Bres* to spot the signal."

"I agree," Moody said. "Sorry, Carys, but it's two against one."

THIRTY-TWO

A high-pitched whistle ringing in her ears, Carys woke and sat up. Blinking, she took in the dull red twilight surrounding her.

She was in the small aliens' abode.

Setia was alive.

What was going on?

Carys vaguely recalled feeling a deep vibration or shock. Dark shapes moved beside her—Sheldrake and Moody were sitting up, also woken from sleep.

Sheldrake turned to her and spoke, but she heard nothing, only the whistling. He put his hands over his ears and shook his head. Moody was speaking too. He got up and walked to the open doorway.

The room should have been completely dark. At night-time, the aliens did something to block out the weird light cast by Polaris Aa from the other side of the planet. The sombre maroon hue of night was only visible outside.

What was going on?!

And why couldn't they hear anything? The whistle didn't seem to be external. It was inside her head.

Sheldrake was speaking again.

Carys lip-read *Where's Moody?*

She looked at the doorway. It was empty. Why had Moody wandered off when it was clear something strange was happening?

"How would I know?" she replied irritably, her voice muffled and indistinct.

She got up unsteadily and limped across the room. As she reached the doorway, six or seven aliens ran in and lifted her from her feet. She barely managed to utter an exclamation of surprise before she was swiftly carried out. Twisting and turning, she tried to prise off the bony fingers grasping her, to no avail. She called out for Sheldrake but it was too late.

The aliens rushed down the passageway, racing through the shadowy habitation. Almost before she realised it, they reached the opening to the vertical shaft and, without slowing down or any kind of discussion, they leapt through it.

Carys yelled in fright, instinct telling her she was about to fall to her death. But in perfect synchrony her bearers beat their wings and ascended. Cool air wafted over her as they went up. The walls of the tunnel sped past and Carys had a brief, insane feeling that she was on the Tube in London, speeding to an unknown destination.

She *was* going to an unknown destination.

Where were they taking her, and why?

She didn't struggle. If she succeeded in freeing herself she really would fall to her death. All she could do was gaze upwards in trepidation, her heart in her throat. Whatever might happen upon arrival at her destination, it surely could not be good.

A dim red disk became visible and rapidly grew larger. It was the colour of night on this planet. The exit to the surface was open and the aliens were taking her there.

An immediate eviction? Was that all this was?

She steeled herself to be ejected onto the rocky slope. Perhaps this was where Moody had gone, and Sheldrake would soon follow. If they were only to be forced out of their shelter of the last few days, she could accept it, but she was worried about Setia. Whether the aliens ejected her too or not, Setia would be in danger.

Carys and the aliens burst into the open. They carried her aloft and then swooped to a soft landing, setting her on her feet with the skill of balancing a pencil on its point. Their delicacy notwithstanding, her ankle couldn't bear her weight unsupported and she dropped to her knees.

Tall figures stood before her. Tall and wide. Three of the larger Polarans balanced on the steep slope with the help of outstretched wings.

One held Moody, who stared at her hopelessly.

A *whoosh* sounded from behind. The whistle in her ears was fading.

One of the unburdened Polarans stepped towards her. She knew what it would do but she was powerless to stop it. Where could she run to on this bare incline? How *could* she run on her injured ankle? How would it be possible to escape a winged pursuer?

Limply, she allowed it to take her in its grasp and walk back to its companions.

The *whoosh* had been Sheldrake's arrival, borne to the spot by smaller Polarans.

Naturally, he was taken captive too.

He also did not resist, and a heavy weight settled on Carys. If *Sheldrake* didn't fight back, if *he* had lost hope of escaping their fate, that had to mean it was over.

She might have heard him if he'd spoken. She could hear the wind now, blowing in from the ocean. But he didn't say a word.

They were about to be carried out across the waves and dropped from a great height. They were not Setia. None of them possessed her supernatural strength and fortitude. They would not be swimming back.

The alien holding her sprang into the air, its massive wings working powerfully to drive upwards into the sombre, red sky. As it swerved, Carys dully noticed a dark, hulking machine on the mountainside. Two long legs propped it upright. Two short legs supported the end nearest the rocks. The front of the machine was hidden within an opening—the second entrance at the upper levels she'd wanted to find. She'd been right about its existence. Not that it meant anything now.

Nevertheless, the presence of the machine puzzled her, though only for a moment. She recalled the shockwave and whistling in her ears that had woken her. The machine had to be responsible.

Too large to enter their smaller cousins' habitation, the large Polarans had invented a device to control them. The machine had to send some kind of pressure blast through the tunnels. If they didn't obey commands, the aliens would suffer the effects of the blaster. It was possible their ears were more sensitive than humans' and the blast was painful.

The journey over the ocean was surreal. How many times in her days of caring for raptors had she dreamed of an experience like this? To fly high in the air, to glide through the upper atmosphere free as a bird. It had been a secret fantasy, something she had never even admitted to her co-workers, fearing she would appear childish. Though, in truth, they probably shared the same private wish. To care for birds, to have an interest in them, had to spark envy and awe of natural flight.

In all her daydreams, she'd never imagined this would be how her wish would come true.

The foam tipping the waves below was red-tinged by the unearthly deflected glow of the hidden sun. The smaller sun was lightening the sky in the east. In the west, maroon clouds gathered. It was in this direction they were headed.

Carys became acutely aware of the grip of the alien's hands around her midriff. Each passing second she anticipated the moment the grip would release. How long would it take for her to hit the water? Would she feel the impact or would it all be over quickly? She hoped so. To die of drowning, her body broken, would be a terrible way to go.

Her captor flew on.

The waiting became a terrible strain. To continue to exist on the brink of death was torturous. She was tempted to prise the creature's fingers from her and get the whole thing over with. But she did not. She turned her mind to the people she loved and to Loki, hoping she could hold them in her thoughts until the end.

Still, the alien did not drop her.

She looked around, wondering what was happening to Sheldrake and Moody. The two larger Polarans flew far off to her left and right. The dim light made it hard to be sure, but they seemed to be carrying burdens—presumably her friends. So they hadn't been dropped either. She looked over her shoulder, craning her neck to see a rear view. The mountain where she and her companions had spent the last few days was lost in darkness.

How far had they flown?

Some birds could fly incredibly fast, reaching over 200 kilometres an hour in a stoop. Even flying horizontally, speeds over 100 kilometres an hour were not rare.

Significant time had passed since her capture, so much that she'd lost all her strength and could only hang like a rag doll. They must have flown a long way. Why hadn't her bearer cast her into the ocean?

Polaris Ab peeked over the horizon and turned the world crimson-gold. It was an achingly beautiful sight. Tears gathered in Carys's eyes and spread over her cheeks, dragged by the wind.

Her neck muscles strained and sore, she allowed her head to sag for a few minutes before gathering the effort to lift it once more. The alien's powerful flight had brought them closer to dark clouds in the west.

Oddly, the shape of the mounded water vapour hadn't altered in all the time they'd been travelling. Having spent much of her life gazing upwards at birds, she knew this was unusual. She wiped her eyes and stared at their apparent destination again.

They were not clouds.

Thirty-Three

The Polaran opened its fingers, and Carys fell.

She'd had the briefest glimpse of a rectangular opening, the interior obscured by darkness, before she was released. Exhausted by the long flight and full of despair and pain, she didn't utter a sound as she plummeted through the cold air. She landed, slamming into a hard surface. By some miracle, she hadn't landed on her bad leg but on her side. Her skull knocked against the floor, dazing her. For long moments she lay still, panting and blinking as she came to terms with her new predicament.

She had been carried through the air for so long, the sensations of the experience continued. She could still feel the passage of the wind, the rhythm of her captor's beating wings, and its grip around her torso. She could still see the scarlet ocean far below and the dark horizon of this strange, alien planet.

Closing her eyes, she turned onto her back and stretched out her legs.

What was this new place?

A vision replayed in her mind. As the alien had flown closer to what she'd mistaken as clouds, the nebulous forms had defined into stronger shapes. The mounded structures were not misty and ever-changing, they were solid and smooth. Their surfaces didn't gently radiate the colours of sunrise, they reflected the rays of rising Polaris Ab like ten thousand mirrors.

When Bujold had mentioned that this planet had aerial cities, Carys had imagined something like Earth's metropolises, only suspended in the upper atmosphere. She'd pictured skyscrapers, office blocks, shopping malls, parks and schools.

She grimaced.

Why the hell would Polaran cities look like anything that existed on Earth?

I'm such an idiot.

Her kidnapper had dropped her expertly into one of several openings right on the city's edge. The rest of it spread out above and below. From her position as she'd approached, she hadn't been able to see its extent, but it had to be huge. It resembled vast columns of cumulonimbus heralding a storm.

She took in a deep breath and exhaled. The air was frigid.

"Ellis?"

The voice was faint but instantly recognisable.

"Sheldrake?! Are you okay?"

"Twisted my knee a bit, but that's it. You?"

"I'm fine. What about Moody? Did he get dropped here too?"

"I don't know. He was behind me."

They both called the scientist's name several times but received no reply.

Sheldrake said, "I guess he's too far away to hear us or they took him somewhere else."

Their voices didn't seem to carry far in the thin air, and the cell walls were another impediment.

"I think you're right," Carys replied. "Do you know what happened to Setia?" She harboured a hope that Sheldrake might have seen her friend being brought here too.

"No idea."

While they'd been talking Carys had climbed to her feet and leaned on a wall for support. She slid down to the floor and rested her back.

Sheldrake said, "I wonder what happens now?"

"Your guess is as good as mine, but one thing strikes me. These cells were built for us."

"Huh? What makes you think that?"

"Because any Polaran could just fly right out of them."

"Right. They've been busy while we were on the mountain."

"Yeah." Carys turned her gaze upwards. The ethereal red of the night sky was fading. Soon, Polaris Aa would rise. As the star passed overhead it would shine directly into the open-roofed prison, heating it up. They could shelter from the worst of the sunshine by moving with the shadows cast by the cell walls, but they would still be slowly cooked.

She decided to not inform Sheldrake of her prediction. Knowing what was coming wouldn't help him avoid it.

They had survived the night—something she hadn't expected, but that was as much as could be said. She recalled Sheldrake's blind faith in her when they'd first arrived at the planet, Bujold's decision to make her an 'advisor' on the aliens, and Robins's invitation to become an apprentice mapper. She curled her lip. How mistaken they'd all been.

"Carys?" Sheldrake called. "You still awake?"

"Uh huh."

"Just wanted you to know, I'm gonna try and get some shuteye. Feeling pretty beat. So if you want to speak to me and I don't answer, that's why."

"Thanks, I might try to sleep too."

"You don't have any ideas on what they plan to do with us?"

How would I know? "No, sorry. I haven't been much use, have I?"

"What are you talking about? You figured out a way for us to eat, and... well, you found Zees."

"And lost her again."

"Quit beating yourself up. You're smarter than you think. I have faith in you. 'Night, Ellis."

"Goodnight, Sheldrake."

She squinted at the sky. It was lighter above one of the cell walls. That had to be the direction where Polaris Aa would shortly rise. She crawled to the wall and lay down at the edge, pillowing her head with her bent arm.

Watching the brightening heavens, she fell asleep.

She was in hell. Demons surrounded her, jabbing her with tridents. Their long tails, tipped by points, flicked, and they bared blood-stained fangs, laughing. Faces loomed from nowhere—faces she recognised: her adoptive mother, Taylan, and Taylan's children, Patrin and Kayla, who she had lived with in the Australian desert, captives of the Crusaders.

"Why did you leave us?" they asked. "What did we do to deserve that? Where are you now? Are you coming home? Come home, Carys. We miss you."

She tried to reply, to apologise, but her lips were stuck together. She couldn't open them. "I'm sorry." Her closed mouth made only incoherent sounds. "I'm so sorry. I miss you too. I would come back if I could."

Aching sorrow gripped her chest.

The friendly faces faded and the demons returned. Their tridents drew closer. They jabbed at her, and there was nothing she could do to get away. The points pricked her skin painfully.

"Stop," she sobbed. "Please stop." She couldn't lift her hands to ward off the attack. She couldn't move.

Carys opened her eyes. Immediately, she shut them again. A brilliant glare had dazzled her. She could still see the glow, stained blood red by her closed eyelids.

Her skin was on fire.

She'd slept for hours, and Polaris Aa had risen and crossed the sky. Now, it shone on her, turning her already burned skin crispy. She was also uncomfortably hot. Gasping in pain, she turned away from the rays and felt for the wall. She was right up against it. She had to crawl in the opposite direction. Hopefully, on the other side of the cell she might find shade.

Keeping her head down, she set off. Her hair hung low, casting a shadow over her face. When had her ponytail band fallen off? She couldn't remember. It must have been days ago.

At least now she could open her eyes without being blinded.

She shuffled slowly forwards, keeping her injured ankle raised and putting all her weight on her knee.

The sun's glare cut out. She'd reached the other side of the cell faster than she'd anticipated.

But there was something wrong with the shade. It wasn't steady. It moved, allowing flashes of light.

She looked up.

A Polaran perched on top of her cell wall, wings outstretched.

She froze.

As she watched, it folded its wings and tilted its head, fixing her with his golden-eyed gaze.

"*Fuck off*," she muttered. "Fuck off, you creep."

Naturally, the Polaran didn't reply.

"Sheldrake?" she called. "Are you there?"

No answer came. He was either asleep and slowly roasting in his cell as she had been, or he'd been taken somewhere else.

"Is that what you want?" she asked the alien. "Have you come to collect me? Or am I only something interesting for you to look at?"

The Polaran leapt down, opening its wing to slow its descent, and landed a couple of metres away.

She moved to a sitting position.

The alien didn't seem to be carrying any weapons and it was alone. She might do it some harm if she tried hard enough.

It walked closer.

She scooted backwards on her behind. "What do you want? Why are you here?"

What if she'd been wrong about why she was here.

What if she wasn't in a prison?

What if she was in a larder?

Was that what had happened to Sheldrake? Was that why Moody hadn't answered when they'd shouted his name?

"Get away from me." She retreated into a corner.

The alien reached into its middle and pulled something out.

Her jaw dropped. The Polaran appeared to have a pouch.

"Half bird, half kangaroo?" she spluttered. "What a bloody freak."

The wall behind her was unremitting. There was no getting away.

The creature pointed a knife at her. The meaning of the gesture was clear.

"Okay, I get it. What do you want me to do?" Using the wall for support, she clambered upright.

The alien tucked the weapon among its feathers and stepped closer.

She allowed it to pick her up and fly with her out of the cell.

Thirty-Four

There was no sign of Sheldrake in the honeycomb of cells. Each of the twenty or so receptacles seemed empty. It was hard to be certain—the harsh glare of Polaris Aa cast deep shadows—but Carys felt sure he wasn't in any of them. That was why he hadn't answered. He was gone. Perhaps Moody had never been in a cell either, carried to another place or even dropped in the ocean.

She braced herself for another gruelling flight, this time exposed to destructive sunbeams. Her sunburn was so sore every movement brought pain, and as her already ragged clothes fell apart, more of her skin was exposed to light. She was also dreadfully thirsty.

She dully scanned the heights of billowing 'clouds' as her bearer carried her upwards. The shell of the aliens' metropolis was pearlescent, effectively repelling the harsh sunlight. Yet it was also translucent. Shadows of flying creatures passed to and fro behind the walls. She was flown so close to the structure it occupied her entire vision. It was vast. She'd read that a storm cloud could grow up to twelve kilometres tall, and this city could easily be that size. It even had the characteristic anvil shape at the top, spreading out over a huge distance.

Why hadn't the Polarans brought the mission team here when they'd first arrived? Why had they dropped their human captives on a small mountainous island nearly devoid of life? It made no sense. Nothing that had happened since she'd left the *Bres* made any sense.

Almost before she knew it, she was out of the sun's glare and passing through an opening the shape of an elongated egg. There was a floor, but it was a dizzying distance below. Galleries surrounded them, tall passageways separated by barriers filled with arched openings, everything made from the same pearlescent substance as the exterior.

And aliens. So many aliens, and all the larger kind.

They flew in every direction like a flock of sea birds disturbed at their nesting site, only the flight of the Polarans was not startled or chaotic, it was as smooth as the glide of an albatross or an eagle riding an updraught.

A strange realisation struck: none of the Polarans they passed as they navigated a passage through the constantly moving bodies took a blind bit of notice of her.

Here, *she* was the alien, and burned and dishevelled as she was, she must have been quite the spectacle. Yet no gazes turned her way. Not that she wanted to be noticed. Attracting attention probably wouldn't be to her benefit. But it was odd.

Her bearer flew up and up until they had to be approaching the anvil. Here, there were few openings between the galleries. Her lungs laboured to extract oxygen from the thin air and she shivered. They passed into a thin cleft, and then swept sharply right.

They were inside a high chamber. Tall, open-topped columns dotted the space, some linked by narrow bridges. Several bridges led to exits. The rays of Polaris Aa pierced the opalescent outer shell and lit the space.

Atop the central column perched three monstrous Polarans. Carys's carrier flew her up to an adjacent column and dropped her onto the flat surface below the bar surmounting it.

She gasped as she landed. Rising gingerly to her feet, she held onto the bar for support and warily regarded the three Polarans. But then, from the corners of her eyes, she saw movement. Turning her head, she was just in time to see two people at the end of a bridge, leaving through an oval portal. Sheldrake and Moody? But one of the couple was female. The other had black, spiky hair.

She knew them!

"Captain Bujold!" she screamed. "Barbier! It's me, Carys Ellis!"

Without reacting, they disappeared through the exit.

"Bujold! Barbier!" Her voice echoed from the walls. "Where are you going? You can't leave me! I need your help. Help me! Get me out of here."

The captain and ambassador were gone. They had to have heard her. They weren't deaf. What the hell was going on?

"Your name is Carys Ellis."

The voice sounded artificial. The intonation was too measured and flat to be natural. She swivelled, trying to figure out where it had come from. The three Polarans regarded her impassively. Had one of them spoken? She peered over the edge of her column at the empty expanse below. No one was here except her and the aliens.

She stared at the middle one, the largest. "Is that a question?"

"Your name is Carys Ellis," the voice repeated.

This time, she saw the mouth of the central Polaran move, though naturally the motions didn't remotely match the words she heard.

Its speech was being translated. So the aliens knew English and they were in contact with the *Bres*.

How long had Bujold and Barbier been talking to them? Had the captain known some mission members were still alive and done nothing to help? Why hadn't she moved heaven and Earth to get her people off the planet?

Carys recalled Bujold's stubborn refusal to fire back when the *Bres* was attacked. The captain was holding on with an iron grip to the protocol of avoiding conflict at all costs, even to the extent of sacrificing her crew.

"Yes, my name is Carys Ellis!" she spat. "Who the fuck are *you*? I demand to be returned to my ship, along with my companions! What have you done with them? Where are they?"

"Carys Ellis, you will reside with my colleague..." A sound followed that the system didn't even attempt to translate. She heard a low, breathy *hushhh*.

The alien to the speaker's right ruffled his feathers.

Carys was reminded of Loki when something had made him uncomfortable. "I'm not going to *reside* with anyone. I want to go back to my ship. Call my captain back right now. I demand to speak to her."

"You will obey, and you will learn. If you fail, you and the rest of your ship's crew will die ignobly."

"We'll... *what*?"

Die *ignobly*?

What did that even mean?

"You can't kill us. If you do, the Interstellar Fleet will retaliate. You might think you can take on the *Bres*, but you're wrong. Our captain didn't return fire when you attacked because she wants you to join an alliance, but if you hurt any more of us, she won't be so nice. And our ship isn't the only one you'll have to deal with. We have two more powerful battleships. They're probably already on their way here, and..." She paused. She'd run out of bluffs. Had any of it had an effect? Reading the Polarans' faces was impossible.

"We are aware of the other ships in your fleet. They are currently collaborating with our enemy. Your lies do not count in your favour." The central alien turned to its neighbour and said something in deep bass tones.

With a shake of his head—it seemed to be an angry gesture—the neighbour opened his wings and stepped into the air. As he swept across the abyss, Carys braced herself, guessing what was coming next. She was grabbed neatly around her middle and carried aloft.

She muttered, "I'm getting really bloody tired of this."

But she didn't fight or resist.

Anger was melting out of her, giving way to sadness and despair. *You will obey, and you will learn.* She understood the first part but not the second. Learn what? And for how long? How much time did she have until the Polarans would kill her and her friends 'ignobly'?

Like it made a difference.

She closed her eyes, feeling nauseated by the constant to-ing and fro-ing in the air, clutched by a monstrous alien.

This wasn't exactly what she'd imagined as her future when she'd signed up to the Fleet. She couldn't remember exactly what she'd envisaged—her thoughts had been focused more on getting away from Earth than what lay ahead—but she vaguely recalled anticipating an easy job caring for the aviary's birds, dealing with the occasional obnoxious visitor, and, at the end of the voyage, a new life on an alien planet. Somewhere she could forget her past and the people she'd left behind.

She'd been naive. Stupid. And now her bad decision-making was biting her on the arse.

Her bearer let go of her.

Carys's eyes snapped open and she released a brief shriek, abruptly cut short by an impact with a hard surface.

Unable to prepare herself, she'd landed badly. She moaned in pain. Through clenched teeth, she growled, "Thanks for the warning."

"You are ridiculously heavy," said Hush. "Listen. You will serve me. I will assess and report on your behaviour. Understand. We do not desire acquaintance with your species. We have no need for the alliance your captain proposes. Your existence is irrelevant to us."

Carys awkwardly pushed herself to a sitting position and squinted up at the creature towering over her. "Uhh, okay."

Thirty-Five

Hush lived somewhere on the outer rim of the cloud metropolis. One side of the dwelling protruded over the ocean, the other faced inwards to a wide, busy corridor, where Polarans flew past day and night.

Carys could not access either place. The ocean-side exit led to a precipitous drop into the water, and while the corridor did contain a floor, it was twenty metres down. The distance was no impediment to a Polaran, but for her it could mean serious injury or death, despite the planet's low gravity.

Her new home was a prison cell without bars. The only way she would leave it was if a Polaran carried her out, and Hush was in no hurry to do that.

What he *did* expect took a while to become clear.

At first, he ignored her completely. After his short explanation of the state of things between them, he didn't utter another word. Taking up a position at the outer exit, he looked over the ocean for an hour or longer. Carys asked him about Bujold and Barbier, trying to confirm that it had been the captain and ambassador she'd seen. She asked what had happened while she'd been on the island, where her companions were and if they were safe. She told him his people had no right to keep her here against her will, and that she demanded to be returned to her ship.

For all the notice he took of her, it was as if she didn't exist.

Finally, in exasperation, she asked him what exactly she was supposed to do in order to 'serve' him, hoping this was the magic question he'd been awaiting all along.

Nothing.

His back and wings confronted her in impassive silence.

She clenched her fists, sorely tempted to shove him off his perch into thin air.

But, of course, that wouldn't hurt him at all. He would only fly, and then probably return to inflict some kind of punishment.

Overhanging the one-sided conversation had been the feeling that she couldn't take things too far. She and the rest of the team were under threat of execution, and they had nothing, absolutely nothing, in their favour, not even help from their captain.

While Carys had been talking to Hush she'd stood behind him. When she gave up trying to get an answer, she slumped to the ground in a corner of the dwelling. Naturally, there were no chairs.

Hush turned from the window, flapped passed her, and flew out into the corridor.

She got to her feet. Leaning out the exit, she peered to the left and right, but she couldn't spot her new acquaintance among all the other Polarans.

"*Bye!*"

Sighing, she regarded the interior once more. It looked like she would be spending some time here. Luckily, Hush's apartment was at a low altitude. The anvil of the cloud spread out high overhead. She wasn't chilled and didn't struggle to breathe. She was, however, hungry and thirsty.

Three doorways opened from the main section. Beyond the first was what appeared to be a place for sleeping. She couldn't call it a bedroom as there was no bed, only a thick bar. This area could be closed off with a curtain.

The second area seemed to be for sanitation. High up on the wall, a spout stuck out over a drain, and there was what might be a toilet. Or maybe this was a kitchen. The room also held shelves filled with large glass jars. Did they contain snacks?

Carys approached the spout. As soon as she got near it, it activated, spraying cold water. She stepped back but not before getting splashed. Angling her head to one side, she managed to get a long drink, though her face and neck were drenched.

She took down a jar from a shelf and, grasping it under one arm, pulled off the lid. Her stomach rumbled.

A gloopy substance filled the container almost to the brim. She sniffed it. The odour wasn't unpleasant. It wasn't appetising either, though it did smell of salt and something savoury. She tentatively dipped in a finger and touched it to the tip of her tongue. It tasted like bone broth but the texture was much thicker.

"Hmmm. Not bad." She scooped out a handful of gloop and ate it, licking the remnants from her fingers.

Within a few seconds, her stomach violently objected. Vomit erupted from her mouth and she sank to her hands and knees. There was nothing she could do to stop puking. Even when there was nothing left to come up, she continued to painfully dry-heave. Minutes later, when the spasm was over, she found herself kneeling in a puddle of puke, eyes watering and throat sore.

It took a while to clean everything up. Scooping the puddle into the drain and washing it away almost started her off again. Then she had to rinse off the splashes on her clothes, leaving her damp and cold.

The event had left her even hungrier, but she didn't dare try to eat anything else. Hopefully, Hush would order her one of the barbecued eels or another food suitable for humans.

Or maybe not.

Carys wandered into the third room. This one contained the now-familiar bar for perching, but there was also a wall screen that looked suspiciously like an interface. She touched it. The screen didn't respond, and there were no buttons or anything else to activate it.

A scraping sound from the main room distracted her. When she looked out, a box had appeared next to the door. After crossing the room she peered out into the corridor. Twenty metres below, a Polaran was walking, towing a trailer stacked with boxes. As she watched, it halted, picked up a box, and flew it up to deliver at the neighbouring portal before returning to the trailer.

The Polaran continued to haul its trailer down the corridor.

Carys returned her attention to Hush's box, picking it up. Thirty centimetres long on each side, it seemed light for its size, and whatever was inside rattled.

Whatever was inside it *moved*.

She hastily put the box down.

It jiggled, as if filled with jumping beans. With a toe, she pushed it well away from the open doorway so it didn't work its way off the ledge.

There was no sign of Hush returning any time soon, and there was nothing for her to do. She seemed to be in for a long, boring wait. At the window overlooking the ocean, she sat down. Then, after a few minutes, she lay down and curled into a ball, listlessly gazing at the view.

Why had Bujold abandoned her? What had happened to her companions? Was Setia even here in the city or was she still with the small Polarans in the mountain? Was she still alive?

Why had she called her a bitch?

The light was rapidly failing. Polaris Aa had to be sinking beneath the horizon somewhere out of sight. Soon, the dull red glow of night would cover the landscape. So many days had passed since Carys had left the *Bres*, and things had only gone from bad to terrible.

Her chances of escaping this living hell were non-existent.

Thirty-Six

"You do not sleep before me."

Carys opened her eyes a slit. She shivered. Every part of her body ached. Her skin was raw. Her ankle throbbed. She had bruises all over. And she was very, very hungry.

It was deepest night and Hush's apartment was bathed in a maroon, ethereal glow. The dark shape of the alien loomed menacingly.

"Were you contemplating casting yourself into the abyss?" Hush asked.

"What? No. I was tired. I fell asleep."

"Good. You do not deserve such a death."

I think I'll decide the death I deserve. "A box arrived for you. It's—"

"I am aware. It is an opportunity for you to begin your servitude. Bring it to me."

Carys took a quick look out into the night. Sighing, she got to her feet and limped across the room. Hush said or did something to activate the lighting. The box had moved from the place she'd left it. She picked it up. "What's inside?"

"Open it, and serve me." Hush had settled onto his perch.

Carys cursed under her breath as she searched for a way into the box. She ran her fingers along the seams, trying to prise them open.

She inspected it carefully for any kind of lock. But the surfaces were solid and uniform.

"Your species is very unintelligent," Hush remarked. "Give it to me."

When she handed it over, he pressed a section identical to the rest. The lid popped open. He handed the box back. "You will feed me."

Carys almost dropped it. The box was filled to the brim with larvae. The length of her hand, the off-white, thin-shelled creatures squirmed and their pale orange legs wriggled. She lifted her gaze to Hush, who had opened his mouth expectantly.

He looked so ridiculous she stifled a giggle. "Can't you feed yourself?"

His mouth snapped closed and he glared at her. "You will obey immediately or your ship and all your people will be destroyed."

"All right, all right." *Keep your hair on.* He didn't have hair. He reminded her of a cross between a feathered T-Rex and a vain old man with a bad comb-over.

She gingerly picked up a larva. Holding it in the tips of her fingers and thumb, she reached up to the tall alien's mouth.

After she popped it in he swallowed it whole. "Another."

She fed him larva after larva until the box was empty. "That's all there is. You've eaten the lot."

"Place the box next to the door for collection. I will wash before I rest. You will help me."

"But... what about my food? When do I eat?" Her stomach growled painfully.

"Your needs are not my concern."

"Hey, you can't just keep me here without feeding me. I haven't eaten properly in days. I'll starve to death if I don't get food. Is that the plan? Kill me with starvation and then tell everyone I failed at whatever stupid thing it is I'm supposed to be learning? Then you'll blow up the *Bres*? Is that what you have in mind?"

Hush's steely gaze fixed on her. "Your species talks too much. There is food. It is not my responsibility to acquire it for you."

"You mean the stuff in your bathroom? I can't eat that. It makes me sick."

"The stuff in my...?" Hush's mouth opened wide, his head

civilisations have advanced. You're a bunch of self-satisfied, useless morons. And..." she added, waggling a finger satisfyingly "... one day, your insularity is going to catch up with you. Another intelligent species will find this planet, and they won't be friendly like we humans. No. You'll be caught with your trousers down even though you don't wear trousers, and then what'll you do? I'll tell you. You're going to regret not helping me when you had the chance. You'll regret not listening to us and joining the Alliance. You'll look around, and there will be no one there to help you. No one!"

Her word vomit made her feel a smidgen better, but it hadn't made the slightest difference to the attitude of the Polarans.

Despairingly, she looked at the floor of the corridor, many metres below. If she could just get down to the floor, she could make her own way around, to an extent. Who knew what she might find if she could only safely make it to ground level?

The more she looked at the floor the more it seemed possible she might be able to get there without hurting herself too badly. The wall leading up to Hush's habitation sloped very slightly outward. It wasn't an entirely vertical drop, so she would slide rather than fall. And if she hung from the edge of the opening by her fingertips before dropping, she would have a little less far to go.

She decided to try.

What did she have to lose?

Hush had made it clear he would not support her in any way. If she was to survive her time in the Polaran metropolis that was up to her. She was on her own.

Carys turned her back to the corridor and knelt down. She lowered herself onto her stomach and eased backwards, dangling her legs over the edge of the doorway. A tremor of fear passed through her as her feet lost contact with a solid surface. Holding on tightly to the edge, she slid farther back until her stomach rested on the hard corner. The surface was smooth, offering no purchase. Her palms were sweaty, too, which didn't help.

Resisting the urge to check over her shoulder—she already knew how far she had to go—she wriggled the final distance, turning her hands so they cupped the edge.

She was hanging free.

Her breaths came fast and shallow and her muscles tensed as she anticipated the pain that seemed bound to follow. She'd been stupid

He put a hand on her shoulder.

She almost cried. It was the first friendly gesture she'd received since arriving in this horrible place. At least, she assumed it was friendly. For all she knew, it could be a precursor to ripping her head off. But she was determined to be positive.

"I'm *really* hungry." She patted her stomach and mimed putting food into her mouth. "Can you help me get something to eat?"

The alien's head tilted.

"Eat. I need to eat. Please." Carys placed her hands together in a praying gesture.

He copied her.

"No, no, no." She flapped her hands in frustration.

This was also copied.

"*Arghhh*!" Why was it so hard to make herself understood? Surely her new friend wasn't *that* stupid. Or maybe he was. After all, he'd been the only one out of scores of passersby to help her. Perhaps in Polaran terms he had the equivalent of a learning disability.

She scrunched up her face in concentration. The only way she was going to get some food was if she could communicate in a way he could comprehend. She thought back to Hush when she'd been feeding him the larvae, and to the small Polarans in the mountain tunnels. One thing popped into her mind. Whenever they ate, they tipped their heads back and dropped the food almost vertically down their gullets. In some cases this was followed by gnashing bones or whatever, but the former seemed the basic method.

She leaned her head so far back her neck was nearly bent double, opened her mouth wide, and mimed dropping something into it.

Understanding seemed to immediately light the Polarans' eyes. But then he turned and leapt into the air, soaring aloft.

"Huh? Where are you going?" In puzzlement, she watched him fly away.

Was he going to get something for her to eat and bring it back?

When he'd gone some distance, he looked over his shoulder and then twisted around to scan the corridor, his massive wings beating hard to hover. This appeared to upset some of the other fliers, who silently roared at him.

Zooming below the main traffic, he flew back and picked her up. His arms folded tightly around her torso he held her close to his chest and resumed his journey.

Had he forgotten she couldn't fly and expected her to follow? That seemed to be the case, but she doubted she would ever find out. Without a translation device like the one Hush used, their communication would be confined to miming and gestures.

Never mind. Nothing mattered as long as she could finally eat.

They flew lower and lower within the metropolis. Her new friend swooped into side passages and main thoroughfares, but all led down. He flew so quickly Carys saw little of what they passed, and the lateness of the hour probably meant that activity was reduced.

The galleried corridors grew narrower and dirtier, and suddenly she realised the passersby were smaller too. They began to resemble the creatures who had helped her and her companions. These aliens fluttered along, rather than beating their wings strongly and confidently.

When the passageways had become so narrow her rescuer struggled to navigate them, and she felt sure they must have reached the very bottom of the city, they glided through a wide, open doorway, and she was finally put down.

She stared in wonder.

The place they'd entered was vast and full of odours. The smaller aliens worked at tables, ovens, benches, over vats, on production lines and within pits. They sliced, roasted, boiled, fried, sorted, killed, washed, chopped, packed and—scores of Polarans bearing boxes exited moments after she arrived—delivered.

This was the food production and distribution hub. Relieved that her meaning had been understood, Carys wondered what would happen next. Was it normal for Polarans to come here to be fed? Would she face the same problems in finding edible food as she had before? How could she communicate what she needed?

As she hesitated, an alarm blared out.

Workers scrambled and flew from a section near a wall, leaving an open space. Lines split along the wall surface, and huge doors swung outward, revealing a view of the ocean and dark red sky. Fresh, sea air swept in, clearing away the smell of food. All attention was on the open portal.

Two large Polarans became visible in the darkness, slowly flapping closer. Another shape hung between them. They were carrying something. As the light from the room lit the object, it became clear it was a fishing net, filled with struggling sea creatures. The Polarans flew in. Simultaneously, they let go of one side of the net and it dropped open, spilling its contents to the floor.

The released animals writhed, jerked, flapped and crawled, glistening with water. Their open mouths gasped as they tried to breathe air, gradually suffocating.

The fishermen were leaving, trailing their net.

Carys blinked in recognition.

That was what the aliens in the mountain had been making. The net looked the same as the ones she'd seen in production in the factory.

Another pair of fishermen arrived, and another, each dropping their catch on the floor. Some lucky escapees slithered from the open doorway, perhaps surviving the drop to their watery home. The processors had already begun to gather the creatures at the edges of the pile, sorting them and killing the annoyingly vigorous survivors with swift, hard blows.

The skinning and chopping started, and the doors swung closed, shutting out the night.

Carys's arrival hadn't provoked much of a reaction. Once more, she was puzzled by the nonchalance the Polarans exhibited towards her. Had an alien turned up anywhere on Earth, there would have been a riot. Police and governments would have been involved. On this world it was just another Tuesday.

What little interest there had been in her existence was gone now the workers had to process tonight's catch. If Carys was going to eat, she would have to figure that out herself.

She wandered deeper into the room, seeking out something tastier and less emetic than Hush's unguents.

Encountering a smell that seemed familiar, she followed her nose. There it was. Someone was taking a roasted eel-like creature out of an oven. The dish was placed on a metal table. Another alien prepared to slice it up and place the pieces in waiting boxes. Carys tentatively picked up an empty box and held it out. Without missing a beat, the alien gave her a slice.

Her mouth watered and her stomach rumbled in anticipation, but she wanted to see what else she could get. She didn't know if she was allowed to be here or how long she could stay. Hush might demand her return any minute. She set off to seek out other food.

The rest of the workers were similarly generous. They seemed to feel their role was just to fulfil the city's nutritional needs, not to question who ate what. Whatever Carys begged for, she received. Soon, her container was full to the brim with fish, vegetables, grains and pulses, all of various kinds, all cooked. In truth, it was rather a mess. Everything was mixed together, and if she hadn't been ravenous the sight would have made her sick.

But it didn't.

Carys found a quiet corner and sat down. She began to eat, dipping her fingers into the box and retrieving pieces of this and that before popping them into her mouth. The knowledge that she should be more careful, that any of these things could either make her vomit or poison her, nagged at the back of her mind, but hunger overrode the thought.

She was quickly full. Days of privation had shrunken her capacity to eat. Carys carefully closed the box. She didn't know when she might be able to come here again. The food might have to last her days. It was time to return to Hush's quarters. She didn't know if she was allowed to leave, and if she was quick she might make it back before he woke up. She didn't want to jeopardise the safety of the *Bres*'s crew. Now she'd eaten, she could tackle the task of convincing the Polarans that humanity deserved their regard.

She stood up and looked for the Polaran who had helped her. All around, the smaller aliens continued to work, processing food for the city's inhabitants.

The exit from the room was empty. The Polaran who had brought her here was nowhere to be seen.

Thirty-Nine

Cradling her precious container, Carys left the food prep section. As she exited she was overtaken by a convoy of aliens pulling trailers. She moved to the side of the passageway, and the burdened food deliverers marched stoically past, ropes over their shoulders. For a species that had invented space travel, it was a remarkably archaic system for feeding the city.

She recalled the arrival of Hush's meal. A small Polaran had flown it up to the dwelling from a similar trailer. These simple vehicles couldn't travel by air, which meant there had to be another method for moving them between floors—presumably a lift of some kind. And she could use it.

The end of the convoy approached. Carys followed, relief flooding her. Not only did she have food, she would be able to make it back to Hush. If he was still asleep he might not even know she'd left.

Though explaining how she'd managed to acquire food would be hard.

She shook her head. She would cross that bridge when she came to it. Maybe he would be impressed by her ingenuity and his estimation of humanity would go up a notch.

The line of aliens pulling trailers went a different route than the one Carys had arrived by. This route led downwards along a sloping corridor, the floor marked by the passage of tens of thousands of trailer wheels. The practice had clearly been going on a long time.

How old was the city? And where did Polarans live before they constructed these places? With land so scarce on the planet, she guessed the cities were needed to house an expanding population.

How did they stay aloft? She hadn't seen any balloons or other containers for lighter-than-air gases. From her experience on Polaran starships it seemed the aliens hadn't invented a-grav. Perhaps they had engines that enabled hovering, like a jump jet. But surely engines the size required to keep a city in the air would be huge and would send vibrations throughout the structure. She *could* detect a soft vibration and faint hum if she concentrated. Maybe that was it. Coupled with the planet's low gravity, she guessed it might be possible.

A couple of aliens had thrown worried glances at her as the troop walked along. She wasn't being *entirely* ignored. When she paid attention, she noticed the furtive looks and chatter that seemed to be about her. It was as if the aliens were curious about the human following them, but something was preventing them from paying her any attention.

The line began to slow. Carys stood on tiptoe to peer over the heads. The aliens at the front had reached the end of the corridor and were arranging their burdens into neat columns and rows. Each new arrival did the same. As Carys walked closer, lines on the floor marking a large square became apparent. All the trailers stood within the lines.

She guessed what was about to happen and pushed forward to step within the lines. But there was no room. The last trailer was slotted into the remaining empty corner of the square, and there was no space to squeeze between them. Carys hesitated. If she climbed onto a trailer, would anyone object? The boxes wouldn't bear her weight. Some meals would be squashed.

The aliens took to the air, flying into the shaft that extended above.

There was a loud buzz. The assembled trailers shook, and the line split. The platform began to rise.

What choice did she have? The aliens might be able to fly to accompany their vehicles, but she could not.

She tensed and tucked her box under her arm as she prepared to leap, but heavy hands descended on her shoulders.

"You should not do that."

She started in surprise and she watched, forlorn, as the platform rose beyond her reach.

Hush had found her somehow. Would he punish her? Would her behaviour spell trouble for the *Bres*'s crew?

Except...

The voice she'd heard sounded different from Hush's.

She turned.

It was not Hush. This Polaran was smaller. Her rescuer? It was hard to be sure, but who else could it be?

"You can speak my language now?" she asked.

"I acquired a translator."

"Cool."

He didn't seem to be wearing any devices, but then again, neither had Hush.

She added, "Uhh... thanks for catching me when I was falling, and for bringing me here."

He stared at her.

"Umm..." She looked up at the meal delivery service, which had risen far beyond her reach. Like a huge dumb waiter accompanied by giant, weird sugar gliders, it was on its way to the upper floors of the cloud metropolis. Her lift back to Hush had gone.

Not that she particularly wanted to return to him, but he seemed to be her only route back to the *Bres*, Loki and her birds.

And there was the whole saving-the-crew-from-being-killed-by-the-Polarans thing.

Her helper was still staring at her.

"Do you think you could take me back to the place you picked me up? I'm not sure I was actually allowed to leave. If we're quick, we might make it before my, er, host wakes up."

"You have food now."

"Yes," Carys replied, relieved to finally receive an answer. "It's all in here." She lifted her box. "So, if you wouldn't mind...?"

"Come with me." He turned and his legs tensed as if he was about to spring into the air.

He turned back. "You cannot fly. I will carry you."

Carys allowed herself to be lifted into the air once more. So he had forgotten she couldn't fly earlier. As she was carried along, firmly gripping her carton of food, she mused that his mistake was understandable. She had to be the only being in the whole place who couldn't fly.

Especially if Bujold and Barbier have pissed off back to the ship!

Seething as she contemplated their betrayal, she tried to wrap her head around it. What had happened since the mission team had left? Had the captain really agreed to the ridiculous proposal that a single crew member had to demonstrate humanity's worthiness to ally with Polarans? And of all the people she could have picked, she'd nominated Carys? What about the flipping ambassador? Wasn't this kind of thing *his* job?

Deep in thought, Carys hadn't been taking much notice of her surroundings, but she suddenly realised she didn't recognise them. She hadn't thought she would be able to tell where she was going—the architecture seemed broadly similar throughout the city—but this section was different. It was older. Fine particles of grime coated the walls. And it was darker. Elsewhere, the metropolis was brilliantly lit at night, mimicking the sunlight that penetrated the translucent walls during the day. Here, darkness invaded, though it was lightening. Daybreak was coming and, presumably, Hush would wake soon and wonder where his human had gone.

"Where are you taking me? This is the wrong way, isn't it?"

"No, it is the right way," her companion replied. "I have lived here many years. This is the correct route. Don't concern yourself."

Don't concern myself?

"But I have to..."

She gave up. It had been several minutes since she'd seen any other Polarans, and they wouldn't have understood her pleas for help anyway. She would have to go wherever she was being taken.

Her bearer swooped into a low entrance and followed the passage downwards. They seemed to be descending even lower than the food prep section.

"Where are we?" she asked.

"We are..." he banked left and entered an open doorway "...home."

He landed and put her down.

They were standing in the only available floor space.

'Home' was very small, perhaps a quarter of the size of Hush's dwelling, which hadn't been large by Earth standards.

But the petiteness of the habitation wasn't the only cause of the lack of standing room. The place was crammed, utterly cluttered with objects. Shelves protruded from every wall, and they were filled to overflowing. Piles of items rose from the floor to the ceiling. Polished stones in brilliant colours or with interesting patterns, odd pieces of dried vegetation, jars filled with mysterious contents, boxes of many sizes, long tail feathers, carvings, and many things she didn't recognise filled the space.

Carys turned a circle. "Wow. You have a lot of stuff."

"You may examine anything. I will explain it if you wish."

"Thanks for the offer, but I should go back—"

"As I said, you don't need to concern yourself. You will not be missed."

"I'm not sure you understand why I'm here." *Or what I am. Or what I'm supposed to be doing.*

"I know. Everyone knows. Don't worry. You have time. Or you may not. Regardless, it will not make any difference."

"I think it might."

The creature tilted his head. "You aren't one of us. You don't understand."

"You can say that again."

"Why do you need me to repeat my statement? Was the translation faulty?"

"It's just a saying."

"I see. We have sayings too. What did you mean?"

"I was agreeing with you. I *don't* understand."

"What exactly don't you understand?"

"Everything, really."

"Maybe I can answer your questions."

"I certainly hope so."

Forty

Carys could not for the life of her figure out how to pronounce her new friend's name. When he stated it, his translator didn't even bother attempting to render it into English. The noise he made instantly reminded Carys of Boots, a cat her adoptive mother had acquired while on active service as a Royal Marine. Boots's favourite habit—apparently—had been to throw up hairballs at every available opportunity.

The Polaran's name sounded exactly like the noise the cat made prior to an evacuation. It was a kind of echoing wail, part distress, part relief that the tummy discomfort would soon be over.

"I-I can't say that," Carys stammered. "Can I call you something else?"

"You may call me a human name if it's easier."

"Okay. How about..." She racked her brains. "Are you male or female?"

"You have different names for each sex? I am male."

"Then I'll call you..." She looked him up and down. "Perseus."

"Perseus," he repeated. At the same time that his translator stated the name, her acquaintance attempted to pronounce it, his lipless mouth forming the word carefully. "I like it. Does it have any significance?"

"He's a character from ancient history who rescued someone."

"Interesting. I would like to hear the story."

"You really would? I thought…" She recalled Hush telling her that Polarans weren't interested in humans, but she brushed the memory aside. She had more important considerations. "Never mind. I'll tell you the story another time. You said before that Hush won't care if I don't go back, and that whatever I do, it won't make any difference. Can you explain?"

"Hush? Who is…? Oh, I understand." Perseus made the '*hushhh*' sound Carys had heard in the Polarans' great chamber. "She has already made up her mind about you and about humans generally. If she is awake and has noticed you left, she can easily discover where you are if she wants to. I made no secret of bringing you here. If she wants you to return she will send a summons. Most likely, she will not."

"Her mind is made up about humans?" Carys swallowed. "It doesn't matter what I do or say, your people will destroy the *Bres*?"

"Most likely."

"But…" Carys's legs weakened, and she found herself sitting on a spiky object. She pulled the thing aside and sat on the floor. She looked up at Perseus. "There has to be something I can do."

"I don't think so. Hush, as you call her, is notoriously stubborn, and unfortunately the Triad has left the final decision to her."

Carys thrust the heel of her hand into her eye, fighting tears, as the enormity of what Perseus was saying hit. Loki, Miriam, Waylis, Mapper Robins, her birds, the crew, Bujold, *everyone*, would die. She blinked as she looked up again. "What about the people who came here with me? Are they still alive or have they already been killed?"

"I don't know."

"Can you find out?" Perhaps there was still a way she could save Setia, Sheldrake and Moody. The Polarans might let the mission team members live out their lives on a mountain somewhere. The aliens held humans in such low esteem, they might not care.

"I can try," Perseus replied, "but I don't have access to secure information."

Forlornly, Carys muttered, "I thought Hush was male."

"My translator didn't pick that up. Please speak louder."

"It doesn't matter."

Perseus slid some of his collection to one side to make room, and squatted down next to Carys. "I am sorry. It may be possible for you to stay here. I can order food for you if you tell me what you can eat."

"I don't want to stay here! I'm not a pet, not another one of your..." She glanced around the cluttered room. Hush's dwelling had been almost empty, and Carys had assumed that was the Polaran way. "What *is* all this stuff?"

Perseus proudly straightened up. "My collections? I have many interests." He picked up a carving. "These are made by juveniles on..." His translator was silent and Perseus's voice took over, saying a word Carys couldn't hope to remember or repeat.

"I think they're beautiful," he continued, "but they're usually tossed into the ocean after a few years. Their makers grow to hate them as they mature. I was lucky to retrieve these before they were discarded."

As he'd spoken, he held out the artefact, motioning Carys to take it. She accepted it without interest, miserable with fear and guilt, and idly inspected the object in her hands. The smooth stone seemed to be something like brown jade, and it had been shaped into the form of a Polaran diving, wings back, body straight, arms at its sides. The level of detail was incredible. If the carving hadn't been cold and rigid to the touch, Carys could have imagined it coming to life and plunging headlong into waves.

"Juveniles carved it?" she asked.

"Yes, on..." Again, an impossible Polaran name.

"That's one of the mountains?"

"What is a mountain?"

"A very high area of land, usually rising to a summit."

"Isn't all land high?"

Her shoulders slumped. "Here, it is."

"But not on your planet?"

"No, on Earth we have mountains too, but many parts of the world are only hilly or flat. Some areas are even lower than sea level, but they're inland or we protect them from flooding."

"Flat land. That seems very strange."

"Imagine if your oceans were much lower and the sea beds were exposed. At some point you would see the bottoms of all the mountains and the surrounding land."

"What a fascinating concept." Perseus's gaze became distant.

Carys returned her attention to the carving. "Why do these get thrown out? They must take months to make, and years to learn how to make them."

"I agree it is a great pity, but as a juvenile grows older he or she begins to understand these things have no value."

"No value?" Carys looked up. "I don't get it. You collect them. *You* appreciate them."

"I do. But I am different. Some of my acquaintances say I never grew up." Perseus did the thing Hush had done when she learned that Carys had eaten her ointments. He was laughing, but presumably at himself. "I love to collect many things that everyone believes have no value. But my collections please me."

"The juveniles..." Some things were beginning to add up in Carys's mind. "I think it was juveniles who looked after me and my friends when we arrived on your planet. Is that right?"

"I don't know. It was only through gossip I found out you were here. There was no formal announcement. You were in another place before you were brought to this city?"

"I was." She told him everything that had happened since leaving the *Bres*.

Perseus was silent throughout her story, though at one point he got up and picked his way through his collections to a window and looked out over the ocean. Polaris Aa rose high as Carys talked, and light flooded in, illuminating the dusty objects filling the space. They were like tiny mountains, a Polaran landscape in miniature.

Carys reached the moment she'd dangled precariously from the exit to Hush's home, starving and desperate.

Perseus turned to face her. "And that was when I saw you fall."

"And saved me," Carys concluded.

"I had heard that a being from another planet was with Hush, and I was curious to see you. It was very surprising to see you simply drop. I was shocked and I was almost too late to catch you before you hit the floor. You are extremely heavy. You would have been hurt."

Carys winced. It wasn't the first time a Polaran had told her she was heavy. In Earth terms she wasn't, yet she couldn't help feeling they were criticising her for being fat. "I know, but I was so hungry I was prepared to do anything."

"It must be very inconvenient to have no wings."

"It wasn't until I came here."

Perseus returned his attention to the ocean, making no comment.

Carys was silent too. It seemed that Polaran society was set up so that the young of the species did most of the work, manufacturing objects, processing and serving food, and so on. Then as they grew older they did less practical work, probably managing and governing. And then finally they attained the high status of creatures like Hush and had the privilege of making major decisions. Somewhere along the way they lost interest in just about anything except themselves. Carys recalled the sparseness of Hush's dwelling, guessing the high-level Polarans spent their days grooming their feathers and chatting amongst themselves.

Yet they did appear to value ideas. Hush had said something about the 'principle of three'. Maybe they fancied themselves to be great philosophers.

"Perseus, can you explain something about Polaran thinking?"

"I can try, but you must understand I am not like most of my species."

"I think I got that already. Can you tell me what it means to die ignobly?"

"That's easy. It means any death that isn't The Great Death."

"What's The Great Death?"

"Humans don't have The Great Death?"

"Obviously not. We spend our lives trying to avoid dying, but when death comes it arrives in many different ways."

Perseus returned to her side and picked up the carving they'd been looking at earlier. "This represents The Great Death. When one of us has achieved all that is possible, when he or she is wise and knowledgeable to the utmost degree, it is time to fly high into the upper atmosphere and then dive into the ocean, bringing the ultimate end to a perfect life."

"You...you *drown yourselves*?"

"If we dive too deeply we cannot resurface. Drowning follows, naturally. But that isn't the point of The Great Death."

"Then what is the point?"

"The point..." Perseus paused. Somehow, his translator had managed to convey a condescending tone, as if he were explaining something to a child. "The *point* is that we achieve perfection in life. Dying of old age or an external factor like a disease or accident is shameful."

"I see," Carys said, though she wasn't sure she did. Recalling

Perseus's assertion that he was different from most Polarans, she asked, "Do you agree with the idea of The Great Death?"

"I agree with the principle, but I don't look down on anyone who dies differently. I mean, it isn't their fault, is it?"

"That's very open-minded of you."

"I like to think so."

Over the course of their conversation, Carys grew to appreciate just *how* different Perseus was from other Polarans. He told her most of his peers valued asceticism over material possessions, and they spent their free time discussing ideas and debating abstract concepts, while he preferred to wander the city looking for anything that might take his interest, or hanging out with 'youngsters' working in food prep, sanitation, construction and other practical professions. He had travelled to many distant mountain islands, but always alone. No one his age wanted to accompany him, and anyone younger didn't have the stamina.

Their talk drew to a natural pause. Perseus glanced at the window, as if considering something.

"I have another question," Carys said.

"Ask it, but I don't have time for a long explanation. I must leave soon to go to work."

"You work? I thought Polarans your age spent their days pontificating."

Perseus's reaction was delayed a beat, but then did that thing Carys assumed was laughing. "Pontificating is how I would describe it too. But few of my people would agree. You are right. It is unusual for someone in my stage of life to be employed. I could resign my position today if I wished and live a simple life, supported by the labour of younger generations. But, I confess, I'm not a thinker, I'm a doer. I would soon grow tired of endless rhetoric, discussion and debate. I need activity."

"What do you do?"

"I'm an engineering supervisor. I coordinate the teams that maintain this city's altitude."

Carys perked up. "You do? I wondered how it floats. We don't have cities like this on Earth. Ours are on the ground."

"On the flat ground. Of course. Cities this size are impossible on my world unless they hover. No landmasses can support them."

"But how does it float? Do you have giant balloons attached to it? I haven't seen any."

"My translator doesn't know that word, but I think it's wrong anyway. Our cities float due to opposing magnetic forces."

"Magnetism?! Whoa. That didn't even occur to me."

"The lower surface of the city is made of a magnetic compound, and corresponding slabs of the same material lie beneath the water directly below us in a shallow sea."

"But how the hell do you create magnetic fields strong enough to suspend entire cities in the air? That must take massive amounts of power."

Perseus gestured outside, where Polaris Aa's powerful beams had washed the colour from the sky. "Also," he went on, "the construction material we use is very light. Furthermore, if *you* are representative of Earth organisms, I suspect that *we* are very light too, in comparison."

"Your gravity is lower than Earth's too." Carys whistled. "Still, *magnetism*." She had a sudden yearning to share her interesting discovery with another human being. But she didn't know where her companions were or even if they were still alive. In a more subdued tone, she said, "The question I wanted to ask was, how are we communicating? You don't seem to have a translator, and I certainly don't have one."

Perseus retched. Carys scooted backwards, eager to avoid anything he might bring up. She hadn't forgotten the 'food' the young Polarans' had offered her and her companions after Sheldrake's unfortunate mime. She couldn't scoot far due to the piles of items stacked behind her.

Perseus retched again. Something shot out of his mouth and he caught it neatly in one hand.

He said something.

"My translator," the translator translated.

He popped the device back into his mouth and swallowed it.

"Uhh, thanks for clearing that up," Carys said. "Look, I have so many questions for you, but you said you have to go to work."

"That's right. I must leave, but I will return later. I have many questions for you too."

"Are you *sure* Hush won't order the destruction of my ship because I came here?"

"Your location within the city is the least of her considerations. In truth, it may benefit your cause to stay out of her way. She's notoriously easy to anger and hard to please."

"I think I already found that out. One last thing. I understand that Polarans look down on humans. We can't fly. We don't know 'the Principle of Three", whatever the hell that is. But if a being from another world landed anywhere on Earth, we would be fascinated. It would be the event of a lifetime. International news for years to come. But your people are utterly uninterested in me. I've travelled through your city a few times and never attracted any attention. To me, that's bizarre."

"I think I can explain. To be Polaran is to be interested only in one's inner self—the process of learning, so that one may achieve the—"

"Great Death. I think I'm getting it."

"I would guess that the workers in the food preparation section were very curious about you, but they would not want to display their curiosity to their co-workers. It would have been shameful. As we age, I believe that we really do turn inward, losing concern for the external world. But I must leave now. Do you have sufficient food to last you the day?"

"Yes, but I was wondering..." Carys scanned the dwelling. "Do you have, er, unguents?"

"Naturally."

"Can I use them? Only, my skin is really badly sunburnt. I think an ointment might help."

"You aren't usually red in colour?"

"Normally, I'm pretty pale."

"You are welcome to use any of my things."

Perseus left.

Forty-One

Firstly, Carys searched Perseus's artefacts. It took several minutes of peering into every nook and cranny, opening boxes and examining their contents, and sorting through piles of unidentifiable objects before she found what she was looking for: something, *anything*, she could wear. At the bottom of a large container made from a papery material, underneath a mound of iridescent, thin-walled glass baubles, lay a piece of woven cloth. She guessed Perseus must have put it there as a cushion for the fragile objects. She carefully picked the baubles out and stacked them in an empty bowl before lifting out the cloth. It was thick and stiff, but it would have to do. The material seemed to be woven from dyed plant fibres.

Perseus's bathroom was mercifully uncluttered. Its only contents apart from the fittings were jars similar to the ones in Hush's apartment. Carys looked in each one but none appeared to contain soap. Never mind.

She stripped. Her crew uniform was little more than tatters, sliced by the Polaran bots on their ship, torn on rocks on the mountain, and begrimed with dirt and sweat. She rinsed it thoroughly under the water spout and then wrung it out before hanging it up near the window in the main room.

Next, she rinsed herself. The cool water stung her sunburned skin, but she bore the discomfort for the sake of being clean. She also rinsed her hair and ran her fingers through it in an effort to break up some of the tangles. She was beginning to shiver when the water mercifully switched to warm air.

Dry and somewhat cleaner, she took down a random jar and experimentally smoothed a little of the contents on her red, sore arm. The effect was mild but it didn't seem to make the burn worse, so she applied the lotion over the rest of the affected areas of her skin.

Finally, she wrapped the woven cloth over her shoulders and returned to the room of curiosities.

Her clothes, stretched out on a decorative screen near the window, were nowhere near dry. She found her food, sat down and took in the view as she ate.

How long would it be until Perseus returned?

Not that he could help her much in her predicament. The information he'd given had improved her understanding of Polaran culture, but she was no closer to knowing how to convince the aliens to not destroy the *Bres*. Perseus had no power or influence within the society as far as she could tell. From what he'd said, he was seen as quite the weirdo. If anything, associating with him might hinder, not help, her cause.

Thoughtfully munching on a deep-fried, salty, leafy vegetable, she went through all she knew about Polarans. They were arrogant, insular, obsessed with their inner mental lives at the expense of all external considerations, focussed on the single goal of a nameless 'perfection'.

What did it mean to be a perfect Polaran?

Carys shook her head, dismissing the train of thought. It didn't matter. Humans were so different in so many ways. The Polarans would never believe the newcomers might be worthy of their esteem. She had to focus on the lesser goal: to save the *Bres*.

A sense of hopeless despair rose up. She felt so utterly inadequate and unsuited to the task. But she set her jaw and pushed the feeling aside. Like it or not, capable or not, this was something she had to do. The memory of Sheldrake's bizarre faith in her came floating into her mind. She grimly smiled. She had no idea why the ex-corporal thought she was so capable, but perhaps she might prove him right. The least she could do was to die trying.

She yawned and stretched. She hadn't slept all night, but she didn't know how much time she had to come up with an idea. Hush hadn't mentioned anything about a deadline. It might only be when she grew tired of the situation.

Deciding the view of the ocean wouldn't offer any useful information, Carys turned her attention to Perseus's many possessions. In her search for something to keep warm in while waiting for her clothes to dry, she'd found a jumble of pictures in a corner. Pulling her blanket over her shoulders, she returned to them. The canvases were crude and uneven, but they enhanced the effect of the drawings and paintings, mostly landscapes and seascapes. Polaris Aa figured heavily in many depictions of the world, unsurprisingly. The smaller, closer sun seemed like an afterthought. The young Polarans had also painted each other. Some subjects had adopted what appeared to be cheeky poses, holding their arms akimbo, their knees apart and their tails curved aloft.

One picture in particular captured Carys's attention. A massive, shallow bowl filled most of the scene. The bowl was full of gigantic eggs, and several had hatched. New Polarans lifted their bald heads on scrawny necks, their eyes still unopened. Tiny arms reached up from the broken shells. Two baby aliens were entirely visible. She looked closer. Though the creatures had wings they were undeveloped, extremely thin, featherless skins stretching between tail, knees and armpits. It was no wonder that the makers of fishing nets had felt protective of the humans who had appeared on their island. To Polarans, humans looked like big babies.

Carys returned the picture to the others and heaved a sigh. The image had reminded her of her impossible task and made it seem even more impossible. What was it Hush had said? Humans crawled on the land like bugs, unable to go up or down unassisted, lower even than the creatures in the ocean. Or something like that. What was worse, Hush was right. Without their technology, human beings *were* confined to the horizontal plane. Carys's ankle ached with the memory of falling and twisting it. Even in this world's lower gravity, her species was hampered by its physical limitations.

As she sat, disconsolate, staring listlessly at the pile of Polaran art, a hum invaded her distracted mind. She looked up, wondering where the noise was coming from. The sound seemed to be floating in from the window.

Carys rose and stepped over to it. Resting a hand on the frame, she peered out. The noise was louder here, but she couldn't see its source. It was coming from all around.

Polaris Aa hung high in the sky, washing the colour from the scene. Though she stood in shade, she could feel the sun's warmth radiating in.

The sound's pitch lowered, and then she couldn't hear it anymore. It had to be coming from the city's inhabitants. They were singing and their voices had gone too low for human hearing. The deep hum resounded once more and rose higher. It vibrated the air. How many were singing? It had to be thousands.

The noise grew louder and louder until it threatened to burst her eardrums. She covered her ears and winced. Why were they singing? Was it some kind of celebration? A horrible thought struck: had the Polarans made their decision about the *Bres*? Had she failed?

But, if she'd learned anything about the aliens, it was that they were profoundly uninterested in anything outside themselves and their world. They couldn't be rejoicing about the destruction of the humans' starship.

Then she saw it.

A single Polaran was flying slowly upwards. It was a large one, at least as large as Hush, though it wasn't possible to be sure at the distance. Carys squinted to follow the figure as it rose into the sky and Polaris Aa's glare. The alien beat its wings rhythmically. As was usual when Polarans weren't carrying anything, its arms hung down. Its head was lifted to the sun.

"*Ohhh*," Carys exclaimed aloud as she realised what was going on.

Her hands dropped from her ears. The city's inhabitants were singing softly now, their voices full of emotion. Despite her terrible predicament, despite the weight of responsibility for so many human lives on her shoulders, Carys couldn't help being moved. Tears filled her eyes as she followed the progress of the solitary creature winging its way steadily into the upper atmosphere.

The voices were rising too, not louder but somehow with more intensity. New notes entered the song. Whereas before they had all sung the same melody, now they began to harmonise. Some sung higher, some lower. The city vibrated with the noise, affecting the floor Carys stood upon and the window frame she touched.

She closed her eyes. She couldn't look upwards any longer. Brilliant red stained her vision.

The singing stopped.

She opened her eyes, holding up a hand to shade them. Unable to look into Polaris Aa, she focused straight ahead.

The falling figure crossed her view. Wings folded into the characteristic raptor's stoop Carys knew so well, the Polaran plummeted, back straight, arms at its sides. In less than a second it hit the water and disappeared with barely a ripple.

A collective sigh seemed to be exhaled. The silence continued.

Carys watched the spot where the Polaran had disappeared, painfully reminded of the moment she'd tried to do the same after Setia's attempted murder. It was easier to do it here. The alien had entered the ocean only a hundred metres away.

Had Hush tried to give Setia a Great Death?

No, that didn't make sense. In order to achieve the pinnacle of Polaran society, one had to be removed from the real world and reach a perfect philosophical understanding of inner reality. Setia's proposed death had nothing to do with that. Dropping her into water had only been for the sake of convenience. The Polarans could tell that humans are not natural swimmers from their anatomy. And they probably thought that Torres's cairn was another example of human inferiority.

Had normality returned to the city? Carys leaned out and looked around. The anvil of the cloud spread out high above and the windows in the billowing walls were empty. But perhaps they'd been empty all along.

She searched the ocean for the place where the suicidal alien had hit, but since she'd taken her eyes off it she couldn't be sure where it was any longer.

Just when she was about to give up looking, the limp form of the dead alien floated to the surface. Waves lifted the lifeless wings.

Forty-Two

Something Carys had discovered over the course of her life was that to persuade another person or being to do something it helped to think from their perspective. When she'd lived as a Displaced Child, a captive of the cultish Crusaders, in order to survive she'd tried to think like a Crusader would think. They were arrogant and entirely convinced of the truth of their beliefs. Central to the Earth Awareness Crusade doctrine was another plane of existence that underlay the physical universe, a more 'real' reality. She guessed it was their go-to justification for their terrible treatment of the kidnapped children. Whenever a Crusader's conscience was twinged, they would tell themselves that exhaustion, starvation and sickness didn't really hurt the kids. It was only their excessive ties to the immediate world that made it seem so.

Not that any Crusader ever subjected themselves to starvation, exhaustion or sickness if they could help it.

So she knew that complaining about being tired or hungry wouldn't result in being allowed to rest or given more food. If anything, it would show the Crusader that the complainer was wedded to a false reality. Instead, she would pay rapt attention during lessons, pretending to absorb all the nonsense she was taught. Even now, she could recite several prayers by heart. This behaviour had resulted in Crusaders paying little attention to what she did, thinking she was a compliant convert.

Her insight had helped her survive, and she'd helped other children. Sadly, it had also meant that when the crisis point came and the Crusaders had to flee, her prediction about what they would do with the kids too small to run had come true. She'd tried to save as many as she could, but only a few had made it.

She applied similar ideas about thinking from the other's perspective when it came to rehabilitating injured birds of prey. They thought primarily through their vision. If you put a bag over the head of a human it would make them panic. But the same action made a bird of prey docile, almost as if you'd turned off their mind. And nearly everything in a raptor's life revolved around hunting and eating. Associating food with a desired behaviour was the best way to train a bird. Most humans were a little more complicated.

Polarans?

She already had an inkling of the way they thought. Perhaps if she understood them better she would find an answer, and though Perseus didn't have any power to sway Hush's decision, he was a portal into the Polaran mind.

Comforting herself with this knowledge, Carys lay down and curled up, covering herself with her makeshift blanket. She could rest while waiting for her portal to finish work.

"Perseus, can I pick your brains?"

The alien's head jerked up and he stared at her.

"I mean, can I ask you something?"

"Of course." He continued eating the meal that had arrived not long after him. Clearly, no Polaran above a certain status ever cooked for themselves. "I thought you meant—"

"I know. Translation's a complete pain the arse, isn't it?"

"I... I don't think that translated well either."

"Probably not. I wanted to talk to you about the war you have going on with the nearest inhabited planet."

"War? There is no war."

"Maybe that isn't the right way to describe it, but you hate each other, right?"

"Polarans do not hate other species. We don't hate humans. We simply have no interest in anyone else and want to be left alone."

This didn't sound correct. Carys recalled what Bujold had told her on the *Bres*'s bridge during the third attempt to make contact. The captain had said the two sides had been sending hostile messages for decades. But then Carys remembered that the information had come from the *Balor*, which was in contact with the other aliens. They'd called the Polarans 'evil freaks' and refused to help the Fleet establish a relationship. The conflict was hearsay.

"We cannot achieve perfection if distracted," Perseus continued. "The Triad fear that if they don't send a clear message to your species, more humans will arrive and divert us from our primary goal in life."

"They could, you know, just tell us."

"As I understand it, we sent a clear signal twice. Both times, we allowed your ship to escape. Yet you still returned."

It was undeniable. Carys replayed the contact attempts in her mind. "So when we re-broadcast your own message back at you, we weren't sending you a threat?"

"That message is a warning, not a threat. It tells the aliens in the next system to stay away or suffer the consequences."

Carys imagined the *Bres*, approaching the Polarans' world, transmitting their own warning in their own language. It was no wonder they had a low opinion of humans.

She asked, "But what about when we transmitted the mathematical formula for lift in flight? Are you saying that didn't make any difference?"

"Some Polarans working in the field of mathematics understood it, but it was not instrumental in the decision to cease firing on your ship."

Carys blinked. Bujold's faith in her was based on an erroneous understanding of what had happened. "Then why *did* you stop firing at us?"

"The decision was made to investigate your species further in order to prove beyond doubt that our assumption was correct—that you have nothing to teach us. I don't agree, but that's the belief of the Triad and most Polarans."

So the odds had been stacked against the mission team right from the start. There wasn't anything they could have done or said, no Polaran with any kind of status was prepared to give them the time of day. The aliens had analysed human anatomy and found it wanting. Then they dropped a few of them in the middle of nowhere, expecting them to quickly die. But the young Polaran netmakers had thrown a spanner in the works by saving them.

And now?

Now, the fate of the *Bres*'s crew hung by a thread. There was no question that the Polarans' reasoning was sound: by killing all the humans who entered their system they could guarantee that none would do the same in a very long while.

"Damn it," she snapped. "What is wrong with you people? You could learn so much, *do* so much, if you would just look outside your little, enclosed world. Our ship arrived from outer space! Hasn't any Polaran ever wanted to leave your system? To see what's out there? We have so much to offer you. Technology, physics, information about the galaxy, so many things. But you insist on living your stupid little lives, working towards 'enlightenment', and then when you achieve it you kill yourselves! I mean, what's the point? What's the bloody point?"

Perseus had watched her in silence throughout her speech. When she paused to take a breath, he said, "Are you angry?"

"Yes, I'm angry. I'm bloody, fucking angry. I'm going to die. Everyone on my ship is going to die. All the birds I've nurtured for months, including one very special bird I love with all my heart, are going to die. And all because some idiotic aliens have heads the size of their own planet."

"I don't think that's possible."

Carys's shoulders slumped. It was hopeless. She'd thought for a moment that she might think of a way out, but there was none. To her shame and fury, tears spilled from her eyes. She angrily wiped them away.

"Are you sad?" Perseus asked.

"Shut up! Shut your face, you big feathered moron. Leave me alone." She stomped to the exit and looked despairingly down at the drop to the corridor floor.

"Do you want me to take you somewhere?" Perseus asked.

"I want you to *leave me alone*."

"I will, if that's your wish. But, first, can I ask a question? What is a bird? We only have your language, nothing else. My translator tells me it is an animal. You were caring for these animals on your ship?"

"Yes," Carys replied tonelessly, "I was caring for them. Birds can fly, like Polarans. There are many different kinds on Earth."

"They sound interesting. It's a pity I will never see them."

She didn't answer. Then, in the silence, the thinnest, most fragile thread of hope appeared. "Perseus, if you really want to see the birds, is there anything you can do to help me? You know Polarans. What can I say or do to save us?"

"I am willing to help, but I fear that your task is impossible to achieve. You cannot demonstrate the worth of your species because humans *are* vastly inferior to Polarans. You have shown me so."

"I've... what? How?!"

"Your behaviour just now was like that of a very young Polaran. Even the workers who initially helped you would never have behaved so."

"But I'm under threat of death? It's normal to get emotional about it."

"Everyone dies. The only sorrow is to die before you have achieved all that you want from life. Even then, showing anger, sadness or other strong emotions and allowing them to influence your actions and state of mind is fruitless and shows a lack of maturity."

Carys replied through her teeth, "You're beginning to sound a lot like Hush."

"I don't deny it. I am, after all, representative of my species. Are you representative of humans?"

"I don't know. My captain seems to think so."

"Then..." Perseus didn't complete his sentence, but his meaning rang clear as a bell.

Forty-Three

Another crimson Polaran night had passed, and Carys's mood was the lowest it had been since embarking on this hopeless mission. Perseus's *Then...* had been ringing in her mind for hours between bouts of fitful sleep. Could he be right? Could humanity really have nothing to teach his narrow-minded, stuck-up species? Had Polarans really reached some sort of pinnacle and no other galactic species could touch them? Did they really have nothing to learn?

It didn't seem possible, yet how could she convince them they were wrong? And how could she do it in the slim period of time remaining before Hush grew tired of the tedious humans besmirching Polaran territory?

Perseus emerged from his room. A new box of food had appeared next to the doorway, delivered overnight. The Polaran picked it up. "Are you hungry?"

Carys sat up and sorrowfully shook her head.

Perseus hesitated.

"No. I'm not hungry." Were the condemned ever hungry? "You said yesterday you were willing to help me. Are you sure?"

Perseus squatted and opened the box. "One thing you should know about Polarans: we speak the truth and rarely prevaricate. If we say something, we mean it."

"Is that one of your steps to perfection?"

"One of the first. Only children lie and obfuscate."

"But isn't it sometimes necess...?"

His frank gaze bore into her soul.

"Okay, I get it. If you *are* willing to help, can you arrange for me to meet with the Triad? I don't want to deal with Hush alone. She hates my guts. I'll never persuade her of anything."

"You don't seem to understand my position. I am not high status. In fact, I am seen as a... a..."

"I think the word you're looking for is weirdo."

"Weirdo. Yes, that's correct. I am a weirdo."

Carys smiled sadly. "Join the club. Look, can you at least try? It's worth trying, right? Otherwise I just sit around and wait for Hush to remember to execute me."

"I will try. But what do you plan to tell them? Have you come up with an argument that demonstrates the worth of your species?"

"Not yet. I'm hoping that the pressure will force something to pop into my mind. One thing's certain—if I don't take the initiative, soon it will be too late."

"I will make the request." He paused, and then said, "It is done. We must await the reply."

"You comm'd them?" Carys frowned and peered at him. "How did you do that?"

"We use an internal device. I will show you." He began to retch.

"No, it's fine," she said hastily. "I don't need to see it."

It wasn't until Perseus was flying her to the meeting the answer came. Carys didn't know why she hadn't thought of it before. Elated, she blurted, "I think I know what to tell them."

"You have the answer?" Perseus replied. "I'm glad. I wouldn't like to lose you. I like you, and there is still so much for me to learn about humans and your planet."

"You'll have to be quick. I think I'll be leaving within the next few days." But if she was right, Perseus would have a huge amount of information at his fingertips.

The reply to Perseus's request on her behalf for a meeting had taken hours to arrive. He'd been forced to take time off work, but this didn't seem to be a problem. Carys guessed his job was probably token anyway, and that there were plenty of lower status Polarans who could fill in for him.

When he'd related the acceptance of the Triad, he'd expressed surprise. Carys was surprised too. Everything that had happened so far indicated that the human visitors were not a priority.

"Perseus, when this meeting is over, could you do me a favour?"

"If it's within my capacity. I have the rest of the day free."

"Being carried around like this is undignified and uncomfortable." Once more, she was being held like a rag doll, dangling from the Polaran's grasp. "Do you think you could carry me on your back?"

"I could try, if that's what you would prefer."

"And..." She took a breath.

"And?" Perseus asked.

For most of her life, ever since she'd become fascinated by birds, she'd dreamed of flying. Not in an aeroplane, glider or balloon, but actually flying like a bird, sweeping the skies, zooming in and out of clouds, travelling to far horizons. Sometimes she had literally dreamed of it, only to wake and realise she was chained by gravity to the ground. "Could...could we go outside and fly over the ocean? Maybe you could take me to an island if there's one nearby."

On the off chance that her plan didn't work, it might be her last moment of freedom, her last few hours of life. She wanted to make the most of them.

"Yes," Perseus replied, "I would like that too."

They arrived at the Triad's chamber. Perseus deposited Carys on top of the column where she'd stood before. He was not permitted to remain.

Hush stood in the middle of the three this time. Carys had begun to be able to distinguish one Polaran from another. Hush's colouring was slightly deeper than her colleagues' and the minor wound on her head was clear.

"You are lucky," Hush announced. "Your request arrived at an opportune moment. In other circumstances it would not have been granted. For your information, I had already come to my decision regarding the presence of humans in our territory, and I was only awaiting a convenient time to carry it out. Can you guess what it was?"

"You decided to kill all the humans on the surface and destroy our ship."

"I see you have learned something about my people and our priorities."

"I have, and that's why I wanted to talk to you." Carys squared her shoulders, but then curiosity about what Hush had said made her hesitate. If there was ever a time to tread carefully, it was now. "Before I make my proposal, can you tell me why you granted me this audience? You said I was lucky."

"A wise question. It happens that this is an extremely important time for me." Hush drew herself upright and smoothed her wing feathers. "After a lifetime of study, reflection, and deep thought, I have nearly achieved the pinnacle of philosophical prowess. I require only one more test, after which I will be judged by a board of my peers. If I pass this test, I will be awarded The Great Death."

Many sarcastic retorts rose to Carys's lips. She kept them to herself. "Sounds amazing. So, whatever you decide after hearing my proposal—and hopefully following through on it—you'll be judged on that?" Her confidence was beginning to waver. If the final say was down to Hush and Hush alone, and her Great Death depended on it, and considering that she already hated humans after one of them had hit her in the head with a rock, things didn't bode well.

"That is correct," Hush replied. "What have you come here to tell us?"

Carys set her jaw. *Fuck it.* Even if her idea was shit, she would go for it. What did she have to lose? "All right. Perseus told me—"

"Perseus?"

"The weir... The Polaran I've been staying with for a couple of days."

"Your absence from my dwelling was noted. It demonstrated to me that you had no desire to learn a better way of life."

"I was just hungry. Anyway, he told me the only information you have about humans is our language."

"That is all the information we require."

"Is it, though? How do you know what we're capable of if you don't know anything about us?"

"That's simple. We have studied your anatomy and your behaviour. Both are poorly developed."

"But you don't know our history. I understand you don't value our science or technology. Philosophy is central to Polaran society, right? Well, did you know that it's important to us too? Humans have thousands of years of philosophical thought. We have many famous philosophers, and their thinking has influenced our societies for millennia." This last comment was somewhat of a stretch. Carys wasn't sure it was true. She was not an expert on the subject, but she was talking for her life.

One of the Triad spoke to Hush and then the other joined in. If it had only been down to Hush, Carys was sure it would all be over. But the other two seemed at least a little interested.

Pushing her advantage, she said, "You must have a way to contact my ship. Ask them to send down everything they have on Earth's most famous philosophers, from Socrates and Confucius right up to Ainsley and Malayali. Read about them. You'll be impressed. You'll see humans are more than emotional, ground-dwelling mammals."

More discussion within the Triad. Carys held her breath. Surely this would work. It had to. She had nothing else to offer.

Finally, and with seeming reluctance, Hush said, "We will study your philosophers. It is not my desire, but I have been overruled."

Forty-Four

"Did it work?" Perseus asked after he collected Carys from the chamber.

"I don't know yet. They're going to request the data from the *Bres*. The captain will give it to them for sure. She wants the Polarans to be the second members of the alliance, after us." Carys recalled the apparently successful contact with the aliens in the Polaris B system. "Or maybe you guys will be the third members. Anyway, our captain has a laser focus on the Fleet's goal. It's an obsession. And the information I want the Triad to study isn't classified or anything. Most of it's ancient history."

"What is the nature of the information?"

"I didn't tell you, did I? Earth has a long and proud record of philosophical thinking too. We started with that stuff aeons ago. We have lots of famous philosophers. Russell, Nietzsche, Marx, Descartes, Locke. Loads of them. It isn't my field, so I can't tell you much about them. But the info will be on the *Bres* for sure. I don't know why I didn't think of it before. It seems so obvious now. Polarans value philosophy above all else, so to demonstrate the value of humanity was to let you know about *our* philosophers. That way, the two sides can achieve mutual understanding and respect." Carys vaguely recalled Barbier going on about something like that. He was an ambassador by profession. He should know about this stuff. It had taken her a little while to get there, but she'd understood in the end.

"Where are we going?" In quiet certainty she'd finally hit upon the solution to her problem, Carys hadn't paid attention to her surroundings. They were in a new part of the city. Judging by the brilliant light beaming through the nearly transparent walls, they were at the very edge. The passageway sloped steeply upward and had few exits.

"You asked me to fly with you outside," Perseus replied.

"Of course. I forgot." Fortunately, Carys had brought along the woven cloth she'd found in his dwelling, like a comfort blanket. If they were venturing into the open, it could serve another, vital, purpose.

Perseus was gripping her tightly around her chest and, as usual, her limbs were dangling while she had to make an effort to keep her head up. "Do you remember I wanted to go on your back?"

"We will have an opportunity to change positions at the exit. I confess, I'm not comfortable with other Polarans seeing you above me while I'm in an inferior position. It would be bad for my reputation, which is already poor."

"I understand. And I appreciate it, Perseus. I really do. You've been a great friend."

"Thank you. It pleases me to hear you say that."

The movement of Polarans in the upper levels was minimal. Few passed by and those that did utterly ignored Carys as usual. She was growing used to being invisible in this strange world.

When they hadn't seen anyone else for a couple of minutes, Perseus flew to a ledge and set Carys down. The wall split open and the harsh rays of Polaris Aa poured in. She winced and squeezed her eyes shut.

"Take care," Perseus said.

"Don't worry. I'm not moving a millimetre until you tell me." Her arms drawn in tightly to her sides, Carys took a peek.

The ledge was only thirty centimetres wide. To one side was a twenty-metre drop to the corridor floor, to the other was an abyss. They were up in the anvil of the cloud city. A strong, chilly breeze threatened to blow her off her platform.

Perseus moved to the edge and crouched, leaning out. "You must hold onto me tightly. If you fall, I don't know if I can catch you."

Looking at the alien's broad back and beyond it to the vast, distant ocean, Carys was beginning to think this was a very stupid idea. How dumb would it be that, just as she'd managed to convince the Polarans not to kill her, she died through pulling an idiotic stunt? And poor Perseus would probably carry the guilt for the rest of his life.

On the other hand, if she was ever going to fly like a bird it was now. Whether the Triad accepted her argument and she returned to the *Bres*, or it didn't and she died, she would never get another chance to fulfil her deepest desire.

She tied the short end of the cloth in a firm knot under her chin, creating a hood while the rest covered her back, protecting her from the sun. Awkwardly, she clambered onto Perseus. By holding onto his shoulders and drawing up her knees, she managed to achieve a fairly secure posture.

"Are you ready?" he asked.

"As I'll ever be."

"What?"

"Yes!"

He leapt into thin air.

The movement nearly broke Carys's hold. She dug in her fingers and knees so hard she thought she must be hurting him, though he said nothing. His wings beat, lifting them higher, and then he spread them wide and glided away from the city.

The exhilaration took Carys's breath away. A wave of joy burst over her. The bright, sun-washed sky was clear to the horizon. The ocean was far below. There was nothing between her and this vast, open space except her alien friend. She was perfectly free.

It was not quite the same as flying herself. She couldn't swoop or soar at will. It was Perseus who controlled their flight, and she had the impression he was flying more evenly and steadily than he ordinarily would due to fear of her losing her grip. But she could feel him ride the air currents, making subtle adjustments to his wings and body. She could sense his deep connection with the air. To him, flying was as instinctive as walking. It was an ability he had learned so young it had become completely internalised. He flew in the same manner that he breathed.

"Where do you want to go?"

"I don't care. Anywhere. This is wonderful. I feel as though I lived all my life just to experience this moment."

"But we're only flying."

"Don't worry. You could never understand."

"I'm glad you like it, but, if you don't mind, I will go to a nearby island. You are surprisingly heavy for a creature your size."

"I think humans are denser than Polarans. Earth's gravity is higher."

"That explains it." Perseus wheeled to the left.

Carys felt herself slipping. She held on for dear life. The amazing trip had suddenly lost some of its leisure and gained more thrill. Her friend altered his posture, re-balancing her.

A mountain peak, rising from the ocean, had come into view. The island was more lush than the net-makers'. Uniform vegetation grew up a gentle incline—a crop of some kind. Perseus headed for the steeper side of the landmass. He circled twice, lowering his altitude, and landed rather clumsily on an outcrop. Carys slid off his back as he bumped down.

"Sorry," he said, turning, "are you hurt?"

"I'm fine. That was nothing. I've got used to being dropped on my arse." She stood up. "What is this place?"

"Just one of many small islets in this area. It's the tip of an archipelago. Only a few people live here, mostly farmers. I come here sometimes when the city is too busy and noisy."

"I like it, but can we find some shade? I'm not built for your sunlight."

"Of course. Even we prefer not to spend too long in the sun." He led her inland along a track until they reached a tall but wizened, spreading plant, bent sideways by the constant wind. There was just enough space to sit beneath its branches.

Carys sat down and untied the knot of her blanket before taking it off. "How long do you think we can stay away?"

"It's hard to say. The Triad will need time to assess the information from your ship and come to a decision. They may only take a few hours or they may need days. Regardless, we should return by nightfall."

"If they want to see it all, it'll definitely take them days, but after that the decision-making should be quick. They're going to leave it to Hush. It'll be her final test to see if she's ready for The Great Death."

"That's what they told you?"

"That's what they said."

Perseus was silent.

"Surely even Hush will see the value of human philosophical thought, and if she doesn't the other members of the Triad will. She has to come to the right decision if she wants to achieve perfection."

"I confess I'm not certain what she will say, but I'm the last Polaran you should ask about these things. Tell me about Earth. I'm interested in the animals you call birds."

"Ha, don't get me talking about birds. You'll never shut me up. But if you *really* want to know..." Carys launched into her favourite subject. She told Perseus about the sparrows, finches, blackbirds, robins, thrushes and tits she'd fed in her parents' garden before the Crusader invasion. She told him of the starlings' murmurations in the evening skies of West BI, of clever corvids and their wily ways, of the songs of nightingales, of graceful swans, deep-diving cormorants, jewel-like kingfishers, cheating cuckoos and the mating displays of great crested grebes, of wheeling, thieving seagulls, summer swallows and ascending skylarks, of silent, ghostly owls and their supernatural calls, of elusive curlews and woodcocks, of pheasants, grouse and quail, doomed to fall to the hunter's gun.

"Those are just a few examples, mostly native to the country I'm from. There are thousands more species, like hummingbirds, parrots, cockatoos, albatrosses and penguins. Don't get me started on penguins! But my speciality is birds of prey. I hardly know where to begin. There's so much to tell you."

Perseus opened his mouth as if to speak, but then he closed it. He settled deeper into his position, folding his arms loosely.

Carys opened with eagles and worked her way down. She spent longest on kestrels, waxing lyrical about their hovering capability—Perseus perked up with interest—and peregrine falcons, fastest living thing on Earth when in a stoop. By the time she reached hobbies and hen harriers, she noticed she was hoarse and the world's largest sun was three-quarters below the horizon.

"Oh dear," she said ruefully. "I did warn you not to get me talking about birds."

"It is no matter. I'm fascinated by everything you've told me. But we should return to the city."

They walked back to the outcrop and Carys climbed onto Perseus's back.

Polaris Aa sank from sight as they flew, bathing the seascape in a ruby glow. Perseus's wide wings swept them higher, and Carys spied the storm-cloud city in the distance. It would take them a while to get there. The few stars visible in this world's sky would be out by the time they arrived. The *Bres* might be one of them.

She had done what she could. She'd tried her best. Whatever decision Hush came to, it was out of Carys's hands. For now, she would relish this magical flight—on perhaps the last night of her life.

Forty-Five

Carys couldn't breathe. Her chest heaved and a stricture fastened around her throat. She tried to speak, but no words came out. Her hands were shaking. She tightened them into fists and gasped, "You can't. You can't! It isn't fair. What did we do? We haven't hurt any of you. Why can't you let us go back to our ship? We'll leave this system and never bother you again. It's not fair! How can you do this?!"

The faces of the Triad seemed expressionless, though Carys couldn't say in truth that she'd learn to read the Polarans' emotions yet, and now she would never get the chance. "Did you study our philosophers and everything they said? You couldn't have. You haven't had time."

As soon as she and Perseus had arrived at the city, he had received a summons to bring her to the Triad's chamber. She'd been optimistic, telling herself that a short perusal of the wealth of human philosophical endeavour must have persuaded the aliens that they'd underestimated their visitors. There couldn't be any other explanation for the speed of their decision-making.

She couldn't have been more wrong. Whatever the Triad had seen, whoever's philosophical works they'd read, they had quickly dismissed them. Or maybe two of the Triad hadn't even bothered. Maybe they'd left it all to Hush, who was already prejudiced against humans.

The alien *seemed* pleased with herself. "We have been more than generous with our time *and* consideration regarding the insignificant efforts of humans in the area of philosophical study. You can't seriously expect us to complete an in-depth examination of the mountains of nonsense your captain supplied. That would take weeks. We fulfilled our side of the agreement and inspected a few samples. Had your specialists any merit, it would have been immediately obvious. It was not."

Did Hush only want to hurry to her Great Death? Had she gone through the motions, and then argued strongly against allowing the humans to live, making her case skilfully and eloquently, purely in order to demonstrate her own 'perfection'? She'd thrown the *Bres*'s crew under the bus to meet her own ends.

"You *bitch*!" Carys screamed, jabbing a finger at Hush. "You arrogant, insane bitch! You're doing this on purpose, just because someone threw a rock at you, just because you want to die in a stupid, last act of superiority." A small voice at the back of Carys's mind told her that displaying her rage was only sealing her and the other humans' fate, that her excess emotion was confirming the Polarans' attitude that her species didn't deserve to live, but she couldn't help herself. And it didn't matter anyway. There was nothing she could say or do, no appeal she could make, that would change their minds.

Hush said something in her own language, not deigning to use the translator. The Triad talked among themselves, ignoring Carys. She looked down from the column and around the chamber, desperation forcing her to seek the impossible: a way to escape.

But she was tens of metres above the floor. The bridge Bujold and Barbier had exited along beyond a yawning divide. The chamber's opening hung suspended in the wall, passable only through flight.

A Polaran flew through it.

Perseus.

She'd recognise him instantly. The tiny squint in his left eye, the patch of feathers on his neck a slightly paler hue than the rest, his chipped tooth.

He flew to the top of Carys's column and plucked her from it. Slowly, he carried her out. The Triad didn't even pause its conversation.

Perseus softly murmured, "Whatever happens, do not struggle."

"Where are you taking me?"

"I am supposed to be taking you to be killed. They don't want to risk dropping you into the ocean, not after your companion survived. They also believe it is a death too similar to the Great Death, and they do not wish to confuse any Polarans who might observe it."

"You're *supposed to be* taking me to my execution?" Hope lightened the leaden weight in Carys's chest. But the feeling was bittersweet. Perseus might be able to save her somehow—maybe he planned on hiding her on a remote island—but he couldn't save Setia, Sheldrake or Moody. He couldn't prevent the destruction of the *Bres*.

How could she go on, knowing all those deaths were her responsibility, eking out a pitiful, hidden existence, the only human on an entire planet?

"It's okay," she said sadly. "Take me wherever we should be going. I appreciate whatever you have in mind, but I don't want it. I failed. It isn't right that I should be saved when so many others are going to die."

"You did not fail. It isn't your fault that my people are blind to anything outside themselves."

"Maybe, but it doesn't matter now. And you'll get into—"

Perseus had abruptly halted. His great wings beat but he began to sink. Kestrels' hovering ability—that he'd been so interested in—was not something Polarans could do.

Ranks of flying aliens were heading for them. Carys had never seen so many all at once, filling the corridor.

Perseus swept around to fly back the way they'd come, but Polarans were converging from behind too. Carys felt Perseus's chest expand against her back as he took a deep breath.

And then he roared.

The sound was almost too deep for her to hear, but she felt it. The air reverberated. Her eardrums smarted. Perseus's body shook.

The sound threw the approaching Polarans into confusion. Some turned, bumping into others. Some took umbrage and roared back, filling the corridor with ear-splitting sound. Some raised their arms and curled their tails, perhaps in a gesture of placation.

"They noticed you weren't taking me to the right place?" Carys asked. She'd covered her ears with her hands and among all the noise she could only hear herself inside her head.

Maybe Perseus didn't hear her at all because he didn't answer. Unable to fly anywhere, he'd sunk a few metres. His grip on her tightened and his wings beat furiously. Carys's stomach lurched as they quickly ascended. Perseus was flying sideways, heading for an opening. He alighted on the lip as the leading Polarans reached them. Swooping into a dwelling, he didn't even touch down. Carys caught a glimpse of a Spartan interior as they passed through, and then they were outside. He'd flown out the window.

The eerie Polaran night surrounded them. Lights penetrating the city's translucent walls turned it into the softly glowing storm cloud she'd mistaken it for at first sight. But the rest was crimson darkness, the deep ocean invisible below.

Perseus flew.

On their previous journey, he'd flown at a leisurely pace and he'd grumbled about her weight. Now, his wings beat powerfully and they raced along. Though Carys had virtually no external markers to gauge their speed, she could feel the wind rushing over her and hear its howl.

Could Perseus really get away?

She assumed that, like birds, he could sense the planet's magnetic field and therefore would have no trouble navigating in darkness. If no pursuers caught him, he might make it wherever he was going. But if he succeeded, what would it mean? Would he be forced to hide with her for the rest of his life?

"Perseus," she shouted over the wind, "stop! Go back. Don't do this."

"I must," he gasped. "It is wrong to kill without sufficient justification. The Triad is wrong. Hush is wrong."

Carys smiled. In so many ways Perseus was typically Polaran. He'd made his decision to try to save her by thinking along philosophical lines. He'd reasoned it out in his head and come to a different conclusion from the Triad, the supposedly near-perfect peak of Polaran society.

She wasn't going to argue about it any longer. He would do whatever he had to do.

"*Unnhhh!*"

Something had slammed into them. Polaran roars filled the air and hands tore at Carys, grasping, pulling, pinching. Wings buffeted her face. Another Polaran or maybe more than one was holding onto Perseus. The aliens whirled and fought. Carys could see nothing except flitting shadows as the creatures spun and tussled. All she could feel was fingers tearing at her and the press of feathered bodies.

She fought and screamed as they plummeted, trying to free herself and Perseus from their attackers. She blindly punched, driving all her strength, all the power of muscles developed on a heavy gravity planet into her angled knuckles. She kicked and kneed the creatures gripping Perseus.

They would not let go.

Something warm and wet ran into her hair. The aliens were biting each other and their blood was dripping down.

How long had they been falling? Surely they would hit the water soon, and then they would all die.

"Release me!" she yelled. "Let me fall, Perseus. It's okay. It's better this way." Her face was wet, not only with the aliens' blood.

"I..." her friend's soft rumble vibrated against her back "will...not."

Steel pincers fastened around Carys's thighs and tugged sharply downwards. She was torn from Perseus's arms. Her back slapped icy water, drenching her, and then she was borne swiftly up. The new Polaran held her around her waist, facing the deep red sky. Her arms flailed and legs drooped.

As far as she could tell, Perseus didn't come after them. Nothing impeded their flight back to the city. She hoped her friend hadn't fallen into the ocean and that no harm had come to him after he'd been forced to give her up.

She saw the city upside down, the black ocean at the top of her vision. They were approaching the lowest reaches of the metropolis.

Should she try to wriggle free and bring her story to a swift end? It seemed the best move. Yet she couldn't bring herself to do it. Something stopped her. Cowardice? Hopelessness? She didn't know.

They entered through one of the lowest portals, perhaps only two or three floors above the base. As they flew into the lighted space, she saw they were not alone. Two more Polarans followed at a short distance. Neither was Perseus.

This place didn't contain the wide galleries with many openings of the upper levels. Nor did it bear any resemblance to the food preparation section. The corridor was long, featureless and barely lit. Carys craned her neck to see where they were heading.

Four large Polarans stood outside something she'd never seen before on this planet: closed doors. Two aliens stood on each side. As she was flown closer, one of the creatures opened the doors. Beyond them was a space even dimmer than the corridor.

Carys's bearer glided in, dropped her and left. The doors closed.

"Burnap's balls," said a voice. "Carys?"

Forty-Six

Figures moved in the half light. One detached from the group and walked closer.

Carys looked up. "Setia?"

"It *is* you! Holy shit. We thought you were dead."

"Ellis!"

Strong arms hauled Carys to her feet and enveloped her in a hug. "Sheldrake? Uhh..." She was crushed against his chest and could barely open her mouth.

"Gentler," Moody admonished. "You could be hurting her."

Sheldrake grasped her shoulders and peered into her eyes. "Are you hurt? Did they torture you?"

"I wasn't tortured. How long have you been here, and who..."

Setia, Sheldrake and Moody weren't the only humans in the room. Fifteen or twenty more sat, lay or slouched against the walls, watching the re-uniting companions.

"Torres's team didn't die?" Carys asked.

"They were brought directly to the planet," Sheldrake explained. "While we were on the mountain, they were here."

"In those holding cells on the edge of the city?"

"You got it. The Polarans made them fast while we were on their ships being relieved of our EVA suits."

"How long were they in the cells?"

"A couple days. Right, guys?" Sheldrake turned to the military men and women for confirmation.

"About that," one replied. "Long enough to get nice and toasty from the sun."

Moody said, "They'd been in this room about the same length of time when we arrived."

"And you've all been here since?" asked Carys.

"We have," Moody replied. "When you weren't brought here too and you didn't turn up, we assumed something awful must have happened to you. There seemed no other explanation for your absence."

Carys's heart sank into her stomach, knowing the reason she'd been singled out. Her expression must have told of her despair.

"Yeah," Setia said suspiciously, "why *were* you separated? What have you been doing while we've been cooped up?"

"I'll get around to that." How much longer did they have? If Carys delayed long enough, maybe she wouldn't have to tell them the dreadful truth. "Setia, I want to apologise. You guessed *I'm* the reason you're here, right?"

"Somewhere on my long swim back to dry land, I figured it out, yeah," Setia growled.

That was why the first word out of her mouth as she had returned to consciousness had been *Bitch*.

"How did you know?"

"Because when you asked Bujold to add Sheldrake to the team, she agreed. Just like that. Like you had some say in the matter. And you knew all about what Arief did to me. You know what I'm capable of. It makes sense that if you knew your life was in danger you would want me around. You didn't get a choice about coming here, but you did get to choose who came with you."

"Like I said..." Carys reached out to touch Setia's shoulder.

Setia shrugged her off. "Whatever. You haven't told us what's been going on while we've been stuck in here gazing at our navels."

"I... I've been..."

I've been screwing up our only chance to get out of here alive.

"Did any of you see Bujold or Barbier?"

"Who the hell's Barbier?" Setia asked.

"The *Bres*'s ambassador. He and the captain were here on the planet. I saw them, but I couldn't talk to them. The Polarans told me they'd come to an agreement." Carys's chest tightened and a hot flush rose to her cheeks.

Moody replied, "None of us has seen anyone who wasn't in the original team. So Captain Bujold and the ambassador negotiated our release? That's wonderful news. I confess my initial interest in meeting aliens has waned somewhat." He chuckled.

Carys swallowed, looking down. "Not that kind of agreement."

"*Damn*," Sheldrake muttered.

"Then *what* kind of agreement?" Setia asked darkly.

"It'll take a while to explain."

"We have all the time in the world."

The night had worn on, and still death hadn't come. After much beating around the bush, Carys had been forced to deliver the devastating news. Unsurprisingly, it hadn't been well-received.

Setia had stared, turned away with a disgusted curl of her lip and gone to a corner to silently fume.

Moody had paled and stammered, "D-d-do you know w-w-when?"

Carys shook her head.

Sheldrake looked devastated but he said with forced confidence, "You did your best, Ellis. I know it."

She only wished she could have lived up to the ex-corporal's image of her.

The soldiers muttered among themselves but did little else.

She understood their reaction. No doubt over the days of their incarceration they'd considered many escape plans. But if they managed to break out of this place, where would they go? They had no way of returning to the *Bres*, no way of leaving the city without wings.

There was no way out. Even if Perseus could gather support in the little time remaining, Carys had experienced first-hand the reaction of most Polarans. Most of them would never allow dissenters to protect the humans, and there were too many to fight against. The sentence conferred by the Triad—or, rather, Hush—had to be carried out. To do otherwise would be to deviate from the path to perfection.

Carys walked over to Setia. She wasn't sure why. She didn't deserve Sheldrake's loyalty and she couldn't bear to witness Moody's anguish and fear.

She slumped down next to her former friend, perhaps hoping for forgiveness, perhaps anticipating well-deserved reproof. Not that either would make her feel better.

To her credit, Setia didn't tell her to piss off.

Carys said nothing. There was nothing to say.

Setia asked, "You're sure they're going to blow up the *Bres* too?"

"That's what they said."

"Maybe she can out-fly their ships."

"With a head start, maybe. But the Polaran vessels must be up close to her by now, and with her nav system jammed she can't escape into the Red Zone. She's a sitting duck."

"*Fuck.*"

Carys couldn't have said it better herself. She rested her elbows on her drawn-up knees and hung her head.

"Somewhere, Arief will be laughing his head off."

"Your alien friend who gave you your powers?"

"I wouldn't exactly call him a friend. More like an extra-terrestrial, arrogant asshole."

"Arrogance seems to be a common trait among intelligent species in this galaxy."

Setia sighed and leaned the back of her head against the wall. "For what it's worth, you're forgiven."

Tears started into Carys's eyes and she tried to take Setia's hand.

Her friend jerked it out of reach. "No need to get all mushy."

"I suppose it says a lot that it takes imminent death for us to be emotional with each other."

"*You're* the one getting emotional."

Sheldrake approached. "The guys are planning something for when the Polarans come to do it. I take it you two are in, yeah?"

Setia looked up from under lowered brows. "What kind of something?"

"Basically, we take as many of the bastards with us as we can."

The men and women of the military contingent were on their

feet, high-fiving and back-slapping each other. They were working themselves up to kill. All they had was their bare hands, but even so Carys had no doubt they could inflict serious damage as they went down fighting.

"Sure," Setia replied, "I'm up for that."

"Me too." Carys was no fighter, but it was a better alternative than meekly accepting her fate.

"Great," said Sheldrake. "I knew we could count on you."

Perhaps the aliens were watching what was going on in the communal cell, or maybe it was only coincidence, but it was at that moment they decided to carry out the executions. The doors opened and a bunch of Polarans entered, carrying knives.

Knives?

In their arrogance, the aliens had assumed that humans were easy to kill. Yet it was strange they weren't going to use an execution method for criminals, like injections or a gas chamber. Perhaps they didn't have any. Polaran society was so tightly structured and controlled by core beliefs, the crime rate was probably extremely low. Perhaps all it had was starships, built to defend the planet from aliens of the Polaris B system.

The soldiers had formed a semi-circle facing the door. Sheldrake joined them. Setia clambered upright and held out a hand to Carys, smiling grimly. "Shame you didn't suck up to them."

"It wouldn't have made any diff..." Carys's mouth fell open.

"Are you going to stand or what?"

Carys stared at the outstretched hand, her mind flipping from how she would die to other, more hopeful scenarios. "*Shit*," she blurted. "You're right!"

"About what?"

Carys leapt to her feet. "We need to suck up to them!"

"Hey, I was kidding."

But Carys was already on her way to the front of the chamber. Knife-wielding Polarans filled the exit, and the soldiers and Sheldrake were edging towards them. Carys got in between the two groups, turned to the humans and raised her hands. "I've thought of someth — *Urghhh*!"

Sheldrake had shoved her out of the way. He launched himself at one of the Polarans, on its way to attack her.

"Stop!" she screamed.

But Sheldrake was already locked in combat with the alien. Carys leapt onto its back and grabbed the arm with the knife. "Perseus!" she yelled at the top of her lungs. "Are you there? Tell them not to attack! I know the answer."

She completed these sentences while being whirled around by the Polaran, trying to get her off its back. She clung on with her knees, thrust into the upper edges of its wings. Both her hands were around its biceps but it still jabbed at Sheldrake.

If growing up on a comparatively high-g planet hadn't made her unusually strong here, she doubted she would have even been able to hold on.

Sheldrake ducked and weaved the bobbing, stabbing knife.

The Polaran swivelled and Carys saw its pals, hesitating. Was Perseus somewhere behind them? Had he heard her shout? Had he said something too low-pitched for her to hear?

The alien swivelled again, nearly jerking her off his back. There were the soldiers, stepping closer, narrowed gazes on the armed Polarans.

"Setia! Keep the team back! I can solve this without bloodshed. I just need a chance!"

Before Carys was whirled around once more, she briefly sighted her friend shouldering through the throng. But could Setia hold them? The military contingent was itching for a fight. They had to know about the death of their commander, and they'd been cooped up for ages.

Sure enough, defiant shouts rang out. Setia yelled back.

There was cursing and grunts from landed blows. But, though Setia was strong and a proficient fighter, she would never beat them all.

The head of the Polaran Carys was clinging to jerked back and smashed into her face. Her nose flashed with pain and hot blood coursed from it. Sheldrake must have got a good punch in. The Polaran staggered and began a slow-motion descent. Carys jumped down and side-stepped out of its path, snatching the knife from its loosened grasp as it fell.

A soldier was running up, heading for the Polarans in the entrance.

Carys stuck out a foot and tripped him. The man face-planted and slid along the floor. "Sheldrake, help me get them under control!" she implored, spluttering through the blood dripping from her nose. "Help me, please!"

He took a single look at her and nodded. Turning to face the soldiers, he lifted his hands. "Stand down, guys! Stand down. It's over."

Forty-Seven

Within half an hour, Carys was back in the Triad's chamber. Perseus had flown her here, and on the way she'd explained her idea. Without committing himself, he'd expressed cautious optimism. If her alien friend didn't think she was deluded or crazy, maybe she was in with a chance.

Nevertheless, as she faced Hush and her counterparts again, Carys's resolve and confidence faltered. So many lives depended on her ability to convince these stubborn, smug arseholes to agree to plan, and it wasn't only the lives of her friends, the only family she had remaining, and the *Bres*'s personnel at stake. If the *Bres* were lost, would that mean the end of the Interstellar Fleet? Would the captains of the *Banba* and *Balor* decide the grand endeavour to unite the intelligent species of the galaxy was too risky?

She swallowed. Her tongue had become an unwieldy lump of flesh cluttering up her mouth.

"My colleagues have deigned to allow you one final opportunity to speak," said Hush. Even the monotonal translator managed to convey her utter rage. "So speak."

Carys guessed that if her pals decided to allow the humans to live after all, it would mean that their previous conclusion had been incorrect, that Hush's judgement was not perfect, and she wouldn't be allowed her Great Death.

"I just need a second to-to..." Carys stammered "...gather my thoughts." If she didn't get this right, if she didn't word her proposal correctly, it was game over.

"You've had more than enough time already," Hush snapped. "You've had days. Speak immediately or accept your fate."

"All right, I've got it." Carys didn't have it. Her brain was refusing to work. She was stalling for time, willing the words to spring to mind.

They didn't come.

They had to come.

She closed her eyes and thought of Loki, who she wouldn't see again. She'd raised him from a chick, and now—that was it!

Hush, Perseus, and the rest of the Polarans were just big birds. They were dinosaurs, evolved to fly. She'd worked with birds all her adult life. She knew their ways inside out. All she had to do was to imagine she was dealing with birds again.

Her terror fell away.

At the same time, something impacted the column she stood upon. Her eyes jerked open. Hush had flown over to her and was reaching down to grab her, perhaps to toss her to the floor. Perseus hadn't been allowed to enter and couldn't protect her.

"Hey!" Carys yelled, slapping away Hush's outstretched hands. "You said I could state my proposal. Back off!"

One of the other Polarans said something in their language. Throwing Carys a look of fury and disgust, Hush swept back to her perch.

Carys began her speech with a deep bow. Would the aliens understand the gesture? Probably not, but it put her in the right frame of mind.

She started with the bullshit. "I apologise for my reaction just now. You're right, oh estimable Hush. I have lived on your wonderful planet and in the company of your excellent species for many days. Yet, in my ignorance, I initially failed to appreciate your wonderful sublimity and supremacy. I wandered your beautiful city, witnessed the lives of its inhabitants, and learned of your wondrous culture and its commitment to ultimate purity and quality of thought. Still, I did not appreciate it and, I'm ashamed to say, I allowed base emotions and instincts to guide my behaviour." She took a breath.

"Hurry up," Hush urged. "You are not telling us anything we don't already know."

"Forgive me. I beg for your patience. I am only a lowly human and unable to match the speed of your perception."

"Again, this is clear."

"I will be as brief as possible. My proposal is..." *here goes nothing* "...that Polarans assume their rightful roles as guiding lights in the forthcoming Galactic Alliance. Your species has achieved the pinnacle of philosophical development. Humans and, I'm guessing, many other life forms, have so much to learn from you. You could be our teachers, our mentors, our advisers. Whenever there is a dispute or uncertainty about how to achieve an aim, Alliance members could approach you for guidance."

Carys paused, her mind racing as she tried to think up more drivel to spout.

The Triad were silent. Even Hush seemed to giving the idea some thought.

Encouraged, Carys sailed to her concluding statements. "In short, if you condescend to help we lesser-evolved species, Polarans could lead the galaxy to a better understanding of how to live perfectly and transcend the trappings of, er, our lack of enlightenment."

She held her breath.

Her pitch to her potential executioners had been hard to make. She was sorely lacking in the charm department, and she was sure that if she'd been addressing fellow humans they would have seen through her right away.

But most humans were not anywhere near as up themselves as Polarans. The species' superciliousness was its greatest weakness.

A murmured conversation started up between the Triad members.

Carys was feeling light-headed. She forcibly exhaled and then took another breath.

Surely...

Surely...

Hush hunched her wings. To Carys, it looked like disgruntlement. It was a good sign that the discussion wasn't going her way.

One of the other Polarans spoke. "We will give your proposal some consideration. You will return with your acquaintance to his dwelling and remain there while you await our decision."

Carys's legs lost their strength and she gripped the platform's perch for support.

Could she really have done it?

Forty-Eight

As Carys stepped down to the *Bres*'s shuttle bay she was sorely tempted to drop to her knees and kiss the deck. The urge to preserve her dignity in front of the ship's personnel stopped her. That, and the fact that a bird fluttered over and landed on her shoulder.

Weeks of association with Polarans made her flinch.

Then she recognised Loki and her heart burst. She gently stroked the bird's head and wept. "I missed you so much. Are you okay?"

He seemed thinner than he'd been when she left, but his eyes were bright, clear and alert. He nibbled her hair.

"You're in the way," Setia complained. "So when you two have had your joyful reunion, if you wouldn't mind...?"

Carys moved away from the bottom of the steps and focused on Loki until approaching footsteps made her look up. Instantly, she started. It was like looking in a mirror, only not quite. Some of the person's features were subtly different. "Waylis?"

Carys-Waylis smiled. "I've started to change back but it'll take a few hours. I thought taking on your appearance might help to keep the birds calm. It worked with most of them, but not him." She nodded at Loki. "I was convinced he knew I wasn't you and he was only tolerating me looking after him while he waited for you to return. I was right. The minute I entered the bay he flew right over to you."

"Of course he did. He isn't stupid. How are the aviary birds doing?"

"They're fine, though Miriam and I had our work cut out. I don't know how you make it look so easy."

Carys suspected the birds had been up to some antics—antics *she* wouldn't have tolerated. "I can't thank you enough for looking after them."

"It was a pleasure. We're just glad to have you back safe and sound."

Miriam was talking with Setia. Mapper Robins was in the bay too, along with Captain Bujold and Ambassador Barbier, here to welcome back the mission team.

One member was missing: Torres. A memorial service was scheduled for him tomorrow.

"If you don't mind," Carys said, "I want to go to my cabin and be alone for a while."

"Won't Bujold want you to debrief?"

"Maybe, but she can go f—"

"Ellis," the captain called. "Debriefing Room. Five minutes."

Waylis, who was already looking more like herself, pulled a sympathetic face. "Sorry."

Carys's shoulders slumped and she replied heavily, "What's another hour or two? Besides, Bujold owes me, big time, and I'm going to make sure she pays."

"I don't think she'll allow you to keep the aviary going, if that's what you're thinking. There are already rumours about concerns over supplies."

"I'm not worried about that. I have a friend on the surface who has promised he'll look after my birds for me."

"Really? One of the Polarans? That'll be a helluva job."

"He wants to do it. He says it'll be his life's work."

Carys could barely keep her eyes open. Now the crisis was over and she was back on the ship, her energy had drained away. All she wanted to do was to spend a little time with Loki and then sleep.

But Bujold wouldn't allow it. She had to dot the i's and cross the t's before she would allow anyone their well-earned rest. And as well as being too tired to put up a fight about it, Carys wanted to keep the captain on her side just a short while longer.

"So," Bujold said, "in conclusion..."

Carys exhaled loudly in relief, drawing some glances and chuckles from the assembled men and women.

"In *conclusion*," Bujold reiterated, "I'm happy to report that Ambassador Barbier has finalised the details of the pact with the Polarans Ab."

"Ab?" queried a voice.

"That's what we're calling them for now. The aliens in the other system will be referred to as Polarans B. It's purely for convenience's sake. As time goes by, I'm sure more suitable names will be found."

"To be clear," said Mapper Robins, who had also come along to the debriefing, "will the Polarans Ab *actually* act as the Galactic Alliance's experts and tutors in the field of philosophical study? I mean, I'm not sure how other species who join up in the future might react. They may find the notion rather patronising and offensive."

"That's what the Polarans Ab believe to be the case, which is what is most important in this context." Bujold's features were characteristically inexpressive, but Carys thought she detected a glint in the captain's eyes.

"I'm sure you're all longing for your bunks," she went on, "so I won't keep you any longer. Well done, everyone. Well done. Ellis, I want to speak to you."

Carys had to clamp her teeth to suppress a groan. Wouldn't the captain ever be done with her? She didn't move from her seat, and as Bujold stepped over between the leaving mission team members, she watched with stony eyes.

"I'm glad you want to talk," she snapped before the captain could get a word out, "because I want to set some things straight."

Bujold's eyebrow lifted. "You do, do you?"

"Yes, I bloody well do. I saved everyone down there and I saved this ship. I deserve a reward. I'm going to tell you what it is, and you're going to agree."

"Er, technically you didn't save the *Bres*. The *Balor* and *Banba* were waiting in the Red Zone, ready to come to her rescue if things got nasty. But I will allow you all the credit for coming up with the answer that saved your team."

The voyage of the Interstellar Fleet continues in...

HEAVEN'S ENVOY

Sign up to my reader group for exclusive free books, discounts on new releases, review crew invitations and other interesting stuff:

https://jjgreenauthor.com/free-books/

Author's Notes

Welcome to the end of *Steadfast Star*. Before I give some background information on the book, I'd like to thank my editor, Liza Wood, Patreon patrons, my Substack reader group and paid subscribers, Instagram followers, YouTube listeners and, last but definitely not least, all the Facebook Starship JJ Green Shipmates. The support of these kind and loyal people is what has made the writing of Interstellar Fleet and all my other series possible.

Polaran Anatomy

The idea for Polaran anatomy was sparked by reading about a strange creature called *Sharovipteryx mirabilis* in the book *Otherlands* by Thomas Halliday. If you're interested in ancient landscapes and the life forms that inhabited them, or just evolutionary history generally, I heartily recommend the book.

Sharovipteryx mirabilis lived during the Triassic Period and, according to extrapolations from the fossil record, the framework for its wings was supplied by its lower limbs. Strictly speaking, this design would be more adept for gliding rather than actual flight as I have portrayed the aliens' locomotion in *Steadfast Star*, but it allowed the creature to hold onto things with its upper limbs—something birds cannot do. Efficient dexterity in the handling of tools is thought to be key to humanity's development, so it makes sense that intelligent extra-terrestrial species would have a similar capability.

Polaris Aa and Polaris Ab

This is where you need to take a humongous pinch of salt. There is a hefty amount of artistic licence used in the stars and planetary system in *Steadfast Star*. In reality, it's very unlikely that any planets orbiting Polaris Ab are capable of supporting life, and if it were to exist, it would have to have figured out how to survive the devastating, life-annihilating conditions depicted so well by Liu Cixin in *The Three Body Problem*.

The brilliance of Polaris Aa in the sky figures strongly in *Steadfast Star*. Would it be so bright in reality? The star is only 5.4 solar masses, and it's 18.5 AU from Polaris Ab (Polaris B is 2400 AU from Aa), but its luminosity is 1,260 times that of our Sun. By contrast, the luminosity of Polaris Ab, the closest star to the planet, is only 3 times that of the Sun. Despite the much greater distance, Polaris Aa would dominate the sky.

Polaran Culture

Inspiration for Polaran culture and society was drawn from my experiences of living in other countries and encountering a wide range of belief and value systems. Is it a little extreme? Perhaps. But one aspect of science fiction is to explore what happens when certain ideas are taken to an extreme. Without pointing fingers, I would argue that, though no single nation closely resembles the Polarans, some individuals live their lives on similar principles.

Carys Ellis

Interstellar Fleet is a spinoff from my Star Legend series, and Carys features as a minor character in book 4, *The Resolute* and book 6, *The Defiant*. To find out more about the Crusader Wars and the long history of aliens interfering in human affairs on Earth, I recommend beginning the story in book 1, *The Valiant*.

If you would like to discuss any aspect of *Steadfast Star* or any of my other books, feel free to post on the shipmates' Facebook page. I would love to see you there.